AS TIME GOES BY

Journalist Delaney Wright is on the brink of stardom when she covers a sensational murder trial for the news. She should be thrilled, yet her growing desire to locate her birth mother consumes her thoughts. And when Delaney's friends offer to look into the mystery surrounding her birth, they uncover a shocking secret... On trial for murder is Betsy Grant, widow of a wealthy doctor who has Alzheimer's. When her lawyer urges her to accept a plea bargain, Betsy refuses: she will go to trial to prove her innocence. As the trial unfolds, Delaney is convinced Betsy is not guilty and frantically tries to prove her innocence – before it's too late.

AS TIME GOES BY

by

Mary Higgins Clark

Magna Large Print Books
Long Preston, North Yorkshire,
BD23 4ND, England.

British Library Cataloguing in Publication Data.

A catalogue record of this book is
available from the British Library

ISBN   978-0-7505-4507-5

First published in Great Britain by Simon & Schuster UK Ltd., 2016

Cover illustration © Ilona Wellmann/Arcangel by arrangement with
Arcangel Images Ltd.

Published in Large Print 2018 by arrangement with
Simon & Schuster UK Ltd.

Magna Large Print is an imprint of Library Magna Books Ltd.

Printed and bound in Great Britain by
T.J. (International) Ltd., Cornwall, PL28 8RW

Acknowledgments

Again and as always, thanks to my forever editor and dear friend, Michael Korda. He has steered me through this journey from page one to those glorious words 'the end.' How blessed I have been to have him as my editor all these years.

I want to thank Marysue Rucci, editor in chief of Simon & Schuster. It has been wonderful working with her these last few years.

My home team is a joy to work with. My son, David, has become a full-time valuable assistant and researcher.

As usual, my other children have willingly been my first readers and sounding boards all the steps of the way.

And as always, thanks to Spouse Extraordinaire, John Conheeney, who has for twenty years listened to me as I sigh that I am sure this book isn't working.

Nadine Petry, my longtime assistant and right hand, is gifted with being able to interpret my impossible handwriting. Thank you, Nadine.

When *Where Are the Children* was published forty-one years ago, I would never have thought that all these many years later I would be blessed enough to still be scribbling away. I relish finding new characters and new situations to put them in.

As I have said, 'the end' are my two favorite words. But they wouldn't be if there wasn't a first sentence that invites you, dear readers, to turn the pages.

Thank you for continuing to enjoy the tales I tell.

Cheers and Blessings,

Mary

For the newlyweds,
Dr. James and Courtney Clark Morrison,
with love

Prologue

The first wail of the infant was so penetrating that the two couples outside the birthing room of midwife Cora Banks gasped in unison. James and Jennifer Wright's eyes lit up with joy. Relief and resignation formed the expression on the faces of Rose and Martin Ryan, whose seventeen-year-old daughter had just given birth.

The couples only knew each other as the Smiths and the Joneses. Neither one had any desire to know the true identity of the other. A full fifteen minutes later they were still waiting anxiously to see the newborn child.

It was a sleepy seven-pound girl with strands of curling black ringlets that contrasted with her fair complexion. When her eyes blinked open they were large and deep brown. As Jennifer Wright reached out to take her, the midwife smiled. 'I think we have a little business to complete,' she suggested.

James Wright opened the small valise he was carrying. 'Sixty thousand dollars,' he said. 'Count it.'

The mother of the baby who had just been born had been described to them as a seventeen-year-old high school senior who had gotten pregnant the night of the senior prom. That fact had been hidden from everyone. Her parents told family and friends that she was too young to go away to college and would be working for her aunt in her dress shop in Milwaukee. The eighteen-year-old boy who was the father had gone on to college never knowing about the pregnancy.

'Forty thousand dollars for the college education of the young mother,' Cora announced as she counted the money and handed that amount to the young mother's parents, her thick arms still holding tightly to the baby. She did not add that the remaining twenty thousand dollars was for her service in delivering the baby.

The grandparents of the newborn accepted the money in silence. Jennifer Wright reached out her yearning arms and whispered, 'I'm so happy.'

Cora said, 'I'll have the birth registered in your names.' Her smile was mirthless and did nothing to enhance her plain, round-cheeked face. Although she was only age forty, her expression made her seem at least ten years older.

She turned to the young mother's parents. 'Let her sleep for another few hours, then take her home.'

In the birthing room the seventeen-year-old struggled to shake off the sedation that had been administered liberally. Her breasts felt as though they were swelling from the impact of holding her baby those first few moments after the birth. I want her, I want her, were the words screaming from her soul. Don't give my baby away. I'll find a way to take care of her...

Two hours later, curled up on the backseat of the family car, she was taken to a nearby motel.

The next morning she was alone on a plane on her way back to Milwaukee.

1

'And now for the usual block of commercials,' Delaney Wright whispered to her fellow anchor on the WRL 6 P.M. news. 'All of them so fascinating.'

'They pay our salaries,' Don Brown reminded her with a smile.

'I know they do, God bless them,' Delaney said cheerfully, as she looked into the mirror to check her appearance.

She wasn't sure if the deep purple blouse the wardrobe mistress had picked out was too strong against her pale skin, but it was okay with her shoulder-length black hair. And Iris, her favorite makeup artist, had done a good job accentuating her dark brown eyes and long lashes.

The director began the countdown. 'Ten, nine ... three, two...' As he said, 'one,' Delaney began to read. 'Tomorrow morning jury selection will begin in the trial of forty-three-year-old former high school teacher Betsy Grant at the Bergen County Courthouse in Hackensack, New Jersey. Grant is being tried for the murder of her wealthy husband Dr. Edward Grant, who was fifty-eight years old at the time of his death. He had been suffering from early onset Alzheimer's disease. She has steadfastly declared her innocence. The prosecutor maintains that she was tired of waiting for him to die. She and his son are the co-heirs of his estate, which has been estimated at over fifteen million dollars.'

'And now to a much happier story,' Don Brown began. 'This is the kind of feature we love to present.' The footage began to appear on screen. It was about the reunion of a thirty-year-old man with his birth mother. 'We were both trying to find each other for ten years,' Matthew Trainor said, smiling. 'I almost felt as though she was calling me. I *needed* to find her.'

His arm was around a heavyset fiftyish woman. Her naturally wavy hair was soft around her pleasant face. Her hazel eyes were shining with unshed tears. 'I was nineteen when I gave birth to Charles.' She paused and looked up at her son. 'In my mind I always called him Charles. On his birthday I bought toys and gave them to a charity for children.' Her voice tremulous, she added, 'I like the name his adoptive parents gave him. Matthew "means gift of God."'

As the segment came to an end, Matthew said, 'Ever since I can remember there was a need in me. I needed to know who my birth parents were, particularly my mother.'

As he gave her a big hug, Doris Murray began to cry. 'It is impossible to explain how much I have missed my son.'

'Heartwarming story, isn't it, Delaney?' Don Brown asked.

Delaney could only nod. She knew that the lump in her throat was about to dissolve into a flood of tears.

Don waited a few seconds for her to answer but then with a look of surprise on his face said, 'Now let's see what our weatherman Ben Stevens has in store for us.'

14

When the program ended, Delaney said, 'Don, I apologize. I got so emotional about that story that I didn't trust myself. I was so afraid that I would be crying like the mother.'

'Well, let's see if they're still speaking to each other in six months,' Don said, wryly. He pushed back his chair. 'That's it for tonight.'

In the next studio, through the glass wall, they could see the national news anchorman, Richard Kramer, on the air. Delaney knew that Don was in line to take that spot when Kramer retired. She got up, left the studio, stopped in her office and changed from the purple blouse to a yoga top. She had been substituting for the usual co-anchor, Stephanie Lewis, who had called in sick. Delaney was especially happy that she was covering the Betsy Grant trial. It's going to be fascinating, she thought.

She picked up her shoulder bag and, responding to a series of 'See you Delaney's,' walked down several long corridors and onto Columbus Circle.

Much as she loved summer, Delaney knew she was ready for autumn. After Labor Day, Manhattan takes on vibrancy, she thought, and then realized she was trying to distract herself from what was bothering her. The feature about the adoption had ripped open the walls that she had always tried to build around herself to keep the same subject from haunting her again.

She needed to find her birth mother. James and Jennifer Wright had adopted her when she was hours old, and their names were on her birth certificate. She had been born with a midwife in attendance. The woman who had arranged the adoption was dead. There was no trace of the name of the midwife. Her birth had been registered in Philadelphia.

It was a seemingly dead end. But she knew she was going to make a decision. She had heard about a retired detective who specialized in tracing the untraceable in cases like hers. She was so deep in thought as she began her one-mile walk home that, almost without noticing, she passed Fifth Avenue.

At 54th Street she turned east. Her apartment in one of the older buildings was next to the one where Greta Garbo, the legendary actress from the 1930s had once resided. Garbo's famous quote, 'I "vant" to be alone,' often ran through Delaney's mind at the end of a particularly frantic day at the studio.

The always-smiling doorman, Danny, opened the door for her. Her apartment was a generous three rooms but certainly a vast difference from the large and beautiful home where she had been raised in Oyster Bay, Long Island. She dropped her bag, took a Perrier from the refrigerator, and, putting her feet on a hassock, settled in her comfortable chair.

On the table directly across the room was a large family picture taken when she was three years old. She was sitting on her mother's lap next to her father. Her three brothers were lined up behind them. Her black curly hair and dark brown eyes so obviously leaped out of the so-called family picture. The others had several shades of reddish blonde hair. Their eyes were varying shades of light blue and hazel.

It was a distinct memory. The first time she saw the picture she had begun to cry. 'Why don't I look like all of you?' she had wailed. That was when she was told that she was adopted. Not in those words, but as best as they could, her parents had explained to her, at that very young age, that they had very much wanted a little girl, and as a baby she had become part of their family.

Last month in Oyster Bay there had been a big family reunion gathering for her mother's seventy-fifth birthday. Jim came in from Cleveland, Larry from San Francisco and Richard from Chicago, with their wives and children. It had been a truly happy time. Her mother and father were moving to Florida. They had given away the furniture they didn't need, telling Delaney and her brothers to pick out what they wanted. She had taken a few small pieces that fit in her apartment.

She looked at the family picture again, visualizing the mother she had never known. Do I look like you? she wondered.

The phone rang. Delaney raised her eyes to Heaven but then saw who was calling. It was Carl Ferro, the producer of the six o'clock show. His voice was exultant. 'Stephanie took the job with *NOW News*. We're all thrilled. She was getting to be a "royal,"' he paused, '"nuisance." She had the mistaken impression that she knew more than Kathleen.' Kathleen Gerard was the executive producer of the News Department. 'Her resignation is coming in the morning. You're our new co-anchor with Don Brown. Congratulations!'

Delaney gasped. 'Carl, I'm delighted! What else can I say?' Then she added, 'My only regret is to

17

miss covering the Grant trial.'

'We still want you to. We'll use rotating co-anchors until after the trial. You're a great reporter. This kind of trial is right up your alley.'

'It doesn't get any better than that, Carl. Thanks a lot,' Delaney said.

But as she put down the phone, she had a sudden disquieting moment. Her former nanny, Bridget O'Keefe, had an expression, 'When things seem too good, there's trouble on the way.'

2

'Willy, I really need a new project,' Alvirah said. They were having breakfast in their apartment on Central Park South. They were on their second cup of coffee, which was the time Alvirah loved to chat. It was also the time Willy had finished reading the *Post* up to the sports section, which he was anxious to devour.

With a sigh of resignation, he put aside the newspaper and looked across the table at his beloved wife of forty-three years. His mane of white hair, craggy face and intense blue eyes reminded older friends of Tip O'Neill, the legendary Speaker of the House of Representatives.

'I know you've been getting restless, honey,' he said soothingly.

'I have,' Alvirah admitted as she reached for a second slice of coffee cake. 'There just hasn't been enough to do lately. I mean I really enjoyed the river cruise through the Seine. Who wouldn't? And to see where Van Gogh lived for the last months of his life. I loved it. But now it's nice to be home.'

She glanced out the window to admire their view of Central Park. 'Willy, aren't we lucky to be here?' she said. 'Just think what a comparison it is to our apartment in Astoria. The kitchen didn't even have a window.'

Willy remembered it all too well. Six years ago he had been a plumber and Alvirah a cleaning woman. They were sitting in their old apartment, Alvirah's feet so tired that she was soaking them in Epsom salt and warm water. Then the winning lottery ticket was announced on television. He had had to read their ticket twice before he realized they had won forty million dollars.

They had taken the money in yearly payments and always saved half of it. They had bought this apartment on Central Park South but kept the one in Astoria in case the government went broke and couldn't continue the payments.

Then the editor of the *Daily Standard* interviewed Alvirah. She told him that she had always wanted to go to the Cypress Point Spa in California. He asked her to write about her experiences there. He had given her a sunburst pin with a microphone in it to record her conversations. The editor said that would help her when she was writing the article. Instead it had helped her to learn the identity of a killer who was at the spa. Since then Alvirah, with the help of her microphone, had solved a number of crimes.

'And I'm looking forward to seeing Delaney tomorrow night,' Alvirah said now. 'She's so lucky

19

to be covering the Betsy Grant trial.'

'Isn't Grant the one who murdered her husband?' Willy asked.

'No, Willy. She's the one who is *accused* of murdering her husband,' Alvirah corrected.

'Well, from the little I've read about it, I'd say it was an open-and-shut case,' Willy observed.

'I agree,' Alvirah responded promptly. 'But as always I'm willing to keep an open mind...'

Willy smiled. 'You better be "open" to the fact that she's guilty.'

3

Fourteen miles away, in her ten-room mansion in Alpine, New Jersey, Betsy Grant was brewing a second cup of coffee in the kitchen and staring reflectively out the window. Subconsciously she registered the fact that the signs of early September were present in the gold tone of the leaves on the elm trees.

The large picture windows made you 'feel as though you were one with nature,' as the overly enthusiastic real estate agent had put it when he showed them this house twelve years ago.

After yet another sleepless night that memory was keen in her mind, as was the memory of the warmth in Ted's eyes as he looked at her for her reaction. She could already see that he wanted to buy it. And what was there not to like? she asked herself. I was so in love with him that any place he wanted to buy was fine with me. I hated the fact that the previous owner was willing to sell at a reduced price because his business was going into bankruptcy. I didn't like to think that we were profiting from someone else's misfortune. But this *is* a beautiful house, she thought.

Coffee cup in hand, she went upstairs. After Ted's death she had gone back to sleep in the master bedroom again. She passed through the sitting room where they had spent so many happy hours together. During the fall and winter they would often turn on the fire in there and watch a television show they both enjoyed or simply sit together reading.

The swift onset of early Alzheimer's when Ted was fifty-one years old had been an unexpected tragedy. Eventually she had blocked off the staircase to keep him from leaning precariously over the railing and had transformed the library on the first floor into a bedroom for him. At first she had slept in the small den next to it but then had turned it over to the full-time aide and moved to the guest bedroom and bath next to the kitchen on the first floor.

All of that kept whirling around in Betsy's mind as she set the cup down on the vanity in the bathroom and turned on the shower.

Her lawyer, Robert Maynard, would be here within the hour. I don't know why he's coming, Betsy thought, with a trace of resentment. I know everything he's going to say. I know everything to expect. As she slipped off her robe and nightgown she thought of the terrible moment when Maynard had informed her that the grand jury had indicted her for murder. The mug shot, the finger-printing, the arraignment, the posting of her bail – all of these were fragments of memory that haunted her daily, no matter how hard she tried to banish them.

She showered, fastened her long, light brown hair in a comb, touched her eyelashes with mascara and applied a dab of blush to her lips. The weather report had said that the day would be sharply cooler. From the closet she selected a long-sleeved hunter-green cashmere shirt and dark brown slacks and put them on her slender body. She had stopped wearing all black four months ago when one of the columnists had commented that the accused murderer of Edward Grant was parading around in widow's weeds. But she did wear only dark colors, even at home.

Before she left the room, she looked around. That had become a habit. There had been occasions when during the night Ted had somehow climbed over the locked gate at the bottom of the stairwell and come up here.

It was easy to tell when that had happened. Every drawer in the chests and night tables had been dumped out. It was as though he was looking for something, Betsy thought now. It was easy for her and Carmen, her daily housekeeper, to put everything back. The one heartbreak was that somehow he must have remembered the combination of the safe in the closet and had taken out the beautiful emerald-and-diamond bracelet he had given her on their first anniversary. She was still hoping that one day she or Carmen would find it, but there was always the worry that

Ted had thrown it in the garbage compactor.

She was tempted to make the bed but knew that Carmen would be coming in any moment. 'Leave it for me, Miss Betsy. That's what I'm here for,' she would always say. But too many years of living with her mother's daily, relentless shining and polishing and vacuuming had made it impossible for Betsy to ever leave a dish in a sink or a robe on a chair.

With an unconscious sigh Betsy went downstairs just as Carmen let herself in. A half hour later the chiming of the doorbell signaled that Robert Maynard, Esquire, was standing on her front porch.

4

Alan Grant, son of the late Edward 'Ted' Grant, stared at his former wife, Carly, and tried not to let the burning anger he felt show in his expression. Their four-year-old son and two-year-old daughter had somehow sensed the antagonism in the air and had scurried into their bedroom to get away from it.

Carly pointed after them. 'Will you please tell me how I'm supposed to put a roof over their heads if I get thrown out of here?' she demanded angrily.

She was a dancer whose Broadway career had come to an abrupt end when she was seriously injured by a hit-and-run driver. Now her startlingly lovely face was showing the strain caused by the back pain following the accident and the financial worries that were part of her everyday existence.

Her ex-husband had no answer for her. In an angry defense, raising his voice, he spat out his reply. 'Look, you know that once this trial is over, the money from my father's estate will be released. And I'll get plenty. There's no question Betsy's going to end up in prison, which also means that the half of his estate that he left to her will be mine. You've got some rich friends. Tell them to lend you money. Pay them interest.'

He reached into his pocket, pulled out his wallet and tossed a credit card on the table. 'This one is caught up. The job in Atlanta photographing those houses paid for it. Use this for food and I'll have the rent by the thirtieth.'

Without bothering to say good-bye to his children, he stalked out of the four-room apartment on West 89th Street in Manhattan, left the building and with swift strides began to walk downtown.

At thirty-five Alan closely resembled his dead father, a fact noted frequently by the media. Six feet tall, with reddish-brown hair and hazel eyes, he looked every inch the privileged Ivy League graduate who had been raised with a silver pacifier in his mouth.

It was all Betsy's fault, he thought. She and Alan were so close, but she was the one who had urged his father to no longer write him a check every time he had a problem but instead put him on a reasonable allowance. 'Alan's an excellent photographer,' she had pointed out. 'If he concentrated less on being the playboy of the western world and

24

settled down, he could make a good living.'

That was when his father had stopped paying his bills and restricted him to a check for one hundred thousand dollars every Christmas. That did not go far enough to support him, an ex-wife with two children, and a ten-year-old son by a former girlfriend.

As he walked, Alan's anger began to fade. It was only a matter of time, he assured himself. There was no possibility that any jury would ever let Betsy off. It became worse for Betsy when it had come out that she had been quietly seeing some guy for two years before his father died. Dr. Peter Benson, the Chair of the Humanities Department at Franklin University in Philadelphia. Although he was weary, Alan decided that it would all come out all right. He'd get the money. Betsy wouldn't inherit a penny. He just had to be patient.

He hadn't wanted to take that job shooting spring fashions for the new designer clothing firm that joke celebrity had founded. But it was necessary.

As he cut over to Central Park West toward Columbus Circle, Alan smiled at the satisfying memory of how his father had attacked Betsy the evening they'd gathered in a pointless effort to celebrate the demented man's birthday. Her anguished cry, 'I can't take it anymore,' had been heard by everyone. And during that night his father had been murdered with Betsy alone in the house.

When she's found guilty, she can't inherit, he thought, so every dime Dad left will be mine.

Then he tried to banish the unwelcome thought that his father's skull had been fractured by a powerful blow to the back of his head.

5

Before having breakfast Dr. Scott Clifton picked up the morning papers on the steps of his home in Ridgewood, New Jersey. A large and athletic fifty-seven-year-old man with a sunburned face and thick head of graying blonde hair, he did not need to be reminded that the lurid headlines were beginning again as the day for the trial approached.

Over the course of twenty years he, Ted and Dr. Kent Adams had developed an extremely successful orthopedic practice. And then Ted had the onset of Alzheimer's more than eight years ago. Since then, he and Kent had severed the partnership and gone their separate ways. In Kent's absence, Scott's surgical practice had declined significantly.

Lisa didn't often get down to have breakfast with him before he left for work. Not that she was a late sleeper, but he was always out of the house by eight o'clock at the latest. He fixed his own cereal and coffee.

But today, unexpectedly, she came into the kitchen.

'What's on your mind?' he asked curtly.

She hesitated, then said, 'You were tossing and turning again last night. You kept mentioning Ted's name. I know the trial is on your mind.'

26

'Of course it is. If I'm disturbing your sleep, I'm sorry.'

'I didn't mean to infer that you were disturbing me. I was just worried about you.' She blinked back tears. 'No matter what I say, you're always snapping at me,' she observed quietly.

Scott did not answer. He knew his marriage three years ago was a mistake.

The ink was hardly dry on his divorce papers when he married her. Now he had three kids in college and an ex-wife who didn't hesitate to call him and say she was a little short, and would he help? Of course, he would. They both understood that.

Lisa, twenty years his junior, had been a drug company representative who made sales calls on his office. He usually didn't have time to speak to detailers, leaving that job to the nurse. But he had made time for Lisa. She was a former Big Ten cheerleader from the Midwest. A great smile and a body to match.

What he had not taken into account was that after the initial attraction had faded, he neither needed nor wanted her.

But the last thing he could handle was to try to get rid of her now. He couldn't let anyone get into an analysis of his finances.

He'd put up with her until the trial was over and things calmed down. He wondered if she suspected anything.

Lisa was holding a coffee cup in both hands. It was the one she had had made with his picture and the words 'I love you, Scott' scrawled at every possible angle. It was enough to drive him crazy.

'Scott,' Lisa said his name hesitantly.

Now she was crying.

'Scott, we both know this marriage isn't working. Are you having an affair?'

He stared at her. 'Of course not.'

'I'm not sure if I believe you, but I still think that we're better off going our separate ways. I plan to see a lawyer next week and begin divorce proceedings.'

I can't let that happen, Scott thought frantically.

'Lisa, listen to me. I know I've been curt and inattentive, but that doesn't mean I don't love you. I don't want to lose you. It's just that Ted's death and Betsy's indictment have put a terrible cloud on the practice. Please.'

Lisa Clifton did not meet her husband's eyes. She did not believe him. She was sure he was having an affair, but she was still hoping that maybe they could work it out. 'Would you go to a marriage counselor with me?' she asked.

Good God, a marriage counselor, Scott thought, then tried to sound enthusiastic. He said, 'Of course, dear, of course.'

6

Delaney and Alvirah were never at a loss for words. They had become fast friends last year when they both covered the trial of a birth mother who had managed to find the couple who had adopted her baby and stole it back from them. While the judge had sympathy for her, he also reminded the birth mother that she was twenty-five years old when she gave up the baby, at the time had the financial resources to take care of the child and had caused great anguish in the two months that the baby was missing.

Because of the nature of that case, Delaney had confided to Alvirah the fact that she was adopted, a subject she seldom mentioned. She knew that Jennifer and James Wright were hurt the few times she ever brought it up. 'Delaney, I held you in my arms twenty minutes after you were born,' Jennifer had told her tearfully. 'I wanted you for years before that. I could visualize a little girl with three big brothers who would always be there for her if your father and I weren't around.'

And they had been. All of them. She had been blessed by being raised in a loving, tight-knit family, but now they were all scattered. Maybe that was why her feeling of urgency to find her birth mother had become so pronounced. Now that her adoptive parents were permanently living in Naples, Florida, it didn't seem so much of a betrayal to begin an active search for her.

When she and Alvirah and Willy were having dinner at Patsy's on West 56th Street, that subject came up again.

Delaney hesitated. Then she said, 'Alvirah, I told you and Willy that I was adopted.'

They both nodded.

'I remember reading years ago about Bob Considine, the newsman, who wrote, "I have four children. Two are adopted. I forget which two." My parents joked that I look so different because

I'm the image of my father's grandmother. She was born in Italy.'

'She must have been a beautiful woman,' Willy observed as he took a bite of his salad.

Delaney smiled. 'Willy, you're really sweet, but the need to know my roots, my birth family, is so strong that I almost cried when we did a piece on the news last night.'

'I was watching,' Alvirah said. 'It was about the birth mother being reunited with her son.'

'Yes. When the son said that he needed to find his birth mother there was such a lump in my throat that I missed my cue. Don had to cover for me and pick up the next story.'

'How about Facebook?' Alvirah asked, then answered her own question. 'But of course your family is bound to find out.'

'Of course they will,' Delaney confirmed. 'My brother Jim's wife is on Facebook all the time. She posts a picture of her kids at least three times a week.'

Alvirah could see that Delaney's eyes were beginning to glisten. 'Exactly how much do you know about the circumstances of your birth?' she asked.

'So little. A midwife delivered me in Philadelphia. Twenty minutes later I was given to the Wrights. They were in the next room from the birthing room with my biological grandparents.

'They were introduced to each other as the Smiths and the Joneses. My parents were told that my mother and father were seventeen-year-old kids who had been intimate the night of the senior prom, that both of them were honor students headed for college.'

Alvirah broke off a piece of crusty bread and dipped it in olive oil.

'I'm a good detective,' she said. 'I'm going to look into this for you.'

As Delaney watched, Alvirah's hand went to the lapel of her jacket. She turned on the microphone in her sunburst pin.

'Oh, Alvirah, you don't have to be bothered recording this. It's sweet of you, but it's hopeless.'

'We'll see,' Alvirah said matter-of-factly. 'Delaney, do you know where in Philadelphia you were born? What was the name of the midwife? What was her address? Who introduced your parents to the midwife? Did the midwife say where your birth mother lived?'

'My adoptive mother...' Delaney's voice trailed off. It was so hard to talk about Jennifer Wright, who had been so loving to her all these years, in those terms.

She began again. 'Six years ago I wrung it out of her, that I was born in Philadelphia, which of course I knew because of my birth certificate. She said the midwife's name was Cora Banks. She gave me the address of her house. The woman who told her about Cora was a friend from her college days. That woman, Victoria Carney, died in a car accident when I was ten years old. I met her a number of times. She was very sweet. She never married and her niece discarded whatever files she had. Mom was so upset that day I asked about it that I told her she was the only mother I ever knew or wanted to know.'

'Alice Roosevelt Longworth's mother died

shortly after she was born,' Alvirah observed. 'Her father was President Theodore Roosevelt. He married again when Alice was two years old. When she asked about her birth mother, that was exactly what she said.'

Delaney's smile was wistful. 'I remember reading that somewhere. Thank God it jumped into my head that day. But I wasn't being honest. I do want to find my real mother.'

She corrected herself quickly. 'I mean my birth mother.'

Alvirah's hand grazed the lapel of her jacket, turning off the microphone. 'Let me put my thinking cap on,' she said decisively. 'And anyhow, the pasta is here.'

They all looked on in anticipation as the waiter brought over steaming bowls of linguini with white clam sauce for Alvirah and Delaney, and spaghetti and meatballs for Willy.

Willy knew that it was time to change the subject. 'To think that this used to be one of Frank Sinatra's favorite restaurants,' he said. 'He'd be one hundred years old now. His songs sound a lot better than what is popular today.' He looked around. 'Speaking of popularity, it looks like this restaurant is doing just fine.'

He changed the subject again. 'Delaney, Alvirah tells me you'll be covering the Betsy Grant trial. What do you think her chances are of getting a not guilty verdict?'

'Slim,' Delaney said. 'In fact I wouldn't be surprised if she's getting pressure to accept a plea deal.'

'Do you think she would take it?' Willy asked.

'Absolutely not. She should take her chances at a trial. I have a feeling that a lot more will come out about Ted Grant's son, Alan, than we know now. The gossip is that he's very, very broke.'

Delaney continued, 'As everybody knows, when there's a murder, the first question they ask is, "who benefits?" His father's untimely departure from this life solves all of Alan Grant's financial problems. And of course the money his stepmother, Betsy, would have inherited all goes to him if she's found guilty.'

'I've thought of that,' Alvirah agreed.

'And something else,' Delaney added. 'The word around the courthouse is that Robert Maynard may have been a hot-shot defense lawyer in his day, but his day is past. He's still traveling on his reputation because of getting some high-profile crooks off and still gets huge fees, but he is leaving the case preparation to inexperienced young lawyers in his firm.'

'We'll find out soon enough,' Alvirah said, as she unsuccessfully tried to wrap linguini around her fork and ended up dropping it back in the bowl.

7

Anthony Sharkey, better known in certain circles as 'Tony the Shark,' looked at the diamond-and-emerald bracelet he was fingering. He was in his small apartment in Moonachie, New Jersey. It was in the basement of a two-story frame house which, like his apartment, had an overall soiled and tired appearance.

The carpet under his feet was grimy, the walls desperately in need of fresh paint, the smell of mildew ever present in the air.

Tony was a heavy drinker and a compulsive gambler. No amount of treatment had managed to curb his thirst or his need to roll the dice. Sometimes after a stint at a safe house he had stayed clean for about a year. But then it would begin again. He'd lose the job he had, manage to find work as a busboy or window washer, and end up broke. That meant going to a shelter, and nothing was worse. Then he'd manage to get sober again and land another crummy job, rent a dump like this and barely have enough cash to feed himself.

His usual solution was to engage in a series of minor thefts, just enough to keep his head above water, pay his rent and head for the casinos in Atlantic City a few times a month. He was usually good at blackjack but lately he'd been having a streak of bad luck and he needed money.

He had a unique system of stealing that was a joke on the people he chose as his targets. There was almost no safe he couldn't open, especially those dopey crackerjack boxes that people kept in their bedroom closet. He never cleaned the safes out. That was because of his keen understanding of human nature and how people think. If somebody opened the safe and it was empty, they would know immediately what had happened and call the police. But when some broad looks in the safe and only one piece is missing, even if it's the best piece, she blames herself and starts trying to figure out when was the last time it was worn, and where it might have been left. After all, no thief in his right mind would leave all the other good jewelry behind, right? Wrong!

Whenever he did a job, he was careful to not disturb anything in the safe. If he had to move some stuff to get to the piece he had selected, he put it back exactly where it was. Most people never even reported to the cops that a diamond necklace or a pair of earrings was missing. They kept hoping they'd misplaced it and it would turn up.

Some of the lucky ones had insurance coverage for 'mysterious disappearance.' They just don't know that I'm 'Mr. Mysterious Disappearance,' Tony thought.

He looked ten years older than his age, which was thirty-seven. His medium brown hair was already streaked with gray and leaving his forehead rapidly. His shoulders were stooped and his light brown eyes were bleary even when he wasn't drinking.

He again counted all of the emeralds and diamonds in the bracelet. A fence once had told him he could get thirty thousand dollars for it. Of course it was probably worth a lot more than that, but thirty thousand was nothing to sneeze at. Tony had told the fence that he'd think about it. But something had warned him to hang on to it. And the initials on the clasp didn't help. 'BG and TG.' How cute, Tony thought.

Now that the Betsy Grant trial was coming up, would it be worth his while to get in touch with her and tell her what he knew about the night her husband was murdered?

The trouble was that if he produced the bracelet, he'd have to explain how he got it, and as sure
as God made little fishes, he'd end up in prison.

8

The offices of Robert Maynard occupied three
floors of the gleaming tower that was the newest
and most expensive building on the Avenue of
the Americas.

When it was obvious that the prosecutor was
treating her as a suspect in Ted's death, Betsy had
asked her estate lawyer Frank Bruno to recommend a criminal defense attorney to her. It was
only later that she realized that Bruno was convinced that she had murdered Ted. That was why
he put her in touch with a seventy-five-year-old
who had the reputation of being one of the best
criminal defense lawyers in the country. And one
of the most expensive.

Betsy stepped off the elevator on the forty-ninth
floor, where a receptionist in a black suit and
pearls received her with a gracious smile. 'Good
afternoon, Mrs. Grant. Mr. Maynard's associate
will be right down to escort you to the conference
room.'

Betsy knew that Mr. Maynard's associate was a
young lawyer whose fee was eight hundred dollars
an hour. She also knew that a second associate
would be in the conference room and that after
she was seated, Robert Maynard would grace her

36

with his presence.

This time he kept her waiting for ten minutes. During that time the young lawyer who escorted her in ... what was his name? Oh, yes, Carl Canon ... tried to make small talk.

'How was the trip in from New Jersey?'

'The usual. It's seldom bad in the middle of the day.'

'I'm from North Dakota. I went to NYU for both college and law school. The minute the plane landed at Kennedy Airport the first time, I knew I was home.'

'My guess is that North Dakota can be pretty cold in the winter.' More meaningless conversation.

'North Dakota was trying to figure out a way to attract more tourists. Someone came up with the bright idea that they rename the state North Florida.'

He is a nice young man, Betsy thought, even though he is costing me eight hundred dollars an hour and the clock is ticking as we discuss the weather.

She turned in her chair as the door of the conference room opened and Robert Maynard, accompanied by his other shadow, Singh Patel, walked in.

As usual Maynard was impeccably dressed, this time in a gray suit with a faint pinstripe. His white shirt, cuff-linked sleeves and subtle tie, a blend of deep blue shades, gave off the appearance of well-groomed success. His rimless glasses enhanced chilly gray eyes. His expression was usually dour, as though someone had asked him to carry an impossibly heavy load on his back.

'Betsy,' he began, 'I'm so sorry to keep you waiting but I am afraid I have to ask you to make an important decision.'

What decision? Betsy asked herself frantically. Her lips could not form the words to ask that question.

Maynard did not help her. 'You have met Singh Patel?' he asked.

Betsy nodded.

Maynard sat down. Patel laid the file he had been carrying on the table in front of him, then took his own seat. Maynard looked at Betsy.

His voice was now measured, as though to let every word sink in. 'Betsy, I know we have discussed this many times, but now that we are on the eve of trial we must address this one final time. You have always insisted on going to trial, but I ask you to listen to what I am going to say. The evidence against you is very strong. There is no doubt that the jury is going to sympathize with all that you endured, including that your husband cursed you and assaulted you at the dinner table the night before he died. But we can't escape the fact that the six people who were there heard you scream and sob that you "can't take it anymore," you "can't take it anymore." These people are going to testify for the prosecutor.'

'He hit me because of the Alzheimer's,' Betsy protested. 'That didn't happen too often. It had just been a very bad day.'

'But you did say, "I can't take it anymore"?' Maynard persisted.

'I was so upset. Ted had been doing comparatively well. That's why I thought he would enjoy seeing some of his friends from the office. But it only enraged him.'

'Be that as it may, Betsy, after the guests left you were alone in the house with him. You claim you may have forgotten to turn on the alarm system, which could be construed as a way for you to suggest that an intruder might have entered the house, but the caregiver is going to testify that the alarm was on the following morning. The caregiver suddenly became ill and had to go home. In the morning she was fine. What caused her too convenient illness? Financially, you stood to greatly benefit by your husband's death. You were also seeing another man while your husband was still alive.'

Maynard adjusted his glasses. 'Betsy, I have to tell you that the prosecutor called me this morning and offered you a very generous plea agreement which I strongly advise you to accept.'

Betsy felt her mouth go dry. Her body stiffened. 'You *strongly* advise me to accept?' Her voice was a hoarse whisper.

'Yes,' Maynard answered firmly. 'I have managed to persuade the prosecutor to allow you to plead guilty to aggravated manslaughter with fifteen years in prison. You would have to serve about twelve years before parole. I know how difficult that would be. But if you are convicted of murder, your minimum sentence is thirty years without parole. And the judge could give you up to life in prison.'

Betsy stood up. 'Twelve years in prison for something I didn't do? I am not guilty of my husband's murder. I would have taken care of him until he died a natural death.'

'Betsy, if you are truly innocent, then of course you must go to trial,' Maynard said. 'We will present the best possible defense that we can. But please be aware that you will be gambling with very grave odds.'

Betsy struggled to keep her voice calm. She and Robert Maynard had been on a first-name basis, but now she did not want that suggestion of warmth to be in what she was about to say. 'Mr. Maynard,' she began, 'I have no intention of saying that I killed my husband. I loved him dearly. I had eight wonderful years with him before the Alzheimer's began and there were still many good days in the early years of his illness. As you may know, the younger a person is when it sets in, the more likely he is to die within ten years. Physically as well as mentally, Ted was slipping rapidly. The doctors felt that it was time to put him in a nursing home. I didn't do that. I kept him home because in his few lucid moments he was so happy to be with me.'

The words crowded her throat. 'I believe I can convince a reasonable jury of that fact. I have already paid you an enormous amount of money to defend me. So *do* it! And don't convey to the jury that you believe that they will come in with a guilty verdict.'

She wanted to slam the door on her way out but did not. Instead she went down in the elevator to the lobby and out to the sidewalk, unaware of the bustling pedestrians going in both directions around her.

It was one hour later before she realized that her seemingly aimless walking had brought her uptown. She was on Fifth Avenue in front of St. Patrick's Cathedral. She hesitated, then went up the steps. A moment later she was kneeling in the last pew in silent prayer. 'I'm so frightened. Please help me' were the only words that went through her mind.

9

Jury selection took five days. Many prospective jurors had been excused because they could not commit to the three to five weeks the trial was expected to take. Others had told the judge that they had already formed opinions about Betsy's guilt or innocence. Most expressed the view that based upon the extensive media coverage they thought she was guilty. In the end, the final fourteen jurors, seven men and seven women, had all indicated that while they had read about the case, they could start from the beginning without any preconceived beliefs and be fair to both sides. The judge had explained to them during the selection process that fourteen jurors would be selected and at the end of the case, just prior to deliberations, two names would be drawn at random and those jurors would be alternates.

It was 8:50 A.M. on Tuesday morning and the trial was about to begin. Eighteen months had elapsed since Dr. Edward Grant had died.

Delaney sat with other reporters in the front row, which was reserved for the press. The court stenographer was already seated at her station.

The door opened and the defendant, Betsy Grant, entered the courtroom, her head held high, flanked by her three attorneys. The lead prosecutor, Elliot Holmes, the chief of the trial section and a twenty-year veteran of the office, was already seated at the state's table.

Delaney had seen television clips and Internet photos of Betsy Grant, but she was still surprised at how young the forty-three-year-old defendant appeared.

Betsy was wearing a navy-blue suit with a light blue camisole. Her jewelry consisted of a narrow pearl choker and matching earrings. Delaney had heard through the grapevine that Robert Maynard had advised her to dress conservatively and had specifically warned her not to wear the forty-thousand-dollar solitaire diamond that had been her engagement ring. He had told her that it would be appropriate to wear her wide gold wedding band, telegraphing to the jury that she was loved by her husband and was in deep mourning for him.

Next Delaney studied Robert Maynard. He carried his seventy-five years well, she thought, with his silver hair and military carriage even while he was seated. His two associates looked to be in their early thirties.

The visitor pews were already packed, not surprising because of the notoriety of the case. Two sheriff's officers stood at opposite ends of the courtroom.

Exactly at 9 A.M., the clerk proclaimed, 'All rise for the court,' and Judge Glen Roth exited from his chambers and stepped onto the bench.

'Good morning, counsel,' he said. 'This is the matter of *State v. Betsy Grant*. We are about to begin the trial. Are you both ready to proceed with your opening statements?'

'Yes, Your Honor,' they both replied.

The judge turned his head toward the sheriff's officer standing by the jury room door and said, 'Please bring in the jury.'

The fourteen jurors filed into the jury box. Judge Roth greeted them and told them that the attorneys would now begin their opening statements. He explained that whatever the attorneys said to them was argument, and not evidence. He told them that because the prosecutor has the burden of proof in a criminal case, the prosecutor would proceed first with his opening statement. Then he looked toward the prosecutor and said, 'You may begin.'

'Thank you, Your Honor,' Elliot Holmes said as he rose from his chair and walked toward the jury box.

'Good morning, ladies and gentlemen. My name is Elliot Holmes and I am a chief assistant prosecutor in the office of the Bergen County prosecutor. During the next couple of weeks I will be presenting to you witnesses and other evidence in the matter of *The State of New Jersey v. Betsy Grant*. The judge has already informed you of the charges, but it is appropriate during the opening statement that the prosecutor read to the jury the indictment that has been returned by the grand jury.'

Delaney listened as Elliot Holmes read from the indictment that, on or about March 22nd, eighteen months ago, Betsy Grant did purposely or knowingly cause the death of her husband, Dr. Edward Grant. 'This, ladies and gentlemen is a murder charge.'

In a conversational tone, addressing the jury, Holmes said the evidence would show that Betsy Grant had married Dr. Edward Grant, a widower, nearly seventeen years ago. 'The state does not dispute that for a very long time it was a happy marriage. Dr. Grant was a successful orthopedic surgeon and the couple lived a very comfortable lifestyle in their home in Alpine. You will hear that the defendant was a high school teacher and took a leave of absence about two years before Dr. Grant died.

'But the evidence will further show that, tragically, about eight years ago, Edward Grant began to display symptoms of forgetfulness and severe irritability which were totally inconsistent with his prior behavior and his prior demeanor. Neurological testing resulted in a devastating diagnosis – early onset Alzheimer's disease.

'It was devastating for Dr. Grant because it quickly advanced, and within months he was no longer able to function as a surgeon. As the years went by, tragically, he was no longer able to function in any independent way. He lived at his home in Alpine with Betsy Grant and was attended to by a caregiver who in his final years bathed him, dressed him, and fed him.

'This diagnosis and steady decline were also, of

44

course, devastating for Betsy Grant. Again, the state does not dispute that this was a happy marriage for a long time. But the evidence will show that this tragic diagnosis and the ever-increasing decline of Edward Grant resulted in Betsy Grant wanting it to end. And when it ended, she would inherit half of his substantial estate as a co-heir with Alan Grant, his thirty-five-year-old son from his first marriage. And she would also be free to pursue a personal life that had so very much changed while he was ill. You will hear, ladies and gentlemen, that during the two years prior to Edward Grant's death, the defendant had been quietly but regularly seeing another man.

'The evidence will further show that on the evening before Edward Grant died, Betsy Grant invited Edward's son and two other doctors, who had been in the surgical practice with him, along with their wives, to have dinner at their home. You will hear from these witnesses that during the evening Edward Grant was agitated and angry and did not recognize his former colleagues. You will hear that as they sat at the dinner table Edward Grant suddenly and without provocation lunged across the table, and as Betsy Grant tried to restrain him, he slapped her in the face. You will hear that Edward Grant was taken to his bedroom by his caregiver and one of the doctors. This bedroom was located on the first floor of the home and the caregiver's bedroom was adjacent to it. During these last months of acute decline Betsy Grant had also moved to a room on the first floor, rather than sleeping upstairs in the master bedroom. They calmed him down and he was given an appropriate sedative. His caregiver then prepared him for bed and he went to sleep.

'You will further hear that Betsy Grant, bruised and shaken from this forceful slap, remained at the table and sobbed, "I can't take it anymore. I just can't."

'You will also hear that the doctors and their wives and Edward Grant's son, Alan, left soon thereafter. The caregiver will testify that she ordinarily would have stayed overnight in a room adjacent to where Edward Grant slept, but that she suddenly felt ill and left to go to her own home at about 9 P.M. She will tell you that Betsy Grant assured her it would be all right if she left and that she would take care of her husband if he needed any assistance.

'Ladies and gentlemen, the caregiver will tell you that she felt better the next morning and that when she went back to the home at approximately 8 A.M. the alarm system was on. She will tell you that she immediately went to check on Edward Grant and that he was lying in his bed as if asleep, but was lifeless and cold to the touch. She immediately dialed 9-1-1 and rushed to Betsy Grant's bedroom to tell her what she had found and that she had called the police.'

Elliot Holmes paused. 'Ladies and gentlemen, the events that morning and in the next couple of days revealed that Edward Grant did not die of natural causes. You will hear from the responding police officer, who will tell you that he did not observe any obvious injuries on Edward Grant and that he had been told by Betsy Grant and the caregiver that his physical and mental condition had recently greatly deteriorated. The officer appropriately reached out to Dr. Grant's primary physician, who confirmed this information.

'You will hear that Edward Grant's body was picked up by Paul Hecker, the director of the Hecker Funeral Home, and transported there. Mr. Hecker will tell you that as he prepared the body for embalming, he noted that at the back of Edward Grant's head his skull appeared to be extremely soft, not bloody, but extremely soft, which he recognized as an indication that there had probably been serious injury to that area, possibly from blunt force. This, ladies and gentlemen, was the first sign that Dr. Edward Grant had not died from Alzheimer's disease, had not died from natural causes.

'The medical examiner will testify that he received the body from the funeral home and conducted an autopsy. He will tell you that in his medical opinion Edward Grant died from blunt force trauma to the back of his head, which in turn caused fatal internal brain bleeding. He will also explain to you that sometimes with this type of injury, there is no actual external bleeding, which is why the injury was not first noted.

'Ladies and gentlemen, Edward Grant died sometime in the hours following the guests leaving and the time that his caregiver found him the next morning. During that night and into early the next morning, apart from Edward Grant, there was one other person and only one other person in that home. And that, ladies and gentlemen,' turning and pointing toward the defendant, 'was Betsy Grant,' he exclaimed.

'Ladies and gentlemen, you will further hear that the home security alarm was on and fully operational the following morning and that there was no sign of forced entry into that home. No broken windows, no broken locks.

'Ladies and gentlemen, you will hear many more details. What I have presented to you is an outline of the state's case. I submit to you that when you have heard all of the testimony, you will be satisfied beyond a reasonable doubt that the defendant Betsy Grant murdered Edward Grant. She murdered him to escape the circumstances that his illness had caused and to go on to a new and much better life.

'I will have another opportunity to address you in my summation at the conclusion of the case. Again, the state thanks you very much for your willingness to serve.'

Holmes returned to his chair.

Judge Roth looked over at Robert Maynard and said, 'Sir, you may begin.'

Delaney watched intently as Robert Maynard got up and walked toward the jury box. That was a pretty strong opening statement, she reluctantly acknowledged to herself.

Robert Maynard began, 'Ladies and gentlemen, if the evidence was as simple and as powerful as the prosecutor just made it out to be, then you might as well just start deliberating now. Just find her guilty and we can all go home.

'What you didn't hear in the prosecutor's opening statement is that Betsy Grant was an utterly devoted wife and companion to her husband, Edward Grant. She certainly had assistance from the caregiver that the prosecutor referenced, but the undeniable truth is that for seven years, during which there was an unrelenting decline in his physical, mental and emotional condition, Betsy Grant was always, always there for him.

'You will hear that she had been advised by doctors and by friends to put him in a nursing home. As his legal guardian she had the authority to do so, but she wouldn't do that to him. You will hear that his illness had caused him to be both physically and emotionally abusive to her well before that last evening. But she had continued to treat him with love and kindness and understanding. After you hear *all* of the evidence, you will be satisfied that when Betsy Grant said, "I can't take it anymore," the last thing on her mind was ending his life. She had this other option when the burden became too great, as perhaps it did that night,' he said softly, 'an option she could have exercised years before, but she loved him and she knew he wanted to be at home. And that option of putting him in a nursing home was still completely available to Betsy Grant when she said, "I can't take it anymore." And no one would have blamed her. So why in the world would she have killed him?

'Ladies and gentlemen, the prosecutor cannot produce one witness who can testify that he or she saw what happened to Edward Grant. If an object was used to strike him, they don't have that object. You will hear that there were four keys that would open the front door of the Grant home but only three have been accounted for. You will hear that there is no way to know for sure how many people knew the alarm code. I submit to you that it is very

49

plausible that someone else went into that home that night, turned off the alarm and later left that home, resetting that alarm.

'I also leave you with one thought that I believe you should keep in your minds during the trial. Betsy Grant was not the only heir to Edward Grant's estate. You will also hear that Alan Grant, who had many crushing financial pressures, stood to inherit half of his father's fifteen-million-dollar estate. If Betsy Grant is convicted, he inherits it all. Either way, the death of Edward Grant makes Alan Grant a wealthy man. And you will hear that the prosecutor's investigation into Alan Grant was negligible at best.

'Ladies and gentlemen, I look forward to speaking to you again at the end of the trial. I remind you that Betsy Grant does not have to prove her innocence, although we will vigorously challenge the state's evidence. As in any criminal case, the state's burden of proof is beyond a reasonable doubt, which means that the jury must be firmly convinced that the defendant is guilty. The evidence that you will hear will not begin to approach that burden.'

10

After Robert Maynard sat down, Judge Roth said, 'Prosecutor, call your first witness.'

The first witness for the state was Alpine police officer Nicholas Dowling, who had been the first to arrive at the scene. Thirty years old and a five-year veteran of the department, he was obviously a little nervous on the stand, this being the first time he had ever testified at the county courthouse.

Of medium height and build, with short brown hair and a boyish face, he wore a uniform that was impeccably crisp. After being sworn in, he sat down on the witness chair.

Responding to the prosecutor's questions, he explained that he had been on motor patrol on March 22nd of last year. A few minutes after 8 A.M., he had been dispatched by headquarters to the home of Dr. Edward Grant. The dispatcher had told him that the caregiver had called to say she believed that Dr. Grant had died in his sleep.

Less than a minute later, he had arrived at the Grant residence.

'Had you ever been to that home before?' the prosecutor asked.

'Yes. A couple of months earlier I was on duty and dispatched at about four o'clock in the morning. On that date, I was met at the door by a woman who introduced herself as his wife, Betsy Grant.'

'How was she dressed?'

'She was wearing a bathrobe.'

'What was her demeanor?'

'She was calm but obviously distraught. She said that her husband had fallen while trying to climb over the gate that led to the upstairs. Mrs. Grant told me that she and the caregiver couldn't lift him up to get him back into bed.'

'Did she tell you at that time what his physical

and mental condition was?'

'She told me that he was in an advanced stage of Alzheimer's disease and his physical and mental health had substantially deteriorated.'

'What did you do then?'

'Mrs. Grant walked me to the staircase area where he was lying on the carpet and moaning. The caregiver, Angela Watts, was crouched on the floor holding his hand and trying to comfort him.

'The caregiver told me she had heard him fall, but that he was more shaken up than injured. I asked her and Mrs. Grant if they wanted me to call an ambulance. They both said no, they didn't think it was necessary. I then proceeded to assist him in getting to his feet and we walked him into his bedroom and put him to bed. I waited for a few minutes to make sure that everything was okay and I was told that he had drifted off to sleep.'

'Do you have any other recollection of the demeanor of Mrs. Grant at that time?' Elliot Holmes asked.

'Well, as I was leaving, she thanked me. She was calm and seemed very sad and tired. She remarked that it was so hard to watch her husband in this condition compared to what he used to be like.'

'Directing your attention back to March 22nd, what happened when you arrived at the home?'

'I was met at the door by the caregiver, the same lady I had met a couple of months before. She told me that she thought that Dr. Grant was dead and that Mrs. Grant was in the bedroom with him.'

'What happened next?'

'She led me into a bedroom which was located on the first floor.'

'Was it the same bedroom you had helped him to a couple months earlier?'

'Yes, it was.'

'What did you observe as you walked in?'

'Dr. Grant was in the bed, lying flat on his back. His head rested on a pillow. The blanket was pulled up to his chest area and his arms were on top of it. He was wearing a long-sleeve pajama top. Mrs. Grant was sitting on the edge of the bed and caressing his hair and face with her hand. She looked up as I entered and just shook her head. I asked her if she could move aside so that I could check his vital signs. She did so.'

'What was your observation?'

'He was not breathing and he was cold to my touch. Based upon my training as a police officer, which includes EMT certification, I concluded that he was deceased.'

'Did you observe any injuries on his face or hands?'

'No, I did not.'

'Did you observe any blood or any other signs of injury?'

'No, I did not.'

'Did you observe any signs of a struggle or other indication of force?'

'No, I did not.'

'Did you examine the back of his head?'

'No, I did not.'

'Did you have any reason to believe that he had any injury to the back of his head?'

'No, I did not. As I said, there was no blood or

any other indication that he had suffered trauma.'

'And you had been there a couple of months before. Is that correct?'

'Yes.'

'And you were aware that he was very ill. Is that correct?'

'Yes.'

'And under all of these circumstances, did you believe that he had died of natural causes in his sleep?'

'Yes, I did. I had absolutely no reason to suspect otherwise.'

'What did you do next?'

'As per my police training and procedure, I asked his wife for the name of his treating physician so that I could contact that person. Mrs. Grant gave me that name and I called Dr. Mark Bevilacqua.'

'Did you speak to Dr. Bevilacqua?'

'Yes, I did. I explained all of the circumstances and then the doctor asked to speak to Mrs. Grant. She got on the phone and said that he had been very agitated before he had gone to sleep the previous evening at approximately nine o'clock.'

'What happened next?'

'I got back on the phone with the doctor and he said that he believed Dr. Grant had died of natural causes and that he would sign the death certificate. I then spoke to Mrs. Grant regarding which funeral director she wanted to contact so that his body could be moved to the funeral home. She told me that she would contact Hecker Funeral Home in Closter.'

'What happened after that?'

'I stayed at the Grant residence for the next hour waiting for the funeral director to arrive.'

'Where was Mrs. Grant during this hour?'

'She stayed in the bedroom with Dr. Grant. For the most part she was on the phone. I remember that she called his son and a couple of other people.'

'Where in the house were you during this hour?'

'I stayed just outside the door of the bedroom so that I could give her some privacy.'

'During the hour that you were waiting for the funeral director, did anyone else arrive at the home?'

'Yes, a lady came in and said that she was the housekeeper. She said her name was Carmen Sanchez.'

'What was her reaction when she was told that Dr. Grant was dead?'

'She appeared to be very sad. She said, 'God rest him. His suffering is over.'

'During this hour, what was the demeanor of Betsy Grant?'

'Very calm. She was not crying, but she was very somber.'

'What did you do when the funeral director arrived?'

'I spoke to him briefly and he said he would take care of the body. I heard him explain to Mrs. Grant and the caregiver and housekeeper that it would be better for them if they waited in another part of the house as he and his assistant prepared the body for removal.'

'Judge, I have no further questions,' Elliot Holmes said.

Judge Roth looked at the defense table. 'Cross examination, Mr. Maynard?'

After a final quick glance at his legal pad, Maynard rose and approached the witness box.

'Officer, you testified that you were at the home a couple of months prior to Dr. Grant's death. Is that correct?'

'Yes, sir.'

'And would it be fair to say that Mrs. Grant was very concerned for her husband that evening?'

'She appeared to be.'

'And did it appear that Dr. Grant was well cared for?'

'Yes, it did.'

'And did Mrs. Grant express to you when you were leaving how sad she was for him that he was suffering like this?'

'Yes, she did.'

'Did she ever say that first time that she was angry to be in this situation?'

'No, she did not.'

'Did she appear to you to be tired in the sense of being worn down?'

'Yes, I would say so.'

'But she never expressed anger or resentment, did she?'

'No, she did not.'

'And she helped you and the caregiver lift him off the floor and get him back to bed, didn't she?'

'Yes.'

'And she was comforting him as you helped get him back into bed, wasn't she?'

'Yes. She was.'

'Now let's go to that morning when you were

again called to the home. You were met at the door by his caregiver, is that correct?'

'Yes.'

'At any time while you were there did the caregiver express to you any suspicion regarding Mrs. Grant or any doubt about his death being from other than natural causes?'

'No.'

'Did you observe the interaction between the caregiver and Mrs. Grant?'

'Yes.'

'Did you observe any apparent tension between them?'

'No, I did not.'

'Would it be fair to say that they were comforting each other?'

'Yes. They were.'

'Did you observe any tension between Mrs. Grant and the housekeeper?'

'No. I did not.'

'Would it be fair to say that they were comforting each other?'

'Yes.'

'You have described Mrs. Grant's demeanor as calm. Is that correct?'

'Yes.'

'Would you also describe her as appearing to be quite sad?'

'She appeared to be.'

'Isn't it a fact that she appeared to be really worn out?'

'Yes, she did.'

'Was there anything whatsoever that suggested to you that she may have been in any type of struggle or encounter?'

'No, I saw nothing suggesting that.'

'Was there anything whatsoever from the appearance of Dr. Grant's body to suggest that he had been injured or in any type of struggle?'

'Nothing whatsoever.'

'One final question. Officer, if you had observed anything out of order, what would you have done?'

'If I had suspected foul play, I would have called the on-duty detective at the police station and he would have contacted the on-call detective from the prosecutor's office homicide unit.'

'But none of that happened because you had absolutely no reason to suspect any wrongdoing. Isn't that correct, Officer?'

'That is correct, sir.'

'Your Honor, I have no further questions.'

11

The next witness for the state was Paul Hecker, the funeral home director. He testified that he had been called to the Grant residence by Mrs. Betsy Grant, who had informed him that her husband, who had been very ill with Alzheimer's disease, had passed away in his sleep. He said that he had immediately contacted his technical assistant, who picked up the hearse and joined him at the Grant home a short time later.

Hecker testified that Betsy Grant met him at the door and escorted him into Dr. Grant's bedroom.

A young Alpine police officer stood just outside the room and nodded to him as he entered.

'Is the person you met and who identified herself as Betsy Grant in the courtroom today?'

'Yes, she is.'

'Would you please point her out.'

'She is seated at the table to my right.'

'Would you describe the demeanor of Betsy Grant at that time?'

'She was courteous, very low-key.'

'Describe what you observed in the bedroom.'

'I observed the deceased lying in the bed. He was wearing pajamas.'

'Did you initially note any indication or sign of injury?'

'No, I did not.'

'What did you do next?'

'I explained to Mrs. Grant that it would be better if she and the caregiver, whose name was Angela Watts, left the bedroom so that my assistant and I could remove the body to the hearse that was parked outside.'

'Did they do so?'

'Yes.'

'Can you describe the demeanor of both women as they left the bedroom?'

'Mrs. Grant quietly walked out. The caregiver was sobbing quite loudly.'

'Did you transport the body to the funeral home?'

'Yes, we did.'

'As of that time did you have any suspicion that there had been any trauma inflicted on Dr. Grant?' the prosecutor asked.

'No, I did not. It appeared that Dr. Grant had died in his sleep.'

'When you had been in his room, had you noticed anything at all that was unusual?'

'I wouldn't use the word "unusual." But I had noticed something out of place, for lack of a better term.'

'And what do you mean by that?'

'Well, I knew of course that Edward Grant was a doctor. On the night table next to his bed, mounted on a granite base, there was an old-fashioned mortar bowl that appeared to be from a mortar-and-pestle set. There was a plate with an inscription on the base. It was inscribed, "Hackensack Hospital, Dr. Edward Grant, Honoree."'

'What did you notice about it?'

'The pestle was missing.'

'Sir, I'm not sure that everyone here knows what a pestle is or what it looks like. Can you please tell us?'

'Apothecaries, who were the early pharmacists, would use a mortar and pestle to grind the drugs they were using. In layman's terms the pestle would be similar in shape to a baseball bat, but only a few inches long. It is a somewhat heavy object, rounded at the top and bottom, but heavier and thicker at the lower end.'

'What kind of material were the mortar and the base that you saw made of?'

'Black marble.'

With both hands the prosecutor then picked up an object that had been on a table behind where he had been sitting. He brought it up to the witness and said, 'Sir, I'm showing you what's been marked "State's Exhibit 25" for identification. Have you seen this object before?'

'Yes, sir. I have.'

'And what is it, sir?'

'This appears to be the mortar-and-pestle set, minus the pestle. I note that the inscribed plate refers to Dr. Grant.'

'Is this in the same condition as when you saw it that morning?'

'Exactly the same, sir. The pestle that I noted was missing is still not there.'

'Is it reasonable to assume that the missing pestle was made of the same material?'

'Yes, it normally would be.'

'And heavy enough to be used as a weapon?'

Robert Maynard was on his feet once again. 'Objection. Objection.'

'Sustained,' the judge said quickly.

'How much would a pestle from this type of mortar-and-pestle set generally weigh?'

'It is a hard marble object, likely weighing about a pound.'

'So the pestle would ordinarily be lying with the thick end down in the bowl-shaped mortar?'

'That's right. Again, the fact that it wasn't there is what drew my attention.'

'Mr. Hecker,' the prosecutor continued, 'did you remove the body of Dr. Edward Grant from his bedroom to your funeral parlor?'

'Yes, I did.'

'When did that take place?'

'Shortly after my arrival.'

'You stated that there was a caregiver on the scene?'

'Yes, I was informed that the caregiver, upon arriving at the house and going into Mr. Grant's bedroom and going over to him, realized he was not breathing. She called 9-1-1.'

'Were you informed that the Alpine police officer on the scene had contacted Dr. Grant's personal physician, who agreed to sign the death certificate?'

'Yes, I was.'

'In your mind, as of that time, was there any suggestion or any indication whatsoever of foul play?'

'No, there was not.'

'What happened after Dr. Grant's body arrived at your funeral parlor?'

'We began our usual procedures to prepare the body for viewing and burial.'

'Did you perform these procedures yourself?'

'Yes, with the assistance of one of my technicians.'

'During this process did you observe anything unusual?'

'Yes.'

'What was it that you observed?'

'The back of Dr. Grant's head was very soft to the touch. It was obvious that he had sustained some type of traumatic injury to that area.'

'At that time did you have any idea about how that type of injury could have occurred?

'I immediately thought of the missing pestle.'

'Given the location and the nature, would it have been possible for Dr. Grant to self-inflict the injury?'

'Absolutely not.'

'What did you do then?'

'I ceased working on Dr. Grant's body and called the medical examiner. He immediately responded that he would call the police and send an ambulance to bring Dr. Grant's body to his facility, the county morgue.'

'What happened next?'

'I understand that an autopsy was performed and two days later the body was returned to my establishment for burial.'

'Thank you, Mr. Hecker. I have no further questions.'

Delaney listened as Robert Maynard asked only one question of this witness.

'Are you in the habit of observing the artifacts in a room when your services are engaged?'

'It is something that I have always done automatically. It is in the nature of my work. When I am removing the deceased, I always closely observe the surrounding physical scene.'

Knowing that he could do absolutely nothing with this witness, Maynard said, 'I have no further questions, Your Honor.'

From her seat Delaney looked at Betsy Grant, who appeared surprised that her lawyer had not asked any more questions.

The prosecutor then called Dr. Martin Caruso, the county medical examiner. After summarizing his extensive medical training and explaining that in twenty years as the medical examiner he had conducted thousands of autopsies, he related what he had observed during the autopsy of Dr. Edward Grant. He testified that the deceased's skull had been fractured in four places causing the brain to swell and internal brain bleeding to begin.

'Is there any way Dr. Grant could have fallen and caused that injury to his head?'

'I would say it is almost impossible to have sustained that kind of injury as the result of a fall.'

'Why is that the case?' the prosecutor asked.

'Because if he had fallen and hit his head, the impact of that trauma would have been so severe that he almost certainly would have lost consciousness. And he would not have been able to get back into bed on his own.'

'Dr. Caruso, I represent to you that the evidence in this trial has indicated that a marble pestle, weighing approximately one pound, was missing from the bedroom where Dr. Grant had been sleeping. In your expert medical opinion, was the injury you observed consistent with the victim being struck in the back of the head with this type of object?'

'Yes. The injury I observed could have been caused by a pestle of this size or other similar object. Let me explain. If the victim had been struck by a larger, heavier object, such as a hammer or a baseball bat, there would have been much more severe external injury and substantial bleeding. An injury from a much smaller object, such as a pestle, will cause internal injury to the brain, but often there is no external bleeding.'

'Was there any external bleeding here?'

'No, there was not.'

As the questioning went on, Delaney tried to analyze the reaction of the jury to the testimony they were hearing. She noticed that the eyes of several of them shifted to look at Betsy Grant. Tears were slipping quietly down her cheeks as she absorbed the reality of the blow to her husband's head.

Delaney listened as Robert Maynard asked just a few questions of the medical examiner. It was clear to her that the witness had undoubtedly established that Edward Grant had died from a blow to his head, not the result under any circumstances of an accident.

When questioning of the witness ended, it was nearly one o'clock. Judge Roth turned to the jury and told them that it was time for the lunch recess. 'Ladies and gentlemen, we will resume at two fifteen. During this break do not discuss the testimony among yourselves or with anyone else. Have a very pleasant lunch.'

When the proceedings resumed, the prosecutor called Frank Bruno, the lawyer handling Dr. Grant's estate. Approximately sixty years old, with a reserved and serious demeanor, he explained that after the death of Dr. Grant's first wife, their son Alan Grant had been the sole heir to his father's estate. Dr. Grant had revised his will after he married Betsy Ryan, then designating both as equal co-heirs except that the home and its contents would solely remain with Betsy. He had also provided that if he ever became incapacitated, Betsy Grant would have power of attorney to make legal, financial and medical decisions for him.

Under further questioning by the prosecutor, he testified that the current value of the estate, apart from the home and contents, was about fifteen million dollars. He further stated that two non-family members, Angela Watts and Carmen Sanchez, had received bequests in the will. Each was left twenty-five thousand dollars. Bruno did not know if either was aware of her bequest before Dr. Grant died.

Robert Maynard then began cross-examination.

'Mr. Bruno, how old is Alan Grant now?'

'He is thirty-five years old.'

'And would it be fair to say that for various reasons he has had over the last many years severe financial pressures?'

'I would say that that is accurate.'

'And is it fair to say that his father gave him a great deal of financial assistance?'

'Yes, he did.'

'Is it also fair to say that a little over a decade ago his father had become very impatient with his lifestyle?'

'Yes, he had. His only employment was as a commercial photographer, and it was not very steady.'

'Do you know if Betsy Grant expressed an opinion on this scenario?'

'Yes, she did. She felt strongly that his annual gift or allowance should be limited to one hundred thousand dollars a year, which was less than half of what he was used to receiving.'

'Did the doctor make that change?'

'Yes, he did.'

'If you know, what was Alan Grant's reaction?'

'He was furious and barely spoke to his father for months after that.'

'What were his feelings toward Betsy?'

'He blamed her for his father's decision and

immensely resented her.'

'Mr. Bruno, you are an expert in estate law. Is that correct?'

'I would certainly hope so after thirty-five years in this practice.'

'If a person is convicted of the intentional killing of another person, can that person inherit from the victim?'

'No, that person may not profit from homicide.'

'So, Mr. Bruno, if Betsy Grant is convicted of murder, Alan Grant becomes the sole heir, is that correct?'

'That is correct.'

Robert Maynard then looked at the jury and half-smiled. 'Mr. Bruno, would you just remind us again what Alan Grant would get if Betsy is convicted.'

'He would receive the entire estate, which apart from the home is valued at fifteen million dollars. He would also receive his father's half share in the Alpine home, which is now worth approximately three million dollars. Finally, he would receive all of his father's personal possessions, such as jewelry and clothing.'

'Thank you very much, sir,' Maynard said.

Prosecutor Elliot Holmes stood up. 'Your Honor, it is now after three o'clock. I know there will be a mid-afternoon break. I request that the state be permitted to call our next witness tomorrow morning.'

'That's fine,' Judge Roth replied. After again cautioning the jurors not to discuss the case and not to read or listen to any newspaper or media coverage, the proceedings ended for the day.

12

Robert Maynard had ordered a car to take Betsy home. 'I'll pick you up at eight o'clock tomorrow morning,' he said, 'but I thought you'd want a little quiet time on the way home this evening.'

'Yes, I would. Thank you,' Betsy said softly. As the door closed, she was aware of cameras taking pictures of her, and they continued as she was driven away. She leaned back and closed her eyes. The day in court seemed unreal to her. How could anyone really believe she would harm Ted? She realized that her mind was always crowded with memories of the early days with him. The day they met when she was his patient after she broke her leg ice-skating. It was a nasty break, and in the emergency room of Hackensack Hospital they had sent for him to set it.

She remembered how he had seemed to fill the room with his presence. He was holding the X-rays of her leg in front of him. 'Well, you really did a job on yourself, Betsy,' he said cheerfully. 'But we'll fix you up as good as new.'

She had been twenty-five then and a history teacher at Pascack Valley High School in Hillsdale and living a few miles away in Hackensack. She soon learned that Ted was a widower living in Ridgewood, also a few miles away. Their attraction to each other had been mutual and strong. They were married a year later.

Alan was in his freshman year at Cornell and had welcomed her with open arms. As much as he missed his own mother, he knew that I was making his father happy again, Betsy thought bitterly. But ever since I persuaded Ted to cut back on the money he was giving him, the truth is he has hated me. He knows perfectly well that I would never hurt his father.

Unconsciously she shook her head. Her mouth went suddenly dry and she reached for and opened the bottle of water in the holder beside her. She again was thinking of the day Ted took her over to see the house in Alpine. When Ted made his cash offer, the realtor said the owner would be willing to close in two weeks. On a beautiful spring morning only twelve days later, it became their new home.

For eight years we were so happy there, she thought. And then it began. The little signs. They started around the time Ted was fifty-one.

The early signs were his forgetfulness. Suddenly Ted became easily upset over trifles. A patient rearranging a scheduled visit irritated him terribly. He began to forget dates they had made socially. He was complaining he had too much on his mind, and it was obvious he was becoming depressed. But it was when he was driving and could not remember the way home, even when they were only in the next town, that she knew something was terribly wrong.

The car had cut over to the Palisades Parkway and they were now approaching Alpine. Betsy knew that Carmen would be preparing dinner. She thought she was looking forward to being without company, but when she arrived, three of her former fellow teachers from Pascack Valley were waiting for her. As each in turn hugged her, Jeanne Cohen, who was now principal, said fervently, 'Betsy, this is going to be ancient history. It's awful that you have to go through it. Everyone who knows you saw the way you took care of Ted.'

'I hope so,' Betsy said quietly. 'I was beginning to sound like a monster in court.'

They had been waiting for her in the living room. She thought of all the good times they had had together here. Outside the shadows were lengthening. It felt as though they were gathering over her. She glanced at the club chair that had been Ted's favorite place to sit. The last time he was in it was the last night of his life. But when they had gathered here before dinner, he had gotten up, come over to her and reached for her hand. He had pleaded, 'Betsy, help me find it.'

An hour later he had become violently upset. But in that single moment of clarity, it had seemed to her that he was trying to tell her something.

13

With rapt attention Alvirah and Willy watched and listened to Delaney's report on the events at the Betsy Grant trial. When it was over, they looked at each other. Willy spoke first. 'It looks like today did not go very well for Betsy Grant.'

'It's only the first day,' Alvirah said hopefully.

'That prosecutor really knows how to lay it on thick.'

'Are you still sorry you're not covering the trial?' Willy asked.

'Oh, I'll start going just as a spectator when the defense part of it starts. But Willy, there's something else I really want to focus on. Delaney has such a terrible need to find her birth mother. And now that her adoptive parents have moved away, she really thinks it's her opportunity to do it without feeling as though she is hurting them.'

'That doesn't make much sense,' Willy said.

'Yes, it does,' Alvirah said. 'When she was back and forth to the house, Delaney knew that Jennifer Wright considered it a personal rejection if Delaney brought up the adoption. They obviously lied on the birth certificate when they put their names in as the parents. So let's see what I can find out. You know I'm a pretty good detective.'

Alvirah still could not get used to using a computer. She had a gift for making mistakes as she tried to do research online. But she was determined to see for herself the wording on Delaney's birth certificate. With some help from Willy, she finally got the information she wanted; only it wasn't nearly enough. It simply said that twenty-six years ago at 4:06 P.M. on March 16th a female named Delaney Nora Wright had been born. The place of birth was listed as 22 Oak Street in Philadelphia. The mother and father's names and address were listed as James Charles Wright, 50, and Jennifer Olsen Wright, 49, living in Oyster Bay, Long Island.

'Willy, the only information the Wrights could

71

give Delaney was the name of the midwife, Cora Banks, and where the birth took place, at 22 Oak Street. Delaney told me there were four listings for Cora Banks in the Philadelphia area. She said she called each one of them, but they were all much younger than midwife Cora Banks would be today, and they all claimed that they had no knowledge of her.'

Willy printed out the information on the birth certificate. Alvirah reviewed it and stared at it, her expression gloomy. 'This is not as helpful as I thought it would be.'

Willy said, 'I think I can look up that address online and see what's there.'

The aerial shot showed an industrial building situated among smaller houses on Oak Street.

'Looks like the house that was 22 Oak Street was torn down,' Willy said.

Alvirah sighed aloud her disappointment. 'Well, that just makes my job harder. But look at it this way, Willy, I've always said that before I die, I want to see Philadelphia again. Let's drive there in the next few days.'

14

At nine thirty the following morning the trial resumed.

'Your Honor,' said Elliot Holmes, 'the state calls Alan Grant.'

The entrance door to the courtroom opened,

and the jury and spectators watched closely as the murdered doctor's son walked slowly toward the witness stand. Handsome, wearing an obviously expensive navy-blue sports jacket and gray slacks, with an open-collar shirt, he was sworn in and took the witness stand.

The prosecutor asked a number of questions about Grant's background. He had graduated from Cornell University, was a professional photographer, was divorced from the mother of his two children and also had a ten-year-old son from a previous relationship.

Holmes then delved into the Grant family relationships.

'Were you happy about the marriage between your father and Betsy Ryan?'

'Very much so,' Alan answered quietly. 'My father was only forty years old when my mother died. For the next two years I knew he was very lonely. When he met Betsy and then married her a year later I was delighted.'

'Were you present for dinner the night your father was murdered?'

'Yes, I was.'

'Who else was there?'

'Betsy, of course. It was my father's birthday and she invited the two other doctors in the orthopedic practice they had started with my father, and their wives. Dr. Kent Adams, his wife, Sarah, and Dr. Scott Clifton and his wife, Lisa, were there.'

'Describe your father's behavior that night.'

'At first it was very calm. He seemed happy to see everyone, even though I don't think he actually recognized us. He may have had flashes of being vaguely aware of who we were. It's hard to say.'

'Did your stepmother comment on his behavior?'

'Yes, she did. She said that for the last two days he had been very upset and opening drawers and spilling their contents on the floor and throwing books off the library shelves. She said that she was going to call off the dinner, but then that morning he woke up and was very gentle and calm so she went ahead with it.'

'When you arrived, did you see a bruise on her face?'

'Yes, I did. She had tried to cover it up with makeup, but it was still discernible.'

'Did you ask her about it?'

'Yes.'

'What did she tell you?'

'That my father had punched her two days ago.'

'Did she seem angry?'

'No, I thought she seemed resigned.'

'Did your father's behavior change during the course of the evening?'

'Yes it did. At first we had cocktails in the living room. Of course he did not have one. But just before we were to go in for dinner, he suddenly became very agitated.'

'What did he do?'

'All of a sudden without saying anything he became very distressed and started pointing at all of us.'

'And then what happened?'

'Betsy went over to him and put her arms around him and tried to soothe him. He immediately became calm.'

'What happened next?'

'We had a very pleasant dinner. He was very quiet and ate quite well. Then just as we were about to have coffee and dessert Dad quickly got up and literally lunged across the table toward where Dr. Clifton and his wife Lisa were seated.'

'What happened then?'

'Betsy grabbed Dad's arm to stop him and he turned and slapped her face. It was a very hard slap. She fell back in her chair and began to sob. Dr. Clifton, Angela, the caregiver, and I took Dad back to his room. He suddenly went limp as though he was exhausted. Angela gave him a pill to calm him down. We got him into his pajamas and put him into bed. After a few minutes, he closed his eyes and his breathing became even. He fell asleep.'

'At that time what did you do?'

'I noticed that Angela was very pale and I asked her what was wrong. She told me she must be getting some sort of bug because she was having terrible stomach pains.'

'What was your response?'

'I suggested that she go home.'

As he spoke, it seemed to Delaney that the pain on Alan Grant's face was too obvious to be faked.

'What did she do?'

'She said that if she didn't feel better soon, she would have to leave.'

'Mr. Grant, were you familiar with the furnishings in your father's bedroom?'

'Yes, I was.'

'On the night table next to his bed was there any display, award or decoration?'

'Yes. There was a mortar-and-pestle set. It was an award he had been given by Hackensack Hospital. I was at the banquet the night he received it.'

'When you were in your father's room that night, do you recall if the pestle was present?'

'Yes, I do. I am absolutely certain it was present. Dr. Clifton, Angela Watts and I were all talking to Dad, trying to calm him down. I very clearly remember pointing to the award and saying to him something like "Dad, it was so much fun that night when we went to the awards dinner. You gave such a great speech." Who knows if he understood a word I was saying. But the whole time I was talking I was looking back and forth between him and the award.'

'And the pestle was present in the mortar bowl?'

'Yes, definitely.'

'Going back, after you suggested that Ms. Watts go home, what did you do next?'

'I went back to the dining room. Dr. Adams had put a cold cloth on Betsy's face. She was still sobbing at the table – holding the cloth.'

'Did your stepmother say anything to you?'

'She said "I can't do it anymore. I'm sorry, I just can't take it anymore."'

'And what was your reaction to that statement?'

'I was sorry for Betsy. My father had just struck her. She was overwrought.'

'Did you in any way consider her statement "I can't do it anymore" as a threat to your father?'

'At the time I did not. Not at all. Later on I began to wonder if it had been a threat.'

'When did you learn that your father had died?'

'The next morning.'

'Who told you of his passing?'

'Betsy phoned me.'

'How would you describe her emotional state based on how she sounded on the phone?'

'Very matter-of-fact.'

'Do you remember her exact words?'

'Yes, I do. She said, "Alan, Dad passed away last night. I'm sure you will believe as I do that it was a blessing."'

'How did you respond?'

'Of course, my first reaction was great sadness. But then I said something like "The father I knew has not existed for the last several years at least. You know how I feel, Betsy. I am glad that his suffering is over."'

'At that time did you suspect there might have been foul play?'

'Absolutely not.'

'What was your reaction when you learned that his body had been sent to the medical examiner's office?'

'I was incredulous. I thought there must be a mistake.'

'When you learned that he had been the victim of a fatal blow to the back of his head, what was your reaction?'

Alan Grant looked directly into the eyes of the prosecutor. 'My immediate thought was that Betsy must have delivered that blow.'

Robert Maynard jumped up yelling. 'Objection, Your Honor, highly improper and prejudicial.'

'Sustained,' Judge Roth immediately responded. 'The answer is stricken. The jury will disregard it.'

'I'll rephrase. Describe your father's behavior during his last six months.'

'His behavior had been increasingly difficult during that time. The night before he died Betsy's words "I can't take it anymore" seemed to me to be an expression of despair.'

'How would you characterize your relationship with Betsy Grant since your father's death?'

'For the first twenty-four hours, very close. We were consoling each other and making plans for the funeral.'

'At what point did that friendly relationship with Betsy Grant cease?'

'When I learned that my father's skull had been crushed by a blow and that the pestle was missing from the set by the side of the bed.'

'When did you learn that your stepmother had been seeing another man?'

'I only learned that after my father's death.'

'What was your reaction?'

'Shock. Outrage. Disappointment.'

'In the months leading up to your father's death, what was Betsy Grant's demeanor toward him?'

'Very loving. Very compassionate. It had been suggested by his doctor that she should consider putting him in a residential facility.'

'Why did the doctor suggest that?'

'He felt that my father was in danger of having a serious accident.'

'Can you give me an example?'

'Dad would wander upstairs to the top floor and lean over the railing. He would pull things out of the drawers in the bedroom.'

'What was Betsy Grant's reaction to the doctor's suggestion?'

'She fenced off the entrance to the second floor and moved downstairs to sleep in the bedroom that had been used as a maid's quarters by the previous owner. In other words, she tried to keep him under her control.'

'Objection,' Maynard shouted.

'Your Honor, I would like to ask Mr. Grant what he means by "keep him under control,"' Holmes responded.

'I will allow him to explain,' the judge said quietly.

'Sir, would you please explain your answer.'

'Of course. What I meant was that she was trying to protect him from being injured.'

'Was it Mrs. Grant's decision to keep your father at home even after receiving the advice from the doctor?'

'Yes, it was.'

'Did she give any reasons for that decision?'

'She said that my father needed her. She said that there were times when he was lucid. At those times he begged her to stay with him. She also told me that someone with my father's diagnosis of early onset Alzheimer's disease usually would not be expected to live much longer than the seven years he had already endured.'

'But then, the night your father was administered the fatal blow that took his life, didn't Betsy Grant wail, "I can't take it anymore"?'

'Objection. Leading question.' This time one of Maynard's associates spoke up.

'Sustained,' the judge said once again.

Elliot Holmes turned to look at the jurors. Delaney could see that he had made the point he wanted to make. 'No further questions, Your Honor,' he said quietly.

'Mr. Maynard,' Judge Roth said, 'you may begin your cross-examination.'

'Thank you, Your Honor,' Maynard replied. 'Mr. Grant, how old are you?'

'I'm thirty-five.'

'When you finished college, did you go to any type of graduate school or did you go straight to work?'

'Straight to work.'

'So that means you've been working for thirteen years?'

'Yes.'

'What type of work do you do?'

'I've always been a freelance photographer.'

'By freelance you mean you are not on salary? You're only paid when you get work. Is that correct?'

'Yes.'

'What is the average annual amount of money you have earned over the years?'

'Typically between fifty and eighty thousand dollars.'

'And is it true that from the very beginning of your career, you were getting financial help from your father?'

'Yes. He loved me. I was his only son and he wanted to help me.'

'So how would he help you? Would he give you money every time you asked or was there some other arrangement?'

'When I got out of college and in the few years after that, I often needed to buy new camera equipment, lenses, filters, etc., to help me get work. Usually when I asked for help my father would say yes.'

'Did that arrangement change?'

'Three or four years after he married Betsy, she persuaded him to help me once a year. At Christmas my father would give me a check for one hundred thousand dollars.'

'And you have received this one-hundred-thousand-dollar Christmas check every year up to and including this past Christmas?'

'Yes, I have.'

'Okay, so one hundred thousand at Christmas and in an average year you earned sixty-five thousand, which means you typically have had one hundred sixty-five thousand dollars per year to address all of your expenses. Is that about right?'

'Yes.'

Delaney scribbled notes as over the next few minutes Maynard delved deeply into Alan Grant's financial life. She found herself wishing she had paid closer attention in the one accounting course she had taken in college. If Maynard was trying to establish that Grant's personal finances were a mess, he certainly succeeded.

In response to Maynard's questions Grant admitted that he had an expensive divorce and alimony commitment with the mother of his two children, and child support payments for his other child. His father had bought him a condominium when he graduated college, but he had taken out a home equity loan. The payments on that loan were due monthly, as were his maintenance on the condo, health insurance payments, and car and garage payments. His rather high routine living expenses included three vacations per year. Grant reluctantly agreed that his expenses of nearly eighteen thousand per month substantially exceeded the one hundred sixty-five thousand dollars available to him each year.

Maynard continued.

'Did your father ever talk to you about changing careers?'

'He told me that the photography did not pay enough and the work was too sporadic. He wanted me to find another career that would insure a stable income.

'Did you follow his advice and seek another career?'

'No.'

'Let's go back to your financial deficits that we identified. To make ends meet, have you taken out any other loans?'

'In addition to the money I borrowed against my condo, friends have also given me loans.'

'Are you paying interest on these loans?'

'I pay interest to the bank for the condo loan. Most of my friends agreed that I could pay the interest and principal on their loans when I got my inheritance.'

'You testified earlier that you received the annual gift last Christmas even after your father's death. Is that correct?'

'Yes. I spoke to the estate lawyer, who requested of the chancery court that this disbursement be approved.'

'And Betsy Grant did not object to this disbursement. Did she?'

'I did not speak to her. The estate lawyer did. He informed me that she did not object.'

'Three months ago did you make an additional application to the chancery court for another disbursement?'

'Yes, I did. Because the estate is frozen pending the outcome of this trial, I cannot receive my inheritance. I was advised that I could make an application for a partial disbursement because of my expenses.'

'And how much did the court approve?'

'One hundred fifty thousand dollars.'

'Mr. Grant, you stand to inherit one half of a fifteen-million-dollar estate if Betsy is not convicted, and you will inherit the full fifteen-million-dollar estate if she is. Is that correct?'

'That is my understanding, sir.'

'Mr. Grant, let me take you back eighteen months to when your father was alive. Is it fair to say that you were in desperate financial straits but also the heir to a multimillion-dollar estate that would be distributed when your father died?'

'Yes, but I loved my father and I had nothing to do with his death.'

Delaney watched Alan Grant squirm in his chair as he answered the questions. He was clearly uncomfortable.

'Mr. Grant, after the birthday dinner for your father, where did you go?'

'I went back to New York City. I had plans to meet someone at a bar close to my home.'

'What time did you get there?'

'About 10 P.M.'

'How long did you stay there?'

'A couple of hours. I left around midnight.'

'You met a former girlfriend there. Is that correct?'

'That is correct.'

'What is her name?'

'Josie Mason.'

'Did you leave together?'

'Yes, we did.'

'Where did you go?'

'We went to her apartment a couple of blocks away.'

'Did you stay that night at her apartment?'

'Yes I did.' Alan's face turned red and angry. 'I know where you are going, Mr. Maynard. My whereabouts are totally accounted for from the time I left my father's home until the next morning when I received the call from Betsy that my father had passed away. The bar has a surveillance camera and so does her apartment building. The prosecutor checked out all of that.'

'Of course he did,' Maynard said sarcastically. 'Tell me, Mr. Grant, did you know the code to the alarm system in your father's home?'

'No, I did not.'

'Is there any reason why you didn't know it?'

'It just never came up.'

'Did you ever have a key to your father's home?'

'No, I did not. Again, it just never came up.'

'So in the event of an emergency at the home, you didn't have a key and you didn't know the alarm code.'

'Like I've told you already, it just never came up. There were always other people there, the housekeeper, the caregiver. There was no specific need for me to have a key or know the code.'

'You saw your father fairly frequently, didn't you?'

'Yes, at least every couple weeks including when he was sick.'

'Your father even in the last couple of years did have lucid moments. Is that correct?'

'Yes, I treasured them.'

'Did you ever ask him in these lucid moments what the alarm code was?'

'Absolutely not.'

'The evidence will show that one of the several house keys has not been accounted for. It was your father's key.'

'I know absolutely nothing about that key.'

'Your Honor,' Maynard said with a tone of sarcasm, 'I have no further questions of this witness.'

'Okay,' the judge replied. 'We'll take the lunch recess.'

15

Delaney had been quietly taking notes throughout the morning. It was always her habit to eat in the courthouse cafeteria, where many of the spectators gathered, and try to overhear their opinions on the testimony they had heard. Neither Betsy Grant and her attorneys nor the prosecutor and his assistants were in the room.

The cafeteria was noisy, but she chose a small table adjacent to one where five women she had seen at the trial were discussing the events of the morning. They all had gray hair and appeared to be well into their seventies. Because of the noise, they were all speaking in loud voices. What she heard was not unexpected. 'I think she did it,' one woman was saying. 'I mean I'm almost positive she did it. My grandmother had Alzheimer's and my mother almost had a nervous breakdown taking care of her. Nana was the sweetest, gentlest, most fun person you would ever know. But toward the end she was suspicious of everybody, thought my mother was trying to kill her, and spitting out her medicine. It was a mercy when she died because then we could remember how wonderful she had been, and have many a laugh over how funny she was.'

'Was your mother ever tempted to kill her, Louise?'

'Oh, of course not,' Louise answered in a shocked tone.

'But you believe Betsy Grant did kill her husband?'

'Yes, I do. I mean, think about it. Her husband got the Alzheimer's when he was about fifty years old. She was only thirty-three. You could tell she was at the end of her rope. If you ask me, Betsy Grant is a really nice person, but she just snapped.'

A third woman at the table spoke up. 'And don't forget, not only would she inherit a lot of money, but she was seeing another guy. I read somewhere that love and money are two of the biggest reasons why people get murdered. And Betsy Grant had both those reasons.'

A fourth woman was shaking her head. 'What about the son? His father spoiled him rotten and then Betsy talked him into limiting his allowance. It sounded like he's in debt up to his eyeballs. He only gets out of debt when his father is dead.'

'But they looked into him, and he was definitely in the city overnight.'

'Couldn't he get someone to do it for him?'

'He would need to know the alarm and he would need to have a key.'

'And he didn't know before that night that the caregiver was going to all of a sudden get sick and go home.'

'He's no prize, but I don't think he was involved.'

'Let's take a vote. Did she do it or did he do it?'

Delaney winced as she heard the vote go four to one against Betsy.

The first two witnesses at the trial that afternoon were the wives of the two doctors who accompanied their husbands to the dinner party the night Edward Grant died. In essence they simply repeated what Alan Grant had testified earlier about that evening.

The third witness was Josie Mason. In her early thirties, she testified that she had been dating Alan Grant on and off for the past two years. On March 21st of last year she met him at a bar in New York City at about 10 P.M. He told her that he had dinner at his father's home earlier that evening. She stated that at approximately midnight they walked to her apartment a few blocks away and that he spent the night with her.

Mason said that she was absolutely certain that he had not left her apartment during the night. She said that he left at about eight o'clock the next morning. She further indicated that detectives from the prosecutor's office had come to the superintendent of her building and had obtained surveillance tape showing them walking into her building that night and him leaving the next morning.

When court was adjourned, Delaney went straight to the office to prepare for the 6 P.M. broadcast. She reviewed the film footage of Betsy Grant entering the courthouse and leaving it. The late afternoon film showed the stress on Betsy Grant's face and the slump of her carriage.

She looks as though she's too tired to stand up straight, Delaney thought with a sudden rush of compassion. I hope to God that some friends will be there for her when she gets home.

16

Betsy's housekeeper, Carmen Sanchez, was the first witness on the stand the next morning. Her hands clammy, her voice quivering, she stated her name and her hometown and answered initial questions about how she came to be the housekeeper at the Grants' home in Alpine.

'I started working for Dr. Ted right after his first

wife died,' Carmen answered.

'How long ago was that?'

'Nineteen years ago.'

'And how many years after you started working for Dr. Ted Grant did he remarry?'

'Two years later.' Without being asked, Carmen said enthusiastically, 'You can't imagine the difference in Dr. Ted. He was so happy. His first dear wife had been ill with cancer for many years.'

'Ms. Sanchez, please answer only the question you are asked,' the judge directed.

'Oh, I'm sorry,' Carmen said apologetically. 'It's just when I think about Dr. Ted and Miss Betsy and the way they looked at each other–'

This time the judge's voice was a little more firm. 'Ms. Sanchez, again please do not elaborate on your answers.'

'Oh, Your Honor, I'm so sorry,' Carmen apologized. She looked at the prosecutor and sighed, 'I knew I wouldn't be good at this.'

'Ms. Sanchez, the evening before Dr. Grant's death, were you all at the house?'

'Yes, Miss Betsy was having a birthday dinner for Dr. Ted and I cooked and served it.'

'At some point during the evening, did Dr. Grant get very upset?'

'Yes, but I was in the kitchen when it happened. I heard the commotion and I ran to the dining room. I could see he was very upset and then Dr. Clifton, Alan Grant and Angela took him to the bedroom.'

'What did you do next?'

'Well, Dr. Ted had fallen against the table and some of the plates and glasses were broken. I cleaned up the mess and I said I would bring out coffee and cake, but nobody wanted it. I finished up and left. By then the guests were starting to say good-bye and I think they left right after me.'

'Were you aware that Angela Watts went home at some point during the evening?'

'Yes, she didn't feel well and wanted to sleep at her own house.'

'Did Mrs. Grant ask you to stay over because Angela Watts would not be there during the night?'

'I offered to stay over, but she thanked me and said it wasn't necessary.'

'Ms. Sanchez, what time did you enter the Grant home the morning of Dr. Grant's death?'

'I always arrive right around eight thirty.'

'Was 8:30 A.M. the time you arrived on the day Dr. Grant was found dead?'

'Well, I got stuck behind a school bus, so it was about twenty of nine.'

Carmen glanced her way and Betsy gave her an encouraging smile. Oh, God help her, Betsy thought.

The prosecutor continued. 'You arrived at the house at 8:40 A.M. the morning that Dr. Grant was found dead?'

Just answer the question, Carmen thought. 'Yes, I did.'

'When you entered the house, who was there?'

'The police officer was in the bedroom. So was Angela Watts, the caregiver. And so was Miss Betsy. Angela told me that Dr. Ted was dead.'

'What did you do then?'

'I went upstairs to the master bedroom.'

'Why did you do that?'

'I wanted to help. It was the only thing I could think of. I was sure that Miss Betsy would want to go back to her old bedroom now that Dr. Ted was gone. I knew she would be much more comfortable upstairs.'

'What did you do in that room?'

'I changed the sheets. Made sure her bathroom was in perfect order. I dusted and I vacuumed.'

'Before the morning when Dr. Ted was found dead, when was the last time you were in that room?'

'Oh, I always went up once a week to be sure that it was kept up.'

'So, when was the last time you actually attended to that room before Dr. Grant's death?'

'I cleaned that room only the day before.'

Carmen paused. She was about to volunteer that she had remembered there had been some dirt on the rug, but she also remembered the judge's warning to only answer the question. I don't know how I missed seeing that dirt on the carpet the day before Dr. Ted died, she thought. But I think I know what happened. The window washing people were in right after I vacuumed the week before.

'After you finished tidying the room, what did you do?'

'I went downstairs and made coffee. I tried to get Miss Betsy to have something to eat, but she would only take the coffee. Angela and I stayed with her in the breakfast room when the funeral director took away Dr. Ted's body.'

'What was Mrs. Grant's demeanor?'

'What?' Carmen asked.

'What was Mrs. Grant's emotional state at that time?'

'She was so quiet. She stood at the window watching Dr. Grant's body being placed in the hearse.'

'Did she say anything to you?'

'She said, "It's over. Thank God it's over."'

I didn't say that, Betsy remembered. I said, 'Thank God *for him* it's over.'

'No further questions,' the prosecutor said.

Robert Maynard stood up. 'No questions, Your Honor.'

Judge Roth turned to the jury and said, 'Ladies and gentlemen, the testimony for this week is finished. We will resume next Tuesday morning at nine o'clock.'

17

At 8 A.M. on Tuesday a juror called the judge's chambers and very apologetically indicated that she was sick with bronchitis. She stated that she thought she would be better by the next day. After discussions with the attorneys about whether to excuse her and continue or cancel the day's proceedings, the judge reluctantly decided to postpone the trial until the following day.

18

The 6 P.M. news that evening was dominated by the breaking story that Steven Harwin, the twenty-three-year-old son of prominent film director Lucas Harwin, had been found dead of a drug overdose in his Soho apartment. The tragedy was compounded by the fact that Steven had survived leukemia when he was in his teens and had become an ardent fund-raiser for leukemia research. He had started a 'Five Dollars a Month' fund that now had three hundred thousand supporters. Only a week before he died, he had spoken at a fundraiser, saying, 'My generation has got to step up to the plate and get involved in helping to find a cure for cancer.'

'What a horrible waste,' Delaney murmured to Don as they sat side by side in the anchors' seats waiting for their signal to go on air.

'I just heard that a guy I went to college with did the same thing,' was Don's quiet answer. 'Thirty-six years old and with two kids. I just wish we could round up all the dealers and ship them to Mars.'

'I do too.'

The commercials were over. 'And now to our sports desk,' Don began as he turned to the sports commentator, Rick Johnson. 'What are the prospects for the Giants this season, Rick?'

When the newscast was over Delaney began her

usual walk home. A lot of times she joined friends for dinner at one of the nearby restaurants, but this evening was not one of them. She wanted some quiet time. Being in her own apartment was always comforting when she was going into one of her 'need to know' episodes of wanting to find her birth mother.

She knew that the periodic craving had resumed when the feature about the reunited son and mother was aired, and it had been deepened by her discussion of the subject with Alvirah and Willy at Patsy's Restaurant. I wonder if Alvirah was serious about doing some of her own research, she thought as she passed Sixth Avenue. Then she smiled involuntarily. If Alvirah Meehan said she was going to do something, she's doing it, she decided. Well, who knows? Maybe she will find some way to trace the midwife.

Immediately cheered by the thought, she turned her mind to the trial. The prosecution was doing a very good job of piling up evidence that certainly seemed to point to Betsy Grant as the murderer of her husband. The defense had a hard sell on their hands with Alan Grant because the prosecution could prove that he spent the night in New York.

But where was the pestle? Delaney asked herself. Granted, Betsy would have had ample time to get rid of it. But where? According to everything that had come out in the newspapers, after he received the call from the funeral director, the medical examiner had contacted the police and reported the suspicious fracture. The police had immediately obtained a warrant and returned to the house, which they searched thoroughly, along with the grounds. But, of course, there had been at least thirty hours between the time that Dr. Grant's body had first arrived at the funeral home, the discovery of his injured skull, the autopsy by the medical examiner, the police application for a search warrant and then the actual search of the home.

What about the housekeeper? There was something about her on the stand. Was it just that she was terribly nervous and trying to rephrase her answers? The way the judge kept reminding her to only answer the questions had obviously rattled her.

As she waited for the light to change, Delaney felt a hand slip under her arm and a familiar voice ask, 'Can I buy you dinner, ma'am?'

Startled, she looked up. It was Jonathan Cruise, whom she had met at a friend's wedding in Boston two months ago. He was an investigative reporter for the *Washington Post,* and they had realized they had much in common. They had gone out to dinner when he was in Manhattan visiting his sister a month ago. He had called to say how much he enjoyed being with her and that had been that. This was the first time she had seen or heard from him since then. But she had thought of him often and realized how disappointed she was that he didn't care enough to call again.

She had changed into sneakers for the walk home and realized how tall he seemed, then remembered that on the two other occasions she had been with him she had been wearing heels, and then he'd been only an inch or two taller. His jet-black hair showed a few slivers of silver, and she remembered that he had told her he probably would have white hair by the time he was forty. 'Happened to my father,' he had said matter-of-factly. 'But maybe it will make me look distinguished.'

All this ran through Delaney's mind as she glanced up at him.

'Jon. Are you in the habit of popping up out of the blue?' she asked.

His smile was warm and easy, brightening a face that in repose could seem stern.

'No, not really. I got in from Washington at five o'clock. I checked the station and knew that you'd be on air tonight. My grand plan was to be waiting outside the studio door when you came out, but the traffic killed that idea. It would have been just my luck if you had plans for tonight. Do you?'

'I guess I do now,' Delaney said with a smile.

19

Alvirah and Willy put 22 Oak Street, Philadelphia, in the navigation system and drove to Pennsylvania.

'Honey, you've got to remember that from the looks of the aerial view, that house is gone,' Willy warned again as the dashboard map showed that they were two miles from their destination.

'That doesn't matter,' Alvirah said, easily dismissing the potential obstacle. 'There's always a way to get information if you just start sniffing around. And don't forget, even if the original buildings are gone, some of the residents from twenty-six years ago might still be in the area.'

It was on the tip of Willy's tongue to repeat the fact that the address was no longer a home but a business of some sort, but he decided against it. It was just that he knew Alvirah was throwing herself heart and soul into finding Delaney's birth mother and knew how disappointed she would be if she failed to do it.

Oak Street turned out to be in a shabby area where older, small one-family homes were gradually being torn down and replaced by warehouse-type businesses.

22 Oak Street was now a three-story building with a sign that read SAM'S DISCOUNT TILE FACTORY. The front window showed displays of tiles of every color and shape. They could see that inside the store there were at least two clerks and four customers.

'Leave it to me,' Alvirah murmured as she pulled open the door.

An older man with thinning hair wearing a pin with the name 'Sam' on it came rapidly toward them.

'Welcome to Sam's Discount Tile Factory,' he said, his voice warm, his smile seemingly genuine. 'What can I do to help you?'

'I'm not going to waste your time pretending to be a buyer,' Alvirah said, 'even though when I looked at those beautiful tiles in the window they made me realize that our kitchen looks outdated.'

Oh come on, Alvirah, Willy thought, we don't

need to redo the kitchen. At least I hope not.

Sam smiled again. 'I hear that from a lot of our customers. They come in because they saw our ad. They think they're just curious but then they decide they really want to redo their kitchen or bathroom. Maybe you're one of those people.'

'Maybe I am,' Alvirah agreed heartily. 'But if you've got just a minute or two...'

Again Sam's agreeable smile. 'Of course.'

'How long have you been here?'

'Sixteen years.'

'Is this the building you bought?'

'No. We bought the two houses next to each other that were for sale, then took them down and put up this building.'

'By any chance do you remember the names of the people you bought the properties from?'

'I remember the name of one of them, Cora Banks. That was some mess.'

'Why?' Alvirah almost could not contain her excitement.

'She had told us that she was an RN. But right after she sold the property to us and before we had taken it down, a policeman showed up with a warrant for her arrest. It seems that she was a midwife who had been delivering and then selling babies.'

'Do you know if she was ever arrested?'

'I don't think she was. She got out of town too fast.'

And that's that, Willy thought.

After thanking Sam for talking to them, Alvirah told him she'd like to take a look at his selection of tiles.

They followed Sam up the stairs to the second floor, where groups of tiles were exhibited, including pictures of how they looked in a kitchen or bath.

It turned out that Sam was a talker. 'Not everyone liked that this neighborhood was changing,' he said. 'Some of them even picketed when they heard that it had been re-zoned for commercial buildings. The woman in the house next door was really upset. She said she'd been here thirty years and didn't want to have a tile factory next door. She was so upset I offered to buy her house too, but she said she would never move out until they carried her out.'

Willy noticed that Alvirah almost dropped the cream-colored tile she was holding.

'Is she still there, Sam?' was Alvirah's next question.

'Oh, you bet she is. Her name is Jane Mulligan. She's a widow now and lives alone. She must be up in her eighties, but whenever I run into her, she tells me again that the neighborhood she grew up in has been ruined.'

Alvirah couldn't wait to see if the neighbor was home. She made herself linger for another few minutes, examining different patterns of tile. She then thanked Sam, promising to think over the several design samples he insisted on giving her.

When they left the store she said fervently, 'Willy, if this Jane Mulligan gives us a lead to Cora Banks, I'll come back here, pick out tiles, and you can redo both the kitchen and the bathrooms.'

When they came to the house next door, Alvirah stopped. 'Willy, in this day and age, if

Jane Mulligan is home, she might be leery about letting people in. You'd better wait in the car.'

Willy knew that Alvirah was right, but he hated to see her go alone into the house, even though there was probably only an eighty-something lady inside it. But knowing that by arguing he would only lose, he reluctantly walked to the curb and got back into their newly acquired, previously owned Mercedes.

After Alvirah rang the bell, she waited a few moments before someone looked through the peephole in the door.

'Who are you and what do you want?' a querulous voice asked.

'I'm Alvirah Meehan. I'm a reporter for the *Daily Standard,* and I am hoping to do a series of articles about changing neighborhoods and the reactions of longtime residents,' Alvirah said, holding up her press card for Jane Mulligan to see.

She heard the click as the door was unlocked. Then Jane Mulligan partially opened the door and looked her up and down. Satisfied, she opened the door wide.

'Come in,' she exclaimed. 'I've got plenty to say on that subject.'

She led Alvirah into a small living room, immaculately clean, with an overstuffed couch, matching club chairs, an upright piano and a round table filled with photographs.

Jane Mulligan invited her to sit down, but first Alvirah took a look at the photographs. Grandchildren, she thought immediately.

'What a handsome group,' she said sincerely. 'Are they your grandchildren?'

'All ten of them.' Now there was pride in Mulligan's voice. 'You couldn't find a smarter and nicer group if you searched the world.'

'I can see why you feel that way,' Alvirah agreed as she settled down.

'What do you want me to tell you about ruining neighborhoods by sticking commercial buildings in them?'

Before Alvirah could answer, Mulligan went into a tirade about how you couldn't find a prettier street than the way this one had been years ago. 'Everybody knew everybody. You left your doors unlocked.'

Alvirah managed to get in a question. 'I understand two houses were torn down to make room for that tile factory. Did you know the people who lived in them?'

'I did indeed. The house two doors over were friends. They sold because they wanted to be near their daughter. She lives in Connecticut now.'

'And the other house?'

'The original owner moved to an assisted living place. The woman she sold it to was a disgrace.'

'What about her?'

'She was a midwife.'

'How long ago was that?'

'About thirty years ago.'

Alvirah did instant math. Then Cora Banks was still in the house when Delaney was born.

'I knew something fishy was going on,' Mulligan said. 'I watched people going and coming, every one of them was the same. One or two people would accompany a pregnant girl into that house and anytime from an hour to eight or ten hours later, they'd come out with the girl, supporting her as she walked to the car.

'It took me a few times to figure out what was going on. The people who left with the baby weren't the same ones who came in with the pregnant girl. At first I thought Cora Banks was running an adoption agency. That went on for fourteen years, but then when that policemen came with a warrant for her arrest I learned that she was selling the babies. I almost died.'

'Do you know where she went?'

'No, I don't. I don't want to know.'

'Did she have any friends who visited her?'

'She pretty much kept to herself.'

Trying to keep the disappointment out of her voice, Alvirah confirmed, 'Then there is no one you can think of who might have been a friend?'

'Who'd want to be a friend to someone who sold babies?' Mulligan asked. 'Cora Banks' social life, if she had any, didn't take place in that house.'

With that Alvirah said good-bye, left and got into the car. 'Let's go home,' she said to Willy.

By the disappointed note in her voice he could tell that she hadn't gotten very far talking to Jane Mulligan. He listened as she gave him a summary of the conversation.

'Then you didn't learn anything that will help Delaney find her birth mother?'

'No, I didn't, but I do know why Jennifer Wright is uncomfortable talking about the adoption with Delaney. She doesn't want her to know they bought and paid for her.'

'Maybe that was the only way they could get a

baby,' Willy suggested. 'They were nearly fifty years old when they got her. Maybe it showed how much they wanted her.'

'I suppose so,' Alvirah admitted. 'But in my opinion it's one thing for a young woman to give up her baby, but it's another thing if she sells it to the highest bidder.'

She paused, then said, 'I'm not going to tell Delaney this. I'll just say it was a dead end.'

'Do you have to give up or are you still going to keep searching for Delaney's mother?'

'Of course I'll keep going,' Alvirah said heartily. 'I know the woman who referred them to Cora Banks is dead, but with any luck she had a big mouth and did some talking to her friends or family.'

'Who are her friends or family?'

'That's for me to find out,' Alvirah said. 'I'll look up her obit notice. It has to name some of her family members. I'll start there.'

They crossed the bridge from Pennsylvania into New Jersey and were on the Turnpike heading into Manhattan when Alvirah suddenly volunteered, 'You know, Willy, I really did love some of those tiles. I mean the pictures of how they'd look in the kitchen and bathrooms were a wakeup call to me. I made myself a promise. If we can track down Delaney's mother, I'm going to do some renovating. But only if we find her.'

Willy sighed. 'Honey, you mean I'll do some renovating and you'll watch.'

Alvirah turned and smiled at him. 'Willy, I've always said you are a deep thinker.'

20

Delaney and Jon walked downtown to Fifty-Seventh Street. Just before they reached First Avenue they went into Neary's restaurant.

'When I was growing up in New York, I came here a lot with my grandfather,' Jon commented as they were escorted to a table. He looked around. 'It's timeless. It hasn't changed.'

'It's my first time,' Delaney confessed.

'Oh, there have been great moments here. It was a favorite place of Governor Carey. He was famous for saying that the Lord changed water into wine and Jimmy Neary reversed the process.'

As Delaney laughed she realized that she felt as though she had known Jon forever. She also realized how absolutely delighted she was that after a month of non-communication, he had suddenly appeared.

It was an evening of getting to know you better. She had told him that she was a court news reporter and absolutely loved the job, but now instead of being the co-anchor fill-in, she told him she was about to become co-anchor of the six o'clock news.

'That's a pretty big promotion,' Jon observed. 'By the way, I remember you like a glass of Chardonnay.'

'And you like a vodka martini,' Delaney volunteered.

She was seated on the banquette. He was across the table looking directly into her eyes.

After he placed the order, Jon began, 'Do I hear a hesitation in your voice about moving full-time to the anchor desk?'

'Not really. It's great. It's just that I've loved being the court reporter. I wonder how many people really understand what it's like to see someone on trial, watching and listening as witnesses put a nail in his or her coffin.'

'You're covering the Betsy Grant trial. I've read about it.'

'Yes, I am.'

'It looks pretty cut-and-dried to me. Alone in the house with her husband. The caregiver suddenly sick, needing to go home.'

'Are you insinuating that Betsy Grant may have slipped the caregiver something to make her sick?' asked Delaney, surprised at the sudden anger that surged through her.

'I don't want to get you mad at me,' Jon protested. 'Delaney, as Will Rogers said, "I only know what I read in the papers."'

Mollified, Delaney nodded. 'Of course you do. I'm overreacting, but being there watching that woman listen to the funeral director and then that stepson of hers, I was cringing for her. When the medical examiner testified about the force of the blow that had killed her husband, she kept shaking her head from side to side as though she was in denial.'

Jon looked at her without answering.

'I can read your mind,' Delaney said defensively. 'Her reaction might be exactly alike whether she was guilty or innocent.'

Jon nodded.

Delaney knew it was time to change the subject. I'm pretty good at being totally objective at a trial, she thought. Why am I going out of my way to become protective of a woman who may very well be guilty of at least manslaughter in the death of a defenseless Alzheimer's victim? There was no answer to the question. The waiter was putting their drinks on the table.

'When I asked you what brought you to New York, you said I did, which is a sweet compliment but not true. What did bring you up from Washington?'

Jon waited until the waiter was out of earshot.

Lowering his voice so much that Delaney strained to hear him, he said, 'Beginning in Washington and up the East Coast to Boston, there is a sophisticated ring of pharmacists who are obtaining illegal prescriptions from doctors and selling them to high-end people like celebrities and Wall Street types. A fortune is being made as doctors see patients for one minute, or not at all, and write them prescriptions for potent opioid pain relievers like Percocet, oxycodone and others. Pharmacists are legally obligated to alert the authorities when they encounter suspicious prescriptions. Some pharmacists just look the other way and make money off filling them. The process creates and supplies thousands of addicts.'

'Were these addicts mostly recreational drug users?'

'Some started that way and got hooked. Others were people taking prescribed medication to relieve pain from real injuries. When their responsible doctors wouldn't write any more scripts, they found other doctors willing to do so. I'm investigating a ring for the *Washington Post*. I know the police have some of the pharmacists and doctors under surveillance in Washington and Boston.'

'You mean they sell to someone like Steven Harwin?' Delaney asked.

'That's exactly what I mean. He was probably on strong pain relief meds during his leukemia treatment. Eventually, he became addicted.'

'Do you have any names in this area?'

'Some. Not too many, but enough for a good start.'

As they were handed menus, Jon said briskly, 'A little more name-dropping. When Bloomberg was mayor, he would phone ahead and tell Jimmy he and Diana were on their way and to put the roast chicken on.'

'That's exactly what I was planning to have.'

After they placed their orders, Jon sipped his martini and Delaney sipped her wine. At their first dinner last month they'd compared their hobbies. When Delaney told Jon that her favorite ones were riding, hiking and skiing, Jon had said, 'The last two I go along with. I never had the opportunity growing up to take riding lessons. Most of the "riding" I did was on subways. My father and grandfather were detectives in the New York Police Department.'

This evening they went deeper, talking about themselves. Jon was two years older. That had come out over dinner last month, but tonight he added, 'I was an identical twin. My brother died at birth. I know my mother has always mourned for him. I see tears in her eyes at my birthday dinners.'

Delaney had told Jon that she was adopted but had not expected to say, 'I wonder if on my birthday my birth mother mourns for me.'

'I'm sure she does.'

It was two hours later that Jon paid the bill and walked her to her apartment. Delaney realized again how comfortable she felt with Jon's arm under hers. While they were at dinner the September evening had become sharply colder.

'Skiing season may be early,' Jon said, satisfaction in his voice.

'I hope so,' Delaney said fervently.

At her apartment building she invited him to come up for a nightcap but he shook his head. 'I'll take a rain check.' He gave her a kiss on the cheek, then as the doorman held open the door for him, he turned and came back to where she was standing.

'Delaney, do you believe in love at first sight?'

He answered his own question before she could: 'I do.'

Then he was gone.

21

Angela Watts, the caregiver, was the next witness. To Delaney she seemed to be just as nervous as Carmen Sanchez had been. After establishing her background and experience as a home caregiver, the prosecutor asked about her relationship with the Grant family.

Unlike Carmen, she answered the questions without embellishment.

'You were the caregiver for Dr. Grant?'

'Yes, I was.'

'How long did you work for him?'

'Three years, two months and four days.'

'What were your hours when you took care of Dr. Grant?'

'I worked six days round-the-clock, then I was off on Sundays.'

'Who took care of Dr. Grant on Sundays?'

'Mrs. Grant.'

'Were you at the house the evening before Dr. Grant died?'

'Yes, there was a small birthday dinner for him.'

'Who was at the birthday dinner?'

'Dr. and Mrs. Grant, Alan Grant and two doctors that Dr. Ted used to work with and their wives.'

'How was Dr. Grant on that evening?'

'During cocktails in the living room, he suddenly became very upset, stood up and started muttering to himself and aggressively pointing around the room.'

'What happened then?'

'Miss Betsy put her arms around him and he quieted down right away. A few minutes later we went in to dinner.'

'Were you seated at the table?'

'Yes, I was. Carmen Sanchez cooked and served the dinner.'

'How was Dr. Grant during dinner?'

'At first, all right. Quiet but all right.'

'Then what happened?'

'He suddenly stood up. His face looked angry and almost twisted. He pushed back his chair so hard it toppled over. He lunged across the table and knocked over a lot of the plates and glasses.'

'What was Mrs. Grant's reaction?'

'She tried to pull him back, but he turned around and slapped her hard in the face. Then the other doctors and his son grabbed him and tried to calm him down. He was very, very upset and crying. As they were consoling him, I suggested that we take him back to his bedroom and get him settled in for the night.'

'And what happened next?'

'Dr. Clifton, Alan and I walked him back to his bedroom.'

'Then what happened?'

'I was about to help him get into his pajamas when all of a sudden I felt sick.'

'Describe your sudden illness.'

'I felt nauseous and light-headed. Really bad.'

'You said this came on suddenly?'

'It hit me like a ton of bricks.'

'What did you do then?'

'Everybody was telling me, "Go home and take care of yourself. We'll get him settled." They asked me if I was okay to drive myself.'

'I told them I was and I left. When I got home I went straight to bed. I fell asleep almost immediately. I woke up at the usual time, 6 A.M. Whatever was wrong with me was over. I felt fine.'

'Do you know if anyone other than Mrs. Grant stayed at the house overnight?'

'Mrs. Grant told me that all of the other guests stayed for about an hour and then they had left when they were sure he was asleep.'

'And that meant that Mrs. Grant was alone in the house overnight with her husband, correct?'

'Yes.'

'Did you come back to the Grant house the following morning?'

'Yes.'

'What time was that?'

'Eight o'clock.'

'Did you have your own key to the front door of the Grant home?'

'Yes, I did.'

'And you knew the four-digit code to activate and shut off the alarm system?'

'Yes, I did.'

'When you arrived at the house the morning Dr. Grant was found dead, was the front door locked or unlocked?'

'Locked.'

'In what position was the alarm system?'

'It was on. I used the code to turn it off.'

'What did you do when you entered the house?'

'I put my coat away and went right to Dr. Grant's room. At first I thought he was still asleep, but then when I went to the bedside, I could see that he wasn't breathing. I touched his neck and face. They were so cold. I knew that he was dead.'

'What did you do when you realized he was dead?'

'I dialed 9-1-1, then I hurried to Mrs. Grant's room to tell her.'

'Was Mrs. Grant still in bed?'

'She was in the bathroom. When I called her name, she opened the door. She had the hair dryer in her hand. She had obviously been drying her hair. I told her Dr. Grant had died in his sleep.'

'What was her reaction?'

'She didn't say a word. She just looked at me. She threw the hair dryer on the bed and brushed past me. I followed her into Dr. Grant's room.'

'What did she do?'

'She put her hands on his face and caressed it.'

'Did she say anything?'

'Yes, she said, "Oh, my poor darling, you won't have to suffer anymore."'

'What was her demeanor?'

'Calm, very calm. She said, "Angela, you said you called 9-1-1?" When I said, "yes," she said, "I had better get dressed." She left Dr. Grant's bedroom without so much as a backward glance at him.'

You make me sound so awful, Betsy thought frantically. I was in shock. For several years I had felt that an axe was swinging over my head. I was watching this wonderful man deteriorate. I had just decided that I had to put him in a nursing home before he hurt himself or me or someone else. I was relieved that he had died before I did that. She bit over the lump in her throat as she remembered how in his rational moments Ted had begged her to keep him home.

'And what happened next?'

'Mrs. Grant got dressed very quickly. She went back into Dr. Grant's bedroom just as the policeman arrived.'

Elliot Holmes paused and said, 'Ms. Watts, let's go back to what happened immediately following the dinner. You testified that you, Alan Grant and Dr. Scott Clifton helped Dr. Grant to his room after he became upset at dinner. Was there any object or decoration beside his bed?'

'Yes, there was.'

'Would you please describe it?'

'It was a mortar-and-pestle set that was part of a plaque that had been given to Dr. Grant as a gift from Hackensack Hospital.'

'And the pestle was an object that could be picked up and removed from the mortar bowl. Is that correct?'

'Yes.'

'Ms. Watts, do you recall if the pestle was on the night table when you helped Dr. Grant into bed after the dinner party?'

'Yes. It was there. It was in the mortar, the bowl.'

'And you are certain of that?'

'Yes, I am.'

'Ms. Watts, I'm now going to ask you some questions in a different area. Did you ever meet a Peter Benson?'

'No, I did not.'

'Were you familiar with that name?'

'Yes, I was.'

'Do you know if Mrs. Grant ever saw Mr. Benson?'

'Yes, I do. I mean she had dinner with him occasionally and she always gave me his cell phone number too in case I needed to reach her and her cell didn't answer.'

'When you use the word "occasionally," what do you mean by that?'

'I'd say it was about a couple of times a month.'

'When was the last time that she had dinner with him?'

'The evening previous to the birthday dinner.'

'Did Mrs. Grant ever talk to you about Peter Benson?'

'No, other than to say that he was an old friend from high school. She never really said much more. But she always seemed to be happy when she was going to meet him.'

'No further questions,' the prosecutor said, the smirk on his face obvious as he exchanged glances with the foreman of the jury.

The courtroom was silent as the prosecutor returned to his seat. Delaney wondered how the defense was going to counteract the testimony from the caregiver. The judge said, 'Mr. Maynard, your witness.'

'Ms. Watts, you indicated that you lived at the home six days a week. You said that this was round-the-clock. Is that right?'

'Yes.'

'When Mrs. Grant went out to meet Peter Benson, what time did she usually leave the house?'

'Usually about four thirty to five o'clock.'

'And what time did she normally return?'

'Usually about ten thirty to eleven o'clock.'

'Was there ever a time that you can remember that she either didn't come home or she stayed out past that hour?'

'Well, to be honest with you, I often fell asleep by ten o'clock. But I'm a very light sleeper and I would usually hear her come in when the garage door went up. But I can't absolutely swear that she never came home later than that.'

'Did she ever tell you that she would not be returning home after one of these dinners?'

'No, she always came home.'

'And she always slept in the little bedroom on the main floor so that she could be close to Dr. Grant if he got up during the night?'

'Yes. She would always help me take care of him if he got up during the night.'

'Ms. Watts, you testified that you had your own key to the front door and that you knew the code to the alarm system. Is that correct?'

'Yes.'

'To your knowledge, did anyone else have a key and know the alarm code?'

'Well, of course Mrs. Grant had a key. So did the housekeeper, Carmen, and they both knew the combination.'

'So that makes three keys. Did anyone else have a key, or were there backup keys?'

'When I started working, there were four keys. Dr. Grant had one. But several years ago he lost or misplaced it. We never found it.'

'Ms. Watts, most modern alarm systems maintain an electronic record that can tell precisely when an alarm was activated and shut off and even which key was used. Could the system at the Grant home do that?'

'No, it was a really old system. It didn't have any of that.'

'Was there ever any talk of upgrading it or replacing it with a new one?'

'I asked Mrs. Grant about that, but she said keeping things the same made it easier for Dr. Grant. When I first started taking care of him, he could unlock the door himself and on good days he could put in the code himself. But in the last couple of years he couldn't do that.'

'Did you ever observe Dr. Grant on a good day put in the alarm code himself?'

'Yes, I did.'

'As he tapped in the four numbers on the alarm box, would he do anything else?'

'Yes. He would say the numbers out loud.'

'Would he say them loud enough for you to hear them?'

'Yes.'

'So you are testifying that during the time you worked in the Grant home there was a total of four keys and the alarm code had been the same for many years. And one of the four keys that could allow someone to gain entrance to the Grant home disappeared several years ago. And Dr. Grant was in the habit of verbalizing the code in a manner that anyone who might have been with him could hear it. Is that correct?'

'Yes.'

Maynard paused for a few moments as he faced the jury. He then turned to the judge and said, 'No further questions.'

22

Steven Harwin's father called a news conference two days after his son's death.

'In his twenty-three years, Steven fought and overcame leukemia, graduated from Bowdoin College with highest honors and started the "Five Dollars a Month" club to get young people involved with giving money for leukemia research. Starting with pain medication during his fight with leukemia, he became a drug addict, a condition he valiantly fought but could not overcome. The pills found in his apartment were potent. I will find the person or people who sold them to him and expose them for the unspeakable swine that they are.'

With that, the director of four Academy Award–winning films choked up and turned away from the cameras.

Delaney was in the studio with Don Brown. Together they watched the on-camera interview.

'I wouldn't want to be the guy who sold the pills to Lucas Harwin's son,' Delaney observed.

'I'd feel the same way if it was my son,' Don said fervently. 'Sean's sixteen, at that age when kids get into trouble. It's a fortune to send him to a private school, and I know that's no guarantee that will keep him away from the drug scene, but last year they expelled a senior from his former school who was selling drugs in the locker room.'

Vince Stacey, the news director, began to count down. At 'one' they were back on the air and Delaney was reporting on the Betsy Grant murder trial.

'The testimony of Angela Watts, the caregiver for the late Edward Grant, was not favorable to Betsy Grant today,' Delaney began, 'particularly when she said that Betsy had had dinner with a former classmate, Peter Benson, the evening before the birthday party.'

She went on to summarize the caregiver's other testimony. 'The alarm was on when the caregiver arrived at the house that morning, a big plus for the prosecution. It certainly makes it much harder for the defense to push the idea that an intruder entered the home.'

'How was Betsy Grant as she listened to that testimony?' Don asked.

'She seemed very calm,' Delaney observed, 'but people do react differently.'

'Great reporting, Delaney. Thanks.' Don turned toward the number one camera. 'Police in New York City are on the lookout for...'

Do they react differently? Delaney wondered as the program went to commercial break. She realized that in her twenty-six years she had not suffered the death of a close family member or friend. Even when her adoptive parents had celebrated her mother's seventy-fifth birthday, she had reassured herself that seventy-five is the new sixty and that both of them might easily live another fifteen to twenty years.

When the program was over, she said that to Don.

'You've had grief in your life,' he answered matter-of-factly. 'Remember how emotional you felt about that segment we aired on the mother and son reunion? What you felt was grief about your own situation, nothing more or less.'

'I guess you're right,' Delaney agreed. 'You're right.'

A thought crossed her mind. It was about a story the network had done six months ago. A two-year-old had wandered out of the house in the middle of the night. The agonized mother had been on camera early the next morning begging help in finding her. The child was found unharmed about a mile away sleeping on a park bench. Delaney vividly remembered the joy of the mother holding the toddler in her arms as she fervently thanked the woman who had found her.

She cheered herself with the hope that maybe Alvirah would somehow, someway bring about that long needed reunion for her.

23

Alvirah had sat in on the trial of Betsy Grant when Dr. Grant's caregiver testified. She didn't get a chance to talk to Delaney, who was rushing back to the studio.

The afternoon had turned warm. She and Willy sipped their five o'clock cocktail on the balcony of their apartment. Reflecting, she looked at the park across the street.

'Willy, how would you feel if you were told that your parents bought you?'

'I guess I'd feel flattered that anyone wanted to pay money for me.'

'But how would you feel if your birth mother, or her parents since she was young, decided to sell you months before you were born?'

'I wouldn't think much of them,' Willy said firmly.

'I wouldn't either. That's what worries me. I mean suppose I do track down Delaney's birth mother. Will Delaney be happy to know that as an infant she was sold like a piece of clothing or an appliance?'

'It's hard to guess. But if her mother was a kid herself, her parents might have thought she'd be too young to take care of a baby.'

'Then why wouldn't they go to a legitimate adoption agency which would screen the adoptive parents carefully?'

'Honey, I agree with you. But on the other hand, weren't the Wrights pretty old when they adopted Delaney? Delaney's twenty-six now and it was just her mother's seventy-fifth birthday. That means she was forty-nine. I know Delaney's father is a year or two older. They've eased the regulations but I'll bet that twenty-six years ago they might have been turned down by a regular adoption agency.'

Willy took a sip of his scotch on the rocks. He

never had a second one so he savored each drop carefully.

Alvirah on the other hand sometimes enjoyed a second glass of wine.

The evening was suddenly turning cooler. 'Instead of a refill here, why don't we go inside?' she suggested.

As always, Willy agreed. When he was seated on his comfortable leather chair, Alvirah took her usual spot on the couch. Willy could see that she was intent on her own thoughts.

A few minutes passed. Willy was keeping an eye on the clock to be sure to watch the six o'clock news and catch Delaney's report on the trial.

Then just before he reached for the remote to turn on the set Alvirah said, 'Willy, I got a good look at Betsy Grant. She's a lovely looking woman but I swear that there was something about her that...' Her voice trailed off.

'What about Betsy Grant?' Willy asked.

'I don't know,' Alvirah said slowly, 'but it will come to me. It always does.'

24

Dr. Kent Adams was the next witness. Sixty-two years old, with every strand of his thinning white hair in place, rimless glasses over mild hazel eyes, his lean frame covered with a gray pinstriped suit, he had an air of poise and confidence.

After he was sworn in, the prosecutor began.

His manner was markedly less aggressive than it had been when he questioned both Carmen and Angela.

Adams testified that he was a surgeon who had been in partnership in an orthopedic practice with Dr. Edward Grant and Dr. Scott Clifton for many years.

'Dr. Adams, did there come a time when you observed certain changes in Dr. Ted Grant?'

'Unfortunately, I did. We all did.'

'What were those changes?'

'Ted had been an outstanding surgeon with a wonderful patient rapport. He was very caring toward all of his patients and he was always cordial and helpful to our office staff. But then there were changes. He started to become forgetful and then he became more and more irritable and impatient with all of us. These changes became more pronounced as the months went by.'

'What did you do?'

'Dr. Scott Clifton and I spoke with Betsy Grant and expressed our concern.'

'What was her response?'

'She was very upset, but not at us. She completely agreed that something was very wrong with Ted and we all decided to speak to him together.'

'Did you do so?'

'Yes, we did. It was very unpleasant.'

'How so?'

'I think it was a mixture of Ted resenting us for raising this issue with him but also a recognition on his part that we were telling him the truth and were very concerned for him.'

'Were you also concerned for the wellbeing of

his patients?'

'Absolutely. Dr. Clifton and I knew that it had to be addressed.'

'What happened after that?'

'Ted reluctantly underwent a thorough series of tests, and the unfortunate outcome was a diagnosis of early onset Alzheimer's disease.'

'What was his participation in the practice, if any, after that?'

'He continued to come to the office on a fairly regular basis, but he did not perform surgery anymore nor was he the primary physician for any patient. As the months went on, the time he spent in the office considerably diminished.'

'Did this affect the rest of the practice?'

'Yes, it did. With Ted no longer an active partici-pant in the practice, it was a time for reevaluation. Dr. Clifton and I had different viewpoints of how the practice should be managed. After much discussion, I decided to leave and set up my own practice. Some of Dr. Grant's patients came with me, and others remained with Dr. Clifton.'

'Approximately how long ago did you split off from the practice?'

'About seven years ago.'

'How did that work?'

'I opened a practice about a mile away, still in Fort Lee. Dr. Clifton stayed in the same location.'

'Did you continue to see Dr. Ted Grant and Betsy Grant after that?'

'Yes, I would visit them at their home.'

'Do you know if Dr. Grant continued to stop in at the original practice where Dr. Clifton had remained?'

'Betsy Grant told me that she still would bring him in to Dr. Clifton's office about once every six weeks. He enjoyed chatting with the staff and just being in his old surroundings.'

'Dr. Adams, I'm now asking you to direct your attention to March 21st of last year, the evening before Dr. Grant was found dead. Where were you on that evening?'

'Well, Dr. Grant's wife, Betsy, had decided to have a birthday party for him that night. My wife and I were invited.'

The prosecutor's following questions elicited the same information that prior witnesses had offered, including the two occasions when Dr. Grant had become extremely upset. Dr. Adams did recall that when Ted Grant had been angrily pointing at everyone during cocktails, he had been shouting something that he believed was the word 'find.'

When asked about Dr. Grant slapping Betsy that evening, he replied that Betsy Grant had been sobbing when she said, 'I can't take it anymore.' He added that it was his perception that when Ted Grant lunged across the table, he had been trying to attack Lisa Clifton.

'Dr. Adams, I have just a couple more questions about that evening. Where was Angela Watts seated at the dinner table?'

'It was a round table. Angela Watts was seated to the right of Ted. His son was seated on his left.'

'Where was Mrs. Betsy Grant seated?'

'Next to Angela on her left and to me on her right.'

'Thank you, Doctor, I have no further questions.'

I can see what he's driving at, Delaney thought. Betsy could have slipped something into Angela Watts' drink to make her sick. But if she were planning to kill her husband, why would she have invited people to dinner that night? But maybe the prosecutor is right. Maybe getting assaulted really did, finally, push her over the edge.

Robert Maynard then stood up. 'Your Honor, I have just a few questions. Dr. Adams, would you say that Betsy Grant was always trying to do something to make Ted happy?'

'Yes.'

'As his health began to steadily decline, would you please describe how she took care of him?'

'She was always concerned and always devoted to him. She was heartbroken by his illness, particularly because for a long time he realized that he was failing. He had been a wonderful husband and an outstanding doctor. But eventually he became completely dependent on Betsy and his caregiver.'

'You have testified that when you were at the dinner party that evening, he assaulted her and that she stated "I can't take it anymore." Did you ever hear her threaten to hurt him in any way?'

'Absolutely not.'

'How did you regard her comment that night?'

'I was so sorry for her. She just seemed weary. She had just been hit very hard. I think she said what anyone would have said under those circumstances.'

Prosecutor Holmes grimaced as Robert Maynard said, 'No further questions.'

Dr. Scott Clifton was the next witness. His testimony was virtually identical to that of Dr. Kent

Adams but it was clear that he was much more reserved and less empathetic in his tone and in his demeanor when he spoke about Betsy. He also stated that he had been very focused on Ted Grant and getting him calmed down and had not taken any notice of the mortar and pestle set. He could not say whether the pestle had been there or not.

When Dr. Clifton was finished, the judge released the jurors until the following Tuesday morning.

25

Alvirah continued on her determined hunt to trace Delaney's birth mother. 'Step two,' she told Willy as they drove to Oyster Bay on the North Shore of Long Island. 'I want to get a good look at the house where Delaney was raised,' she said, speaking over the voice of the navigation system.

'That was "turn right in five hundred feet."' Willy hoped he was right, as he tried to concentrate on directions in the unfamiliar area.

He made the turn and could see the map depicting a straight line for at least a mile even as the mechanical voice said, 'One mile to right turn.'

'I mean this is a lovely area,' Alvirah said admiringly. 'Remember years ago I was offered a Monday-to-Friday cleaning job in a house in Oyster Bay, but it was too inconvenient to get there without a car and you needed our car to get around to your jobs.'

'I remember, honey,' Willy confirmed. 'In those days I never would have believed that we would ever win the lottery.'

'Neither would I,' Alvirah sighed as she visualized her days as a cleaning woman, vacuuming and dusting and dragging heavy sheets and towels down the stairs to basement laundry rooms.

The last turn was to Shady Nook Lane. It was a dead end street with homes on an acre or more of property. The trees were still rich with leaves, and azaleas and chrysanthemums lined the driveways. Several of the houses were handsome brick-and-stucco Tudors, others very large manor-type dwellings with front porches.

Willy had been watching the mailboxes for numbers. 'It's this one,' he said as he slowed down and stopped in front of a long two-story residence.

'That house reminds me of Mount Vernon,' Alvirah said approvingly. Then she added, 'You can tell it's not occupied because there are no curtains. But Delaney told me that it was just sold, so I guess the new people will be moving in soon.'

'I would guess that Delaney was lucky to be adopted by people like the Wrights,' Willy observed. 'With that kind of private adoption it was hit or miss as to the kind of parents she was given.'

'I agree, and now let's go talk to Delaney's old nanny. We're lucky that she still lives on the Island.'

Thirty minutes later they were parking in front of a ranch-style house in Levittown, a community built after World War II for returning veterans.

Bridget O'Keefe, Delaney's former nanny, opened the door herself. A vigorous-looking

127

seventy-eight-year-old with a pear shape and short white hair, she greeted them with hearty warmth and invited them into her living room, where a tray with cups and a plate of cookies was on the coffee table. 'It's always nice to have a cup of tea,' she announced. 'You settle yourselves and I'll be right back.'

She disappeared into the kitchen.

'No wonder Delaney liked her so much,' Willy whispered.

Bridget returned a few minutes later carrying a teapot with steam wafting from the spigot. 'I don't have any use for those teabags,' she announced, 'and when you make real tea you can always read your fortune in the leaves.'

When she had poured the tea and passed the creamer, sugar and cookies, she went directly to the point. 'You are trying to trace Delaney's birth mother.' It was not a question but a statement.

'That's right,' Alvirah confirmed. 'We did manage to find a woman who lived next to the midwife but she has no idea where she is now.' Deliberately she did not mention that the midwife was selling the babies she had delivered.

'I started working for the Wrights the day they brought Delaney home,' she said. 'You couldn't have seen a more beautiful newborn. Most of them aren't that attractive until they fill out but she was beautiful with those gorgeous brown eyes and ivory skin.'

'What did they tell you about her background?'

'Mrs. Wright's friend, Victoria Carney, who had arranged the adoption, had told Mrs. Wright that the mother was very young and that she was of

Irish descent on both sides of the family.'

'You never knew more than that about her real mother?'

'Never. I don't think the Wrights knew more than that either. But from the time she was three years old and knew she had been adopted, Delaney started daydreaming about her mother.'

'Yes, that's pretty much what she told us,' Alvirah said. 'What about the friend who helped arrange the adoption?'

'Victoria Carney was a very nice lady. She died when Delaney was ten years old. I know the Wrights felt terrible about that.'

'That's what Delaney told us. She got in touch with Victoria Carney's niece, but she said that her aunt never talked about any details of Delaney's birth and that she had gotten rid of any papers she had when her aunt died.

'We knew that much,' Alvirah continued, a trace of defeat in her voice, 'and we know that she expressed concern over the midwife who arranged the adoption. Is there anyone else you can think of we may talk to who might have some information about Delaney's background?'

'I've been thinking about that ever since you called me,' Bridget said. She put down her teacup and walked over to the upright desk in the corner of the room. From a drawer she took out a picture. 'I dug this out. I wasn't sure I'd kept it. One day Miss Carney came to the house. She asked me to take a picture of her and her friend Edith Howell, who'd come with her, with Delaney. She told me she had bragged so much to Miss Howell about how beautiful Delaney was, that Miss Howell wanted to take a picture with her.

'Anyway, I took the pictures with Miss Carney's camera, one of Miss Carney holding Delaney and one of Miss Howell holding her. She was nice enough to send me a copy of both pictures. She wrote on the back of them.'

Eagerly Alvirah reached for the pictures. On the back of one was written, 'Delaney and I,' and the date; on the other, 'Delaney, Edith Howell and I.'

The other woman was obviously much younger than Victoria Carney.

'Have you any idea where Edith Howell lived?' Alvirah asked.

'I only know she was Miss Carney's neighbor in Westbury,' Bridget said. 'I looked her up in the phone book. If it's the same Edith Howell, she still lives there.'

It was a slim lead to follow, Alvirah thought with resignation. But if Edith Howell was a neighbor of Victoria Carney, there was always the hope that over a cup of tea or a glass of wine Victoria had confided something about the adoption to her.

She thanked Bridget O'Keefe profusely, then on the way out paused and stopped. 'Bridget, you speak to Delaney regularly, don't you?'

'Yes, I do.'

'Please don't tell her about Victoria Carney's neighbor yet. I mean if she hears about her, she'll get her hopes up and then be so disappointed if it doesn't amount to anything.'

Bridget made the promise, then laughed. 'When we were kids and promised something, we would say, "Cross my heart and hope to die."'

When they were back in the car, Willy said,

'Honey, why not just call this lady now and see if we could drop in for a few minutes?'

'I thought about that,' Alvirah said, 'but I decided it wasn't a good idea. You just heard Bridget say that my call jogged her memory. If I get to talk to Edith Howell, I want to give her time to jog her memory after I tell her why I'm calling.'

'That makes sense,' Willy said even as he noted that the westbound traffic was already thickening. Resigning himself to a long drive home, he turned on the radio and learned there was a traffic accident on the westbound Long Island Expressway and to expect heavy delays.

26

After discussing on the phone the fact that they both liked northern Italian cooking, Jon and Delaney met at Primola's restaurant. It was only their third date but Delaney realized how totally comfortable she was with Jon.

She asked him how the investigation into the drug dealers was going.

'I paid a visit to Lucas Harwin, the father,' he said. 'I told him that I was conducting an investigation for the *Washington Post* about a drug ring in Washington, New York and New Jersey that we believe is selling prescription pills to high-end people. He assured me that he would keep that confidential.'

'How was the father when you talked with him?'

'If you ever wanted to see the face of grief, he was the one to look at. His wife was there. Of the two she seems to be bearing up better, although that isn't saying much. Steven was an only child.

'She told me that she had so looked forward to having grandchildren someday and now it would never happen. She said the overdose didn't just kill Steven, but also the next generation and the ones after that.'

'Did Lucas Harwin have any idea where their son might have gotten the pills?'

'Well, as he said in that statement, these were not the kind you can ordinarily get on the street corners. He almost certainly had a prescription, but the ones that were found in his apartment were in medicine bottles without labels. That suggests that the pharmacy he went to knew enough to keep its name off the bottle. The police are undoubtedly checking Steven's cell phone to see if they can trace any calls to or from a doctor or pharmacist. The Harwin interview will be my first column in the *Washington Post* and will come out tomorrow. It will focus on Steven's life and the impact of his loss on his family, but of course, it's not going to reveal our investigation.'

'What then?'

Jon lowered his voice. 'I'm going to start going to a couple of those clubs where some minor-league celebrities are known to go.'

'Celebrities who use drugs?'

'Exactly. The word gets around among the up-scale users. Some of them are names you would recognize but not the kind who go somewhere with an entourage of bodyguards. I'll try to get on a friendly basis with one or a couple of them in that group and see what happens.'

As the waiter cleared their dishes, Jon asked, 'As much as I could, I've watched your coverage of the Betsy Grant trial on television. Of course, you were objective, but what are your thoughts about her now?'

Delaney paused, then looked directly at him. 'It's like watching a coffin being nailed shut with her in it. The testimony sounds so devastating, every word of it. I mean her outburst after Ted Grant slapped her hard. The caregiver suddenly taking ill. The security system being on. Then Professor Peter Benson, the boyfriend. She had dinner with him the night before her husband's birthday gathering.'

'Is there any chance that he might have done it?'

'Zero. He can absolutely confirm that he was in Chicago at the time of the murder. He was meeting with professors he was recruiting for positions at Franklin.'

'From what you tell me, it doesn't sound as though it's going well for Betsy Grant.'

'It isn't. But Jon, if you were to see her, she's so pretty. She's forty-three but she doesn't look it. She's very slender and sitting next to that big hot-shot lawyer of hers, she looks so–' Delaney paused. 'What is the word I'm looking for? I know, so vulnerable. My heart aches for her.'

'I read that she was a history teacher at a high school in New Jersey.'

'Pascack Valley. I phoned the principal there. Her name is Jeanne Cohen. She told me in no uncertain terms that Betsy Grant was a marvelous teacher, that the students loved her, and that she was loved by the other teachers and the parents. Cohen said that Betsy had taken a leave of absence to care for her husband about two years before he died. She was adamant that Betsy Grant would no more have taken another life, especially the life of the husband she loved dearly, than the sky would fall on top of all of us.'

'Pretty vehement,' Jon observed.

'And Jon, I don't think that Robert Maynard is passionate about her defense. For example, if she had killed Dr. Grant, and I say "if," why would it be a blow to the back of the head? From all accounts he was given extra sedation after he made such a scene at dinner. Supposedly, she goes to his bedroom, manages to get him in a sitting position, hits him with the pestle on the back of his head, and then just goes back to bed? It doesn't make sense.'

'Delaney, it sounds as if you should be Betsy Grant's lawyer.'

'I only wish I could be. There's a little problem though. I don't have a law degree. But I do think I could do a better job.'

They both smiled, then Jon said, 'Delaney, do you remember what I said last week about "love at first sight"?'

'I'm sure that it's little more than hyperbole. But it's a good line.'

'Actually not, but probably much too soon to have said it. I mean I wish I had waited a month or two.'

Delaney laughed. 'That line gets better and better.' For a brief moment the images of the men she had dated since college ran through her mind. A couple of them had been mildly interesting, but not enough to go deeper into any steady kind of dating.

'It's not a line,' Jon said, 'but we'll leave it at that.'

For a long moment they looked across the table at each other. Then Jon reached over and for a brief moment touched the hand Delaney had unconsciously reached out to him.

27

Alan Grant often did the nightclub scene in SoHo with his buddy Mike Carroll. They had grown up together in Ridgewood and had much in common. Mike was also divorced and that had 'freed him from bondage' as he liked to put it.

Like Alan, he lived on the west side of Manhattan near Lincoln Center. Unlike Alan, he was a partner in an engineering firm, and even after supporting his ex-wife and two children, he was able to live comfortably.

A ruddy-faced, slightly overweight thirty-seven-year-old, his quick humor and winning smile made it easy for him to pick up women at bars. As he had joked to Alan, 'You look classy; I look sexy. Way to go.'

But friends though they were, Mike had been upset when he read in the *Post* that Alan had received a one-hundred-fifty-thousand-dollar disbursement three months ago. When they met, Mike immediately pulled a folded sheet of paper from his wallet. 'Pay-up time, buddy,' he said cheerfully but firmly.

Alan's eyes widened as he saw the total amount of the loans and interest, sixty thousand dollars. 'I didn't know it had piled up so much,' he said.

'It sure has,' Mike said. 'Don't forget you've been underwater for years. I helped bail you out. And you promised to pay me back as soon as you got any of your father's money.'

Alan's sense of euphoria after receiving the check from the estate was rapidly receding. Why did that have to come up at the trial? he asked himself. After reading the *Post's* article about how much he had received, Justin's mother had immediately called him and demanded back child support. His ex-wife Carly had phoned the same day. She had seen it too.

When he received the disbursement, he had paid Carly the arrears of fifty thousand dollars, but he had not paid her in the three months since then. He had just paid Justin's mother eight thousand dollars in arrears. Besides that, he was behind on the bank loan and on his condo maintenance and had bills all over the place. After his personal expenses of the last three months and now paying off Mike, he'd have a measly ten thousand dollars left to live on. And he didn't know if it would be weeks or months after the trial before he could get the rest of his money.

I'll have to find more jobs, he thought, as he wrote out a sixty-thousand-dollar check to Mike and shoved it down the bar to him. Not that many magazines were offering to hire him. He knew his reputation in the business was that he was very good but unreliable.

'It looks to me like your stepmother is going to get convicted,' Mike said as he signaled the bartender for a refill. 'I read in the paper that she had a boyfriend. That sure won't help her any. Did you know about him?'

'No, I didn't,' Alan said vehemently. 'I mean she was always doing the sweet, loving wife routine with Dad. Then she goes out and was probably having a fling with the guy. When I found that out, I felt like I'd been kicked in the gut.'

But the question buoyed him immensely. Mike was a smart guy and that was his take on the boyfriend issue. Great! When Betsy's found guilty, I get everything, he thought, every last dime.

The bartender was putting Mike's drink in front of him. Suddenly upbeat, Alan shrugged off the fact that his cash supply was dwindling rapidly. 'Don't forget me,' he told the bartender as he pointed to his empty glass.

Three hours later, somewhat unsteady on his feet, he was back in his apartment. The light on his phone was blinking. 'Call me first thing in the morning' was the brief message.

'What's that about?' Alan wondered nervously.

He slept fitfully that night. At eight o'clock the next morning he placed the call.

When the conversation was over he buried his face in his hands and began to sob.

28

By this point in the trial, Delaney could see the ever-increasing stress on the face of Betsy Grant. Her complexion was pale to the point of pallor and she walked into court as though she was forcing herself to enter the room instead of fleeing from it. On every court date day she wore the same kind of subdued clothing, a jacket and skirt in either dark blue or dark gray. And the same single strand of pearls, pearl earrings and her wide gold wedding band.

It seemed to Delaney that in even these few weeks Grant had lost weight, so that instead of looking slender, she had a distinct aura of fragility about her. Even so, she sat straight in her seat, her expression calm except when the blow that killed her husband came up in testimony. Delaney could see that when that happened, Betsy closed her eyes as though trying to shut out the mental picture that she was seeing.

The courtroom remained packed every day. Delaney began to identify some of Betsy's supporters, parents from the school where she had been a teacher and friends from the community. At the lunch break she interviewed some of them and without exception they heatedly declared that it was impossible to conceive of the thought that Betsy Grant was a murderer.

She knew that she had to report on the six

o'clock news what had happened, not express an opinion that she could not shake, her growing feeling that no matter what the evidence suggested, Betsy Grant was innocent.

'The thing I noticed,' she told Don Brown after they went off the air, 'is that Betsy does not seem to have any family supporting her at the trial. I did find out that she was an only child, and that her mother died about twenty years ago, and that her father lives in Florida and is remarried. Wouldn't you think that he would be up here to be with Betsy at this time?'

Without hesitation Don replied, 'You bet I would be.' He paused. 'Unless of course the father is too old or too sick to make the trip.'

Delaney slid her laptop over to allow Don to view the screen.

'This was on Facebook yesterday. It's Betsy Grant's father, Martin Ryan, with his grandsons at a football game at their high school in Naples.'

The picture was of a vigorous-looking, seventyish man broadly smiling with his arms around two boys who appeared to be about fifteen and sixteen. The message under the picture was, 'As proud as I can be of my grandkids. Both on an undefeated team. How lucky I am!'

Don Brown read the post and then, incredulous, turned to Betsy. 'His daughter's on trial for murdering her husband and this jerk is bragging about his grandchildren?'

'Step-grandchildren,' Delaney corrected him. 'And his daughter, his flesh and blood, his only child, doesn't have a single relative there to support her.'

She waited while Don reread the Facebook post with increasing disbelief, then said, 'Don, I have a hunch that this obvious estrangement between Betsy Grant and her father may be a part of a whole scenario. I'm going to do some background investigating on my own time.'

29

Jon Cruise, dressed casually but expensively, was making the rounds of the hot nightclubs in SoHo. His good looks, an expensive Rolex watch prominent on his wrist and a handsome tip to the greeters – or non-greeters – at the door insured his welcome even at places where he was told, 'no table available, but you're welcome at the bar, sir.'

Within a week he began to see the pattern of celebrities, some of them on the A-list, and also regular patrons, many of whom appeared to him to be on drugs. Discreet inquiries resulted in a question about what he wanted and being told to meet someone in the men's room to conclude a deal.

With money bankrolled by the *Washington Post*, Jon made two transactions. An analysis of the pills by a private laboratory showed that what he had bought was diluted, and not the high quality that he was interested in obtaining.

Ten days after his interview with Lucas Harwin and his wife, Jon was surprised to receive a phone call from the film legend asking him to come to his office as soon as possible.

'I'm in the middle of producing a documentary,' Harwin explained. 'It's on a tight deadline which actually is a good thing. But I have to go to the set in Massachusetts this weekend, and I don't want to go until I show you some possible leads to Steven's supplier.'

Jon knew what he meant. The best way to handle grief was to be busy.

When he arrived at the office, he was surprised to find that it was relatively small and plainly furnished. But then he remembered that Harwin Enterprises' main headquarters was in Hollywood.

The receptionist greeted him by saying, 'Mr. Harwin is expecting you. Come right in.'

Lucas was dressed casually in an open-neck shirt and long-sleeved sweater. His desk had all the signs of a hands-on producer, with scripts scattered on top, their pages heavily annotated with Post-it notes.

Jon could see glossy pictures of familiar faces hanging on the wall. He wondered if they were in the documentary.

The deep lines on Harwin's face and the sadness in his eyes were evident, but he greeted Jon with a brisk handshake. From a corner of his desk, Lucas picked up a pile of papers and slid them across. 'I've been going through Steven's things,' he explained. 'I was hoping that I would find something, anything that might be a tie to his supplier.'

'And did you?' Jon asked quickly.

'I don't know. This may mean nothing but these are the last three months of Steven's E-ZPass statements. Also the E-ZPass bill for the month he overdosed and nearly died a year and a half ago. Read them and see if anything jumps out at you.'

Carefully Jon read line by line the bill for the last month of Steven Harwin's life and then read the bill for the month prior to his earlier overdose.

With a start he saw what Lucas wanted him to find. In the three weeks before his death, Steven's E-ZPass showed two trips to New Jersey. On the bill before his previous relapse, he had gone over the George Washington Bridge three times in less than three weeks.

Jon looked up and asked, 'The trips to New Jersey?'

'Exactly. Sure, Steven had friends in New Jersey, but why would he have gone there so frequently in the short period before he lapsed into using drugs again?'

'You think his supplier might have been in New Jersey?'

'Yes, I do.'

'Have the police told you anything about his cell phone records?'

'Yes. They told me they got a court order and went through the last year of his calls and there is nothing to a doctor or pharmacist. They did say that it's entirely possible that he also had one of those disposable phones where you just buy the minutes and there's no name attached to the phone. Let's face it,' Lucas said wearily, 'the supplier was selling the pills illegally and Steven was buying them illegally. He didn't want to leave a trail.'

142

'Do you have anything else that points to New Jersey?'

'Yes I do.' Lucas Harwin opened the top drawer of his desk. 'This Visa bill just came in and it may narrow it down. Steven ate at the Garden State Diner in Fort Lee. Only one week ago.'

As he passed the bill across the desk to Jon, he said, 'Steven used a credit card for every purchase right down to a coffee at Starbucks. He'd joke that if he paid cash, he'd miss out on the rewards points for free airline flights.'

As Jon looked at the bill, Harwin again reached into the drawer and pulled out two bank statements, one from the month of his son's earlier relapse and the second covering the last several weeks. 'Jon, take a look at these and tell me what stands out.'

Jon's eyes scanned the transactions and then were drawn to the section of the earlier statement which showed two cash withdrawals of six hundred dollars each. They were on the day before and on the day he had actually driven to Fort Lee, one day prior to his earlier relapse. The second statement showed thirteen hundred dollars being withdrawn just before his final visit to Fort Lee, three days before he died.

Harwin's voice had become agitated. Jon could see that he was choking with anger.

'My son wouldn't have any reason to go to Fort Lee, New Jersey, twice in the short time before he died, and absolutely no reason to have a lot of cash in his pocket, unless that was where his supplier lived or worked.'

'The trail does appear to be leading to Fort

143

Lee,' Jon agreed. 'But it may not help us all that much. I know that Fort Lee is full of large, up-scale condo buildings. People like overlooking the Hudson River. It also has plenty of one-family homes and businesses.'

'There's another point that might help us. Steven was very faithful about going to meetings for addicts. His counselor called me yesterday. When he had the previous relapse, the counselor had warned him that these pills under any circumstances are dangerous, but if he's getting them from a street dealer, he has no idea what's in them.'

Lucas' lips pressed together as if he was trying to suppress a flood of expletives. 'The counselor said that Steven had told him that that was one thing he didn't have to worry about. His supplier was a doctor.'

'That's not uncommon, I'm afraid,' Jon said quietly. 'Unfortunately we frequently find that a doctor is the supplier.'

'Have these doctors ever reminded themselves that they took the Hippocratic oath?' Lucas asked sarcastically.

'Mr. Harwin,' Jon said firmly, 'the *Washington Post* research staff is the best in the business. I'm going to call in what you suspect, that a doctor in Fort Lee is the supplier. We'll check the list for any suspected doctor dealers we may have there and we'll especially focus on any of them that are in close proximity to the Garden State Diner. There's always the chance that we'll be able to come across some connection.'

As he got up to leave, Lucas reached out his

hand. 'Jon, as I told you last week, I don't want anyone else to become the victim of the despicable swine who killed my son.'

30

As soon as they got home from seeing Bridget O'Keefe, Alvirah made the call to Edith Howell, the neighbor of Victoria Carney.

'Oh, Victoria felt so guilty about that adoption,' she told Alvirah. 'She said that even as a tiny girl, Delaney was asking about her birth mother. Victoria blamed herself for arranging the private adoption. If the Wrights had been able to adopt Delaney through a reputable agency, she would have been able to trace her birth mother. I do know Victoria went back to that house in Philadelphia a short time before she died to see if she could get any information.'

'How long ago was that?' Alvirah asked quickly.

'It was just after the house where Delaney was born was taken down for the tile factory. Victoria was so terribly disappointed. I know that she told me that she rang the neighbors' bells on either side of the new building to ask about that midwife. Victoria did speak to one of them. She told her that Delaney was born on March 16th, what would now be twenty-six years ago. The neighbor remembered something about the day Delaney was born, but it wasn't enough to go on. Victoria never told me exactly what it was.'

'She spoke to a neighbor?' Alvirah exclaimed.

'Yes, she rang a couple of bells on the street but only one of the neighbors was home. I don't know the name. That isn't much to tell you.'

Alvirah fervently thanked Edith Howell. 'If that neighbor is still there, it might give us a lead,' she said hopefully.

Two days after speaking to Edith Howell, Alvirah and Willy put the Oak Street address back in the navigation system. 'Well here we are again,' Alvirah said cheerfully when they saw the WELCOME TO PHILADELPHIA sign.

'Yes, we are,' Willy agreed, 'and let's hope this time we get a little more information.'

'I blame myself for not ringing the doorbell of the neighbor on the other side of the factory,' Alvirah said.

It did not occur to Willy to say that he was inclined to agree. Although the Yankees were his first love, he had been swept up in the excitement as the Mets were battling down to the wire with the Philadelphia Phillies for the division title. He knew he could have asked Alvirah to wait a few days to make this trip, but he sensed that she was red-hot anxious to follow this particular lead.

It was an overcast day and drizzling on and off. When they turned onto Oak Street it looked as dreary as both of them had remembered.

They parked outside the tile factory and once more Alvirah suggested, 'Willy, you'd better stay in the car again. This neighbor, if she's still there, might be nervous if the two of us arrive on her doorstep.'

This time Willy had no objection to staying in the car. He immediately turned on the radio.

Alvirah got out of the car and walked past the tile factory to the house next door to it. It was the kind of house she often cleaned, a Cape with a dormer. It could have used a coat of paint, but the lawn was trim and the plants under the front window were obviously well tended.

Well, let's hope whoever lives here doesn't slam the door in my face, Alvirah thought, as she rang the doorbell. But a moment later the door was opened by a seventyish man wearing a Philadelphia Phillies jersey.

Alvirah spoke first. 'I'm Alvirah Meehan and I'm helping a young woman who was born next door who is trying to trace her birth mother. And I'm also a columnist.'

Through the partially opened door she saw a woman approaching. She had obviously heard what Alvirah had said. 'Joe, it's okay. This woman was interviewing Jane Mulligan last week. Jane told me about her.'

It was obvious that Joe resented being told what to do. 'Okay, come in,' he said reluctantly.

As Alvirah entered the house she could hear the baseball game on in the living room. It was very loud and she guessed that Joe was hard of hearing. 'You've got the game on,' she said. 'I don't want to interrupt.'

'I'm Diana Gibson,' his wife said, her attitude day-and-night different from her husband's. 'Come into the kitchen and we can talk.'

Gratefully, Alvirah followed the woman into a small but neat kitchen.

'Sit down, sit down,' she was urged. 'Don't mind my husband. He's the biggest baseball fan on the face of the earth.'

'My husband is too,' Alvirah said, 'and with the Mets battling for the playoffs, he's happy as a clam.'

For the moment she felt guilty about Willy sitting in the car listening to the game instead of being in his comfortable chair in the apartment watching it with a can of beer in his hand. Then she dismissed the idea. She began, 'I know your neighbor, Mrs. Mulligan, isn't happy about the warehouse being built next door. How do you feel about it?'

'I'm okay with it. Our taxes went down and that's a big help, and Sam, who owns the factory, is a very nice man. When it snows he has his plow guy do our driveway too.'

'Did Mrs. Mulligan tell you that I asked her about Cora Banks, the woman who owned the house that was torn down for the factory?'

'Yes, she did. Cora's leaving was no loss to the neighborhood. I guess Jane told you that she was a midwife and that cars were regularly parked in front of the house. Pregnant girls would arrive in one car; hours later people in another car would leave with a baby in their arms. I thought Cora was running a private adoption service, but then when the police came with a warrant for her arrest, I realized that she was selling babies. Isn't that awful?'

'Yes, it is,' Alvirah agreed. 'A regular adoption service would look into the adoptive parents and screen them carefully. I guess Cora was selling them to the highest bidder. Do you remember meeting Victoria Carney, a lady who years ago came looking for information about a baby being adopted here?'

'Yes, I do. The reason I remember is because that woman told me the baby was born on March 16th, ten years before. March 16th is our wedding anniversary. And sixteen years ago, when the lady came, was our thirtieth anniversary. That's why it's very clear to me. I told her that the day the baby was born I had been walking the dog when I saw a couple arrive with a pregnant girl who was crying. They had her by both arms and were hustling her into Cora's house. She was a very pretty girl and obviously in labor. Their car was an old black Ford with Jersey plates.'

Alvirah held her breath, then asked hopefully, 'By any miracle do you remember the license plate number of the car?'

'Oh, no. I'm so sorry.'

Alvirah found it hard to hide her disappointment. No wonder Victoria told Edith Howell that whatever information she got wasn't helpful, she thought, as she got up to go.

After thanking Mrs. Gibson profusely, she left and started to walk to the car. Just as she passed the tile factory, the owner, Sam, opened the door.

'Hey, am I glad to see you,' he said. 'After you left I thought of something. I have a copy of the closing papers from the sale of the house from Cora Banks to me and I remembered that her lawyer's name was on it. I wrote it down in case you ever came back to buy something. I have it right inside.'

He went behind the counter, took a folded sheet

of paper from the drawer and held it out to her.

Alvirah tried not to grab it out of his hand. The name on the paper was Leslie Fallowfield.

'Leslie Fallowfield,' she exclaimed. 'There can't be too many of them around.'

'That's what I thought when I met him,' Sam agreed

'Sam, do you know if he was from around here?'

'I'm pretty sure he was. He wasn't much to look at. He was short, skinny and balding.'

'About how old was he?' Please, God, don't let him be so old that he might be dead by now, Alvirah prayed.

'Oh, I'd say he was about fifty. I think he may have been Cora's boyfriend because he said something to her about meeting for drinks at the usual place.'

Alvirah wanted to kiss Sam but held back. Instead she pumped his hand. 'Sam, I don't know how to thank you. I just don't know how to thank you.'

When she got back in the car, Willy asked, 'Any luck?'

'Willy, if what I just heard leads to anything, we are going to tile all the floors and walls and ceilings in the apartment.'

31

'Your Honor, the state calls Peter Benson,' said Prosecutor Holmes.

The back door of the courtroom opened and everyone turned around to watch him enter. A strikingly handsome man, flecks of gray in his dark brown hair, about six feet tall, he walked to the well of the courtroom, raised his right hand and swore to tell the truth. He settled into the witness stand and the prosecutor approached him.

The jury watched intently as the questioning of this highly anticipated witness began.

Elliot Holmes had handled many witnesses like Peter Benson in the past. Sometimes it was necessary to call a witness who was very close to the defendant and basically hostile to the prosecutor in the case. But he had no choice because it was the only way to bring out certain information.

Holmes also knew that he had to be careful because sometimes these witnesses would look for any opportunity to give an answer that would sandbag his case. And Peter Benson, Ph.D., was a very smart and educated man.

The prosecutor's initial questions established that Benson was the Chair of the Humanities Department at Franklin University in Philadelphia. His wife had been fatally injured in a car crash nearly five years ago. They had been married for almost thirteen years and had not had children. His wife had been an adjunct professor at the same university.

'Sir, how long have you known the defendant, Betsy Grant?'

'We both grew up in Hawthorne, New Jersey, and we both attended Hawthorne High School. We graduated twenty-six years ago.'

'During your high school years, how much contact did you have with her?'

'I did see her quite often. Actually, we dated in our junior and senior years.'

'After you both graduated, did you continue to see her?'

'Only a few times. She had skipped a grade in elementary school. And I remember that her parents felt that she was too young, just having turned seventeen, to go away to college. They decided that it would be best if she went to Milwaukee to live with her aunt for a year and work in her dress shop before starting college. So, around mid-summer she left for Milwaukee.'

'In the next couple of years, did you see her at all?'

'No. I went to Boston College and my father's company relocated to North Carolina so that's where I went on school breaks. So we just kind of lost contact.'

'When is the next time that you saw or had any contact with her?'

'We met quite by accident at an exhibition at the Metropolitan Museum of Art in Manhattan. That was about three and a half years ago. As I walked by her, we looked at each other, did a double take and immediately recognized each other.'

'After that, did you rekindle your friendship?'

'If by rekindle you mean did we become friends again, yes, we did.'

'Did she tell you that she was married?'

'Yes, she told me that her husband was quite ill with Alzheimer's, and of course, I told her that my wife had been killed in the car accident.'

'Now you live in Philadelphia, is that correct?'

'Yes.'

'And she has lived in Alpine, is that correct?'

'Yes.'

'And about how long does it take to drive from Philadelphia to Alpine?'

'I wouldn't know. I've never driven from Philadelphia to Alpine.'

Holmes paused and then continued, 'How often have you seen her in these last three and a half years?'

'About once or twice a month up until Dr. Grant died.'

'And where would you meet her?'

'We would usually have dinner at a restaurant in Manhattan.'

'Did you ever have dinner in New Jersey?'

'No, we did not.'

'Why not?'

'No special reason. We just enjoyed going to the city. There were a few restaurants we liked there.'

'Did you drive directly to Manhattan?'

'Yes, I did.'

Holmes' voice became sarcastic. 'So you never once had dinner in New Jersey, anywhere near her home?'

'As I said, we had dinners in New York.'

153

'And in going to New York, is it fair to say that it was far less likely that you would run into people that either of you knew?'

Peter Benson hesitated, then said quietly, 'Yes, that is fair to say.' Then he added, 'However, it was not a secret that we were having dinner. Mrs. Grant always gave my cell phone number to the caregiver as a backup in case there was a sudden change in Dr. Grant's condition.'

'In those three years did the caregiver ever phone you?'

'No, she did not.'

'Now, Mr. Benson, you just indicated that you stopped seeing Betsy Grant after her husband died. When was the last time you actually saw the defendant?'

'Until I walked into the courtroom today, it was the evening of March 20th of last year.'

'And Dr. Grant was found dead the morning of March 22nd?'

'That is my understanding.'

'Mr. Benson, were you having an affair with Betsy Grant?'

'No, I was not.'

'Were you in love with Betsy Grant?'

'I respected her for her devotion to her husband.'

'That was not the question I asked. Mr. Benson, were you in love with Betsy Grant?'

Peter Benson looked past the prosecutor and directly at Betsy as he answered the question. 'Yes, I was and am in love with Betsy Grant, but I must adamantly add that she was devoted to her husband.'

'So are you telling us that you have not seen her since her husband died?'

'Yes, that is what I am telling you.'

'And why have you not seen her since her husband died?'

'Mrs. Grant called me on March 22nd and told me that her husband had passed away. The next day she called me again and told me that the funeral director had discovered a suspicious injury to her husband's head and that now the police were looking at her as having caused it.'

'And what was your reaction?'

'I was utterly startled when Betsy said that the police were investigating her. I knew that she had nothing to do with his death.'

Holmes stopped. 'Your Honor, I ask that that last comment be stricken because it was not responsive to my question.'

Judge Roth nodded and turned to the jury. 'Ladies and gentlemen, you will disregard that comment. Is that understood?'

All of the jurors nodded their heads and looked back at the prosecutor.

Holmes resumed. 'What else did Mrs. Grant say to you?'

'She told me that she did not want me to be drawn into this whole terrible scenario. She told me that we could not see or even speak to each other until everything was over. She said that she had no idea when that would be. I read within a couple of weeks thereafter that she had been arrested.'

'And again, you are telling us that there has been no communication since then?'

'I am telling you exactly that.'

'Mr. Benson, I will ask you again. Prior to Dr. Grant's death, had you been having an affair with Betsy Grant?'

'Absolutely not. I just told you, no, absolutely not.'

'And you just admitted that you were in love with her, correct?'

Peter Benson again looked at Betsy as he answered the question. 'When we first started having dinner, I was still in deep mourning for my wife. As time went on, I knew that I was developing strong feelings for Betsy. I think that the tragedy of her husband's illness and the tragedy of my wife's death were a shared bond between us. And now, to specifically answer your question, I repeat, yes, I was and am in love with Betsy Grant, but I must adamantly also repeat that she was utterly devoted to her husband.'

'Have you asked her to marry you since her husband was murdered?'

'I told you, I have had no communication.'

'Did you ever discuss marriage with her at any point in your relationship?'

'No, we did not.' Peter Benson shifted in his chair and his face reddened with anger. 'Mr. Holmes, Betsy Grant loved her husband deeply and took care of him in their home when he could no longer care for himself. She is completely incapable of hurting anyone. When she is cleared of this horrendous and false accusation, then yes, I will ask her to marry me.'

Elliot Holmes momentarily considered asking the judge to strike those comments, but he understood that the jury had heard the words and he could not undo that. He would deal with it later in his summation.

'No further questions, Your Honor.'

The judge turned to Robert Maynard. 'Mr. Maynard, you may begin your cross-examination.'

To the surprise of everyone in the courtroom, he answered, 'I have no questions, Your Honor.'

As Peter Benson stepped down from the witness chair the only sound that could be heard in the otherwise hushed courtroom was Betsy Grant's uncontrolled sobbing.

32

The day that Peter Benson testified at the trial, three neighbors were Betsy's loyal supporters in the courtroom. They wanted her to join them for dinner at one of their homes, but she firmly turned them down. 'You're all so good,' she told them, 'but I'm absolutely exhausted. I'm going straight to bed.'

Once again the media crowded around her as with her defense team she made her way to the car. Peter had not exchanged glances with her after he left the stand. Without his telling her, she knew that he was desperately afraid that his testimony might have been harmful to her.

In her mind she could see him as though he had been beside her when he told the prosecutor that he loved her and would ask her to marry him.

And if they ask me that same question when I am on the stand, I will have to answer that same way, she thought, because it's true. It has been true since I bumped into him in the museum. She knew that Peter would call her tonight. It had been eighteen months since she had seen or heard from him, and they desperately needed each other. The minute she realized she was under suspicion of having murdered Ted and hired Robert Maynard, he had warned her not to have any contact with Peter until the trial was over.

For some reason she thought of the brief time she had lived in New York City when she was in her early twenties. I used to rent an apartment on the West Side, Betsy recalled, but then when I knew I was not cut out to work at a PR firm, I went for my master's at night. Then I was hired to teach at Pascack Valley and moved back to New Jersey.

And met Ted.

For the rest of the way home she closed her eyes and willed herself not to think about what would happen if she was found guilty of murder.

She had told Carmen not to worry about preparing dinner for her, but when she got home, Carmen was there.

'Miss Betsy, I can't have you not bothering to eat,' she said. 'And this morning you told me that you absolutely were not going to accept a dinner invitation.'

'Yes, I did,' Betsy said and realized that the scent of baking chicken probably meant that Carmen was preparing a chicken pot pie, one of her favorite dishes. She went upstairs to change into slacks and a long-sleeve shirt. As always in the bedroom she glanced around hoping that somehow she would think of a place where Ted might have hidden the emerald-and-diamond bracelet. But, of course, that was useless. She and Carmen had ransacked not only this room but the whole house looking for it. I might as well put in a claim to the insurance company, she thought.

When she went downstairs Carmen had a glass of wine poured for her. She sipped it in the den as she watched the end of the five o'clock news. There was only a small reference to the trial on that one, but over dinner she watched the six o'clock news, when Delaney Wright reported on it.

Betsy had noticed Wright in court and sensed that she was constantly being studied throughout the day by her. Of course, that was to be expected because she was being paid to report on what was going on. When Delaney Wright was on camera, she said that Peter Benson, the Chair of Humanities at Franklin University, had testified under oath that he was in love with Betsy Grant and was going to ask her to marry him. She finished the report by saying that the prosecutor looked like the cat who had swallowed the canary when he heard that statement.

Then when the anchor asked Delaney her thoughts about how the trial was going, she said, 'Don, I certainly don't think that today was a good day for Betsy Grant. I was really surprised when the defense attorney said, "No questions, Your Honor." I guess it was because he didn't want to keep hitting on the fact that she was

159

dating a man who was in love with her, but on the other hand I could tell that the jury expected him to ask questions of Peter Benson to try to soften the impact of what Benson had said.'

Betsy pushed the off button on the remote. She knew that Carmen must have been watching the broadcast in the kitchen, because when she removed the barely touched pot pie, she did not urge her to try to eat a little more.

She was almost finishing her coffee when the phone rang. It was her father calling from Florida. 'How are you doing, Bets?'

He knew that she hated being called 'Bets,' but he always forgot that or pretended to forget it. Even before she said hello, she finished the thought. He continued to call her 'Bets' not to annoy her, but because he simply didn't bother to remember to not call her 'Bets.'

'Hi, Dad. How are you doing?'

'Oh, I'm doing okay. Not bad for a guy on Social Security for ten years.'

Betsy knew that was his way of saying she had forgotten that last Sunday was her father's seventy-fifth birthday.

'Oh, belated happy birthday,' she said unenthusiastically.

'Thanks. I've been reading about the trial. Believe it or not it's in all the papers here. I'm glad you haven't been asked about your relatives. Or were you?'

'I said that my mother was dead and that my father was elderly and lived in Florida. They didn't ask any more than that.'

'To tell you the truth I'm glad. I haven't said

160

anything about it and I wouldn't want the grand-kids to be asked questions about it in school.'

The grandkids! Betsy wanted to slam down the phone. Instead she said, 'Dad, I hate to cut you short but I'm expecting a call from my lawyer.'

'Oh, I'll get off. Keep your chin up, Bets. Everything is going to be okay.'

When Betsy hung up the phone she tried to push down the familiar rush of anger she had always felt for her father. He had remarried twenty years ago, within months after her mother died, then taken early retirement, sold the house and moved to Florida with his new wife. She had wanted to be near her grown children, and now Betsy was sure it was as though neither her late husband nor his late wife had ever existed.

Or me, Betsy thought. Or me.

If I see one more picture of him on Facebook grinning with his grandchildren, I think I'll go mad. Then why do you look at their posts on Facebook? a voice in her head asked.

Carmen came in from the kitchen to say good night. 'Try to get a good night's sleep, Miss Betsy,' she said.

The bedroom had become her sanctuary. She walked through the house turning off the down-stairs lights that Carmen had left on. The living room, the hallway, the den, the library that was now completely back to what it had been before she made it into Ted's room. Before she snapped off that light, she looked at the shelves with their rows of medical books. He had pulled them out a number of times when he woke up in the middle

161

of the night and Angela didn't hear him. It was the same way he pulled out drawers all over the house whenever he got the chance.

Once again Betsy wondered if Ted in his mind had been looking for something, or had it all been meaningless, random outbursts?

Peter phoned at nine o'clock. She was already in bed, trying to concentrate on the book she was reading. When she heard his voice, the icy calm that had protected her emotions shattered, and she could only sob, 'Oh, Peter, how will this end? How *can* it end?'

33

Jon had phoned Delaney to say that he would be waiting on the sidewalk when she came out of the studio at a quarter of seven.

When she opened the door, he was observing the traffic on Columbus Circle. For a moment she studied him. His black hair was neatly trimmed, as opposed to so many men his age. His hands were in the pockets of his zip-up jacket. His stance was relaxed and comfortable as though he was completely at ease with himself and at peace with the world.

She walked over to him and tapped him on the shoulder. 'Are you available to be picked up, sir?'

As he turned, his arms reached out to give her a brief hug and he kissed her on the lips.

'I'm afraid not. I'm waiting for a beautiful,

intelligent, charming young lady. No one can possibly ever compete with her.' They both laughed and he said, 'I have one of my excellent ideas. It's a perfect evening to eat out and I passed the former Mickey Mantle's place on Central Park South. They have tables on the sidewalk.'

'Love it. We can watch the passing parade.'

As they walked across Columbus Circle, he asked, 'How did it go in court?'

'I don't think it went well at all for Betsy Grant. The guy she had been dating was on the stand and the prosecutor got him to admit that he was in love with her and planned to ask her to marry him.'

Jon whistled. 'Not good.'

'No, it isn't. And as I just said on air, I was amazed that the defense attorney didn't ask him any questions. I know he may not have wanted to belabor the fact that Peter Benson had been a serious boyfriend in the past, but I could tell that the jury was expecting something more from him. I've said from the beginning that Robert Maynard is not worth his Park Avenue fees.'

They walked in silence down Central Park South until they reached the restaurant Jon had selected.

When they were settled with glasses of wine in front of them, Delaney said, 'Jon, I'm a reporter and I know I'm supposed to be objective, but I am convinced in my heart and soul that Betsy Grant is innocent. In my head I can't picture her murdering anyone, never mind a husband who everyone agrees she treated with tenderness.'

'Delaney, I'd like to agree with you that it seems illogical, but on the other hand the courts have

163

been filled with people who wouldn't dream of committing an act of violence being driven to the point when they snap.'

'I know it,' Delaney acknowledged, 'but, Jon, from his pictures Ted Grant was a pretty big man, not fat but certainly big. While he was asleep, did Betsy pull him to a sitting position and hit him in precisely the spot where his skull would be fractured and there wouldn't be any blood?'

'Does she have any medical knowledge, as far as you know?'

'Nothing that has come out, but from what I understand his library was filled with medical books,' Delaney admitted.

Jon did not press the point any further. 'Let it unfold, Delaney,' he said.

Delaney realized there was no point in more speculating. On the other hand her mind and heart were filled with the tormented expression on Betsy Grant's face when she had listened to the funeral director describe the blow that killed her husband.

She forced a smile. 'Jon, catch me up on your investigation.'

'Very interesting. Let's look at the menu first. I only had a pretzel from a street vendor for lunch and I'm hungry.'

'I had a cold grilled cheese sandwich at the courthouse cafeteria for lunch. Let me correct that. The sandwich was fine, but I was so busy trying to eavesdrop again on the people sitting around me that I forgot about it.'

'What kind of reactions did you hear?'

'Pretty much the same as last week. "You can

understand why she did that, but on the other hand how could anyone crush that poor sick man's skull? You just can't get away with something like that no matter how stressed you are.'" Delaney sighed. 'Okay, now let's look at the menu.'

They both decided on salmon and a salad.

'A guy I dated last year hated salmon,' Delaney observed. 'He insisted on telling me that it was a very heavy fish and probably filled with mercury.'

'A lady I dated last year ate only salads. Then one night she started lecturing me on why I should never eat red meat. Just for spite, I ordered a hamburger.'

They exchanged a smile. Jon reached across the table and took Delaney's hand. 'So far we seem to agree on a lot of very important subjects.'

'Like the menu.'

The waiter took their orders, then Jon said, 'You were asking about my investigation. I got a real break when Lucas Harwin, the director whose son overdosed last week, called me. I met with him and he gave me Steven's E-ZPass statements, which showed two trips to New Jersey in the three weeks before he died and three trips in the three weeks before he relapsed almost two years ago. There were two credit card charges at the same restaurant in Fort Lee, New Jersey, and both times unusually large cash withdrawals from his bank account just before the Jersey visits. Lucas said that Steven had told his counselor that he got his drugs from a doctor.'

'What are you going to do with that?'

'I'm getting a list of all the doctors in Fort Lee

with a ring around the ones closest to the diner.'

'Any interesting names on it?'

'Yes– This is strictly between us. Included on it are the offices of Dr. Grant's former partners, Dr. Kent Adams and Dr. Scott Clifton. And they're both within walking distance of the diner.'

Delaney ignored the fact that the waiter was placing dishes in front of them. 'What is the next step?'

'Continue the investigation, of course. Check the backgrounds of the doctors in that area. See if I can find out if any of them have been writing an unusually high number of prescriptions for opioid drugs.'

'Jon, we're both investigators, although in a different way. Is it only a coincidence that Doctors Clifton and Adams are in the same area you're investigating?'

'Sometimes truth is stranger than fiction.' Jon smiled. 'Eat your salmon. Don't let it get cold like your grilled cheese sandwich.'

34

It was not too difficult for Alvirah to locate Leslie Fallowfield. A disbarred lawyer, he had served ten years in prison for buying and selling newly born infants. His most recent address was a post office box in Rowayton, Connecticut.

'We're getting close, Willy,' Alvirah said exultantly when Willy managed to dig up the information. 'And wasn't he the one? He must have been in on Cora Banks' terrible racket.'

'There's no question. They're both the lowest of the low,' Willy agreed. 'But it won't be easy to find the guy if he just has a PO box. For all you know, he may keep his mailing address there but be living in California.'

'One step at a time,' Alvirah said confidently. 'If we were lucky enough to have Sam spot us the other day when we were in Philadelphia, we're going to be lucky enough to track this guy down. We'll head for Connecticut tomorrow.'

This time Willy had no problem agreeing. The Mets and the Phillies had identical records and were heading for a season-ending three-game series. It was an off day for them. Otherwise he would have been forced to put his foot down and say, 'No way.'

The September weather continued to vary, one day warm as it had been yesterday, and now again turning chilly. But as Alvirah said, 'God made four seasons for a reason, so don't complain that it's too hot in August and then complain again when the temperature starts to drop.'

When they were on their way, Alvirah was silent for nearly half an hour, which, as Willy knew, was highly unlike her.

'Honey, anything wrong?' he asked her anxiously.

'What? Oh, no. I'm fine. It's just that I have my thinking cap on. We know that Delaney's adoptive parents must have paid money for her, maybe a lot of money. But I bet even if we're lucky enough to find Cora through Leslie Fallowfield,

167

do you think she bothered to keep records of the people who sold babies and the people who bought them? I mean, apparently she was doing it for years. The neighbors in Philadelphia said that pregnant girls were going into her house at least every few days. And Delaney is twenty-six years old. Even if we find Cora, she may just tell us she has no idea of the real names of either set of parents, that they were always called "the Smiths and the Joneses." In that case, we'll really be at the end of the line.'

'Alvirah, honey, it's not like you to look forward to being disappointed.'

'Well, I'm not exactly looking forward to it, but naturally it's a worry.' Alvirah sighed, then looked around as they turned off at exit thirteen from Route 95 North. 'Oh, Willy, didn't I always say that Connecticut is the most beautiful state? I know we only get to see a little of it when we're driving up to the Cape, but remember when my Thursday job, Mrs. Daniels, moved to Darien when her husband got the great new job, and I came up for a few days to help her get settled? I got to see it then.'

'Oh, of course.' As he answered, Willy searched in his mind for that occurrence and when it was. He had spent those few days fixing the plumbing for the nursing home run by his sibling Sister Pauline.

Willy also remembered that it was one of the few occasions in their married life that he and Alvirah had been apart for a few days, and he hadn't liked it. Now he told Alvirah that.

'I agree,' she said. 'And with all the work I did,

Mrs. Daniels only paid me to the penny, not a red cent extra for all the heavy lifting I did for her. You know I don't like to brag, but she was one of the first I called to tell we won forty million dollars in the lottery.'

'I remember that.'

'I could hear her teeth grinding when she said, "How wonderful." It made me feel so good. Oh, here's the sign for Rowayton.'

Ten minutes later they were in the post office talking to one of the postal clerks who introduced himself as George Spahn. A small man with sparse hair, he had a nasal condition which caused him to clear his throat frequently.

'Sure, sometimes we get to know the people who have boxes,' he said. 'Most of them come in once a week for their mail. The others, who may travel a fair amount, like to have a box so the mail won't pile up on the stoop and alert any crooks that the house is unoccupied.'

'Very sensible,' Alvirah said encouragingly. 'Now, how about Leslie Fallowfield?'

'That's not the kind of name you forget,' the clerk said and smiled. 'Oh, sure I know him. A very quiet gentleman, but very pleasant. He comes in once a week like clockwork.'

Alvirah tried to keep sounding casual. 'Oh, then he lives nearby?'

George Spahn suddenly looked concerned. 'Hey, why are you asking me so much about Mr. Fallowfield?'

'Only because a very dear friend of mine is looking to find her birth mother. Mr. Fallowfield is the lawyer who arranged the adoption. He's her last hope of getting the information she needs.'

Spahn studied Alvirah's face and seemed satisfied by what he saw. 'I can understand that. But it may be better if I check with him and get back to you.'

He'll never want to see us, Alvirah thought despairingly.

Willy stepped in. 'My wife has worn herself out getting this far. If we meet Mr. Fallowfield, one of two things will happen. Either he will be able to provide the name of the birth mother or he won't. How would you feel if you had been adopted and had this need to learn your roots? Haven't you ever been curious about your family tree?'

'I've spent time on Ancestry.com,' Spahn announced with pride. 'My great-great-grandfather was a Civil War veteran.'

'Then understand why a twenty-six-year-old woman needs to know who her parents are.'

There was a long silence. Then Spahn looked at them and away from them. 'Tell you what,' he said. 'Mr. Fallowfield comes in every Wednesday at one o'clock on the dot. Why don't you be here at that time? I'll give him a big "good afternoon, Mr. Fallowfield," and you can take over from there. But keep me out of it.'

'That's very fair,' Alvirah said enthusiastically. 'Willy, isn't that wonderful?'

'Absolutely,' Willy confirmed as with a sinking heart he realized that the Mets were scheduled to start at precisely that time.

35

Despite Scott's feeble attempts to act attentive and loving, Lisa knew that it was a useless effort to try to save their marriage. Or excuse for a marriage, she corrected herself.

She knew the reasons, or at least some of them. Ted Grant's death had had a profound effect on Scott. The thought that Betsy Grant could have dealt such a vicious blow to a helpless man seemed to have impacted him to the core. His dreams about Ted, when he would mutter his name in his sleep, were occurring regularly.

His habit of waking up after those dreams and going downstairs to watch television, or so he said, was increasing.

Lisa knew that the financial pressure on him was mounting. It had been bad enough that Ted had been blasted with early Alzheimer's, but then a few years before she married Scott, he and Kent had ended their partnership. From what she gathered, it was Adams who opted out, and the majority of the patients had left with him.

And of course Scott had three kids in college. The twin boys had just started their senior year at University of Michigan and the daughter was a junior at Amherst.

The tuition was a heavy burden, but the end was in sight. Certainly when Scott was courting her he had seemed pretty comfortable.

But there was one factor that was clearly evident. No matter his protests, there was no doubt in her mind that Scott was having an affair. Too often after dinner he claimed he had to check on a patient.

One time when she called the hospital to speak to him, she was told Dr. Clifton currently had no patients at the hospital.

Lisa had left a very good job in J&J Pharmaceuticals when she married Scott. Now realizing she had to think about her future, she called her former boss Susan Smith. She went straight to the point: 'Susan, by any chance do you have a job open for me?'

'For you, of course I do. Your timing is perfect, but the opening I have will involve a lot of traveling every week.'

'The travel part won't be a problem.'

'How will Scott feel about that?'

'It's not going to matter very much. The marriage was a mistake and it's absolutely pointless to pretend it was anything other than that. I'm making an appointment with a divorce lawyer and filing immediately.'

'I'm so sorry. You seemed so happy.'

'"Seemed" is the best word. It was so obvious almost from the beginning that Scott had a rush of emotion for me that wore out pretty quick.'

There was a long silence, and then Susan said, 'If you're that definite about it, then I have a suggestion to make. How much of your personal stuff is in the house?'

'Besides my jewelry, quite a lot. Some paintings that my grandfather collected that I know have

gone up considerabl   d my grandmother were antiqu   two Persian
carpets, boxes of chi   seventeenth-
century desk, tables   some original
Shaker chairs that s

'Scott bought his   f the house and
she left most of the   re here. For the
last three years I've   living in another
woman's house. H   at we'd buy a different house and p   n the market, but it
never happened. I   to mix my things in
with the leftovers o   Mrs. Clifton.'

'Well, take a piec   ce. Before you breathe a word to Scott about your plans, get everything you have out and put it in storage. Remember the old expression, "possession is nine-tenths of the law." That house is in his name. You could go home one day to find he had the locks changed and it will be a long road to getting your stuff back.'

'Oh, God, I hadn't thought of that. In the next few days, I'll drive down and see if I can find an apartment or condo near Morristown again.'

When Lisa ended the call, she felt deflated and sad. She had so hoped that her marriage to Scott was going to be a happily-ever-after. He had been so ardent, so anxious to marry her. That emotion had been over in a year.

She knew it wasn't her fault. She had sympathy with him about his failing practice, put up with his restless sleeping habits and tried to be patient with the fact that he constantly demeaned her in public.

My self-esteem at the moment is zero minus,

173

she thought. Thirty-seven years old and about to be divorced. She knew that any feeling she had for Scott had been destroyed by his attitude, and maybe there was a third Mrs. Clifton waiting in the wings.

Good luck to her, Lisa thought, as she got up from the chair where she had made the call to Susan. She was in the living room of the Ridgewood house. It was a large, pleasant room, but she was not into its stark monotone décor. Scott had said that his wife had redecorated the living room and dining room before she left. I bet the only reason she left the new stuff, Lisa thought, was because she realized it lacks any warmth. It would fit better in the waiting room at his office.

At the Ridgewood Country Club she had met a divorce lawyer and his wife. Even though Paul Stephenson and Scott were fellow members, she hoped he would take her case. The 'prenup' was a simple one: 'What's yours is yours; what's mine is mine.' She would not ask for or need alimony. Just get the paperwork done. She'd make the call later.

But now she felt a sudden urge to look at the beautiful desk, tables, lamps and paintings she had grown up with.

Feeling slightly better, she took the first step up the stairs to the attic.

36

At twelve thirty Alvirah and Willy were in the post office in Rowayton, Connecticut. Alvirah was so anxious not to miss Leslie Fallowfield that she insisted on arriving half an hour earlier than George Spahn had told them the usual time was for him to pick up his mail.

A worried-looking Spahn greeted them with barely a nod, and they busied themselves putting stamps on empty envelopes for bills that would not need to be paid for three weeks.

Of course all of those bills could have been paid by automatic deductions from one of their bank accounts, but Alvirah was having none of it. 'Nobody takes money from our accounts except two people, Willy. One of them is you; the other is me.'

As one o'clock approached she kept glancing at the clock. 'Oh Willy, suppose he doesn't show up?' she sighed.

'He will,' Willy replied encouragingly. And then on the stroke of one the door of the post office opened and a skinny man in his late sixties, with thinning hair, came in.

Alvirah did not need Spahn's hearty 'Hello, Mr. Fallowfield' to know that the man she desperately wanted to meet had arrived. As she approached him, the thought crossed her mind that she should have let Willy stay in the car in case Fallowfield brushed her off and drove away.

Too late, she thought, as with a warm smile she walked over to Fallowfield, who was pulling mail from a box, and said, 'Good afternoon, Mr. Fallowfield.'

Startled, Fallowfield spun around and faced her. 'Who are you?'

'I'm Alvirah Meehan and my good friend is a young woman who is desperate to find her birth mother,' Alvirah said hurriedly. 'Please talk to me. Cora Banks was the name of the midwife and you were the lawyer when she sold her house to the owner of Sam's Tile Factory sixteen years ago.'

Fallowfield looked incredulous. 'You mean you found that out?'

'I am a good detective.'

'I guess you are.'

'Do you know where Cora Banks is now?'

Fallowfield looked around. The post office was becoming busy, with people on line to mail packages and others to buy stamps. 'This is no place to talk,' he said. 'There's a diner down the block.'

He closed and locked his post office box and shoved the small amount of envelopes into the pocket of his jacket.

'That's my husband, Willy,' Alvirah said as she pointed.

'Then obviously bring him along too.'

Five minutes later Fallowfield was sitting across from them in a booth in the nearby diner. After they ordered coffee Fallowfield said, 'You told me that a child Cora delivered is looking for her birth mother.'

'Yes, she needs to find her,' Alvirah said vehemently. 'I know that Cora Banks may not have kept records but we can only pray that she did.'

Fallowfield looked amused. 'I can guarantee you that Cora kept records.'

It took Alvirah almost a minute to absorb the stunning impact of the words. Then she repeated, 'She kept records?'

'Cora is a very smart woman. Obviously that kind of information has great potential value.'

'Do you know where Cora Banks is now?'

'Yes, I do.' Fallowfield took a sip of his coffee.

'Can you give me her address?'

'Of course. She's residing at the Danbury Prison for Women; however she is being released tomorrow.'

'Where will she go?'

'Oh, right here to my house in Rowayton. Cora has been my close friend for many years. I can arrange for you to meet her.'

Fallowfield reached into his breast pocket for a small pad. 'Give me the specifics of the birth mother you are looking for; where it took place, the date of the birth, the sex of the child.'

The sex of the child, Alvirah thought. Does that mean she helped deliver more than one baby in one day? She made an effort to keep her face from showing any expression of shock. 'Then can you arrange for us to meet Cora when she gets here?'

'Oh, of course I can,' Fallowfield said. 'But you must be aware of something. Cora has been in prison for ten years. When she gets out she is going to have a lot of expenses. She is going to have to get health insurance. She is going to have to buy clothes and have some money in her pocket. She can never go back to her practice as a midwife. She lost her license and has a lifelong injunction against reapplying for it.'

Willy had been taking in the conversation. This is downright extortion, he thought. It was obvious that Alvirah did not share that concern. 'How much?' he asked.

Fallowfield turned to look directly at him. 'You are a man after my own heart,' he observed. 'And I noted that you are driving a very expensive automobile. I would say that fifty thousand dollars cash, all in twenty-dollar bills, would make it worth Cora's time to go through her records.' Fallowfield's tone continued to be mild, as though they were discussing the weather.

'You'll have it,' Alvirah said emphatically.

'Excellent,' Fallowfield exclaimed. 'And of course we all agree that this is a confidential transaction. The only ones who will ever know about it are the three of us and Cora.'

'Of course,' Alvirah said.

Fallowfield turned and stared at Willy. 'Agreed,' Willy spat out as he rose from his chair.

Ten minutes later they were on the way home. 'Honey, I'm trying to figure out how we're going to put together fifty thousand dollars cash without looking suspicious,' Willy began.

'It'll be all right,' Alvirah said briskly. 'I believe I read that if you deposit or withdraw more than ten thousand dollars cash, the bank has to file a report. But after we won the lottery we put our money in ten different banks. We'll withdraw five thousand dollars from each of them.'

'Honey, we're careful about money. Do you really want to give that much to those jokers?'

'No way. But what I want more is to give Delaney this information. Who knows? Her birth mother may be looking for her too. I just hope I'm there when they meet.' With a happy sigh Alvirah settled back in her seat.

37

Dr. Mark Bevilacqua was the final witness for the prosecution. Delaney listened as the prosecutor initially questioned him about his academic training and experience. He testified that he was sixty-six years old, had graduated from Harvard Medical School, and for the past twenty years his practice had specialized in the diagnosis and treatment of Alzheimer's disease. At the prosecutor's request, the judge then accepted him as an expert in the area of Alzheimer's.

The judge then turned to the jury and explained that the evaluation of the expert's testimony was entirely up to them.

The prosecutor resumed his questions. Dr. Bevilacqua then explained to the jury the nature of Alzheimer's disease and the variations of its impact on those afflicted.

'Dr. Bevilacqua, under what circumstances did you first meet Dr. Ted Grant?'

'It was eight and a half years ago. Dr. Grant's wife had made an appointment with our office. She and Dr. Grant's physician partners were concerned about a series of behavioral changes they had observed in Dr. Grant and wanted to find out what was causing them.'

'And were you able to provide an answer?'

'Yes, after a series of tests my diagnosis was that Dr. Grant was suffering from early onset Alzheimer's disease.'

'Doctor, would you please explain what that means?'

'In the vast majority of cases, Alzheimer's disease is diagnosed in patients over sixty-five. Ten percent of Alzheimer's patients are diagnosed at an earlier age. These patients are classified as early onset. Dr. Grant was fifty-one years old when I diagnosed his condition.'

'Did you continue to see and treat Dr. Grant after his diagnosis?'

'Yes, I was his physician up to the time of his passing a year and a half ago.'

'Dr. Bevilacqua, how were you treating him?'

'There is no specific treatment that can actually stop the progression of Alzheimer's disease. I did prescribe various drug therapies that can help to delay the progression of symptoms such as sleeplessness, agitation, wandering, anxiety and depression. Treating these symptoms makes the patient with Alzheimer's more comfortable and usually makes their care easier.'

'And were these therapies helpful to Dr. Grant?'

'They certainly did help in the earlier years of his illness. Particularly in his final year, not withstanding these treatments, he was suffering more acutely with depression, agitation and sleeplessness.'

'Dr. Bevilacqua, I want to go to the morning of

March 22nd last year, when Dr. Grant was found deceased in his bed. By that point you had been treating Dr. Grant for almost seven years?'

'That's correct.'

'How were you contacted that morning?'

'I received a phone call from an Alpine police officer who informed me that it appeared that Dr. Grant had died in his sleep.'

'What was your reaction at that time?'

'I was somewhat surprised.'

'What do you mean by "somewhat surprised"?'

'Dr. Grant had been to my office for an examination four weeks prior to that date. Alzheimer's disease attacks both the mind and the body. Although his mental condition was steadily deteriorating, his vital organs appeared to be in relatively good shape at that time.'

'But when you agreed to sign the death certificate, were you satisfied that he had died of natural causes?'

'Based upon the information I was given at that time, yes I was. Let me explain. Medicine is far from an exact science. There are many examples of patients who undergo physical examinations that indicate no signs of imminent problems, and they die of a heart attack or stroke later the same day. When an individual who has been suffering from Alzheimer's disease for seven years dies suddenly, even if that patient appeared to be in relatively good physical health, that is not all that unusual.'

'Dr. Bevilacqua, evidence has been presented at this trial that has indicated that Dr. Grant's death resulted from a blow to the back of his head, and not from natural causes. In your expert medical opinion, if Dr. Grant had not suffered that injury to his head, how much longer might he have lived?'

'Every Alzheimer's disease case is different. The average life expectancy after diagnosis is eight to ten years.'

'You said "average." Is there a wide variation?'

'Yes. Some patients live as little as three years, while others survive as long as twenty years after their diagnosis.'

'So, would it be fair to say that Dr. Grant could have survived at least several more years?'

'I say again, every patient is different. But based upon Dr. Grant's condition when I saw him a month before his death, and the high level of care he was receiving, it is more likely than not that he would have lived a few more years, perhaps as many as five years.'

'No further questions, Your Honor.'

Robert Maynard stood up. 'Dr. Bevilacqua, you have testified that you were somewhat surprised to receive the call on March 22nd of last year that Dr. Grant had passed away?'

'Somewhat surprised, but not shocked.'

'And you also testified that most victims of early onset Alzheimer's disease, on average, do not live more than eight to ten years. Is that correct?'

'Yes.'

'And at the time of his death, how many years had Dr. Grant been suffering from the disease?'

'I had been treating him for seven years. And by the time I diagnose the disease in a patient, in most cases it has been present for at least a year.'

'So while on average patients with this disease live eight to ten years after diagnosis, in all likelihood, by the time of his death, Dr. Grant had been afflicted for at least eight years. Is that correct?'

'Yes.'

'Doctor, you also testified that despite the medications you were prescribing and despite the high level of home care that he was receiving from Betsy Grant and his caregiver, the depression and agitation and sleeplessness had significantly increased in his final year. Is that correct?'

'Yes, that is correct.'

'No further questions, Your Honor.'

Prosecutor Elliot Holmes stood up. 'Your Honor, the state rests.'

The judge looked at Robert Maynard. 'Judge, we request an hour recess. The defense will be ready to begin at that time.'

'Very well,' the judge said.

38

When Alvirah and Willy started up to Rowayton for the third time, Alvirah was tingling with excitement. 'Oh, Willy, to think that we will know the name of Delaney's mother and probably even her father too. I just hope that the mother hasn't moved to Japan or China.'

'Highly unlikely,' Willy said dryly. He thought about how he had spent the previous day visiting ten banks making withdrawals. He had used the same line at each bank, 'I sure hope I get lucky in Atlantic City.' To his relief the tellers had just smiled as they counted the bills and wrapped the bundles.

They were scheduled to meet Cora at Leslie Fallowfield's house on Wilson Avenue at two o'clock. They had both been surprised when he had said, 'his house.' He caught their exchanged glances and quickly added, 'the house I'm renting.'

Now Alvirah looked anxiously at the navigation map, which showed that they were only a mile away from the address Fallowfield had given them. A few minutes later the mechanical voice said, 'Your destination is five hundred feet ahead on the right.' Then seconds later it said, 'You have arrived at your destination.'

They were in front of a ranch house, the kind built in the post-war 1940s. It had a small front lawn and only a few sparse shrubs under the front window. 'Depressing,' Willy muttered as he turned off the car.

Willy popped the trunk lid, got out and removed an old suitcase from the trunk. The fifty thousand dollars, in fifty bundles, was jammed inside.

Alvirah got out and they began walking up the stone pavement to the front door.

Obviously Fallowfield had been watching for them, because the door opened as Willy was about to ring the bell.

'Right on time,' Fallowfield said, as if he were greeting old friends as he held open the door. Alvirah noticed that he was quick to eye the suitcase Willy was carrying.

Fallowfield led them into a small den. 'Sit right

184

here and I'll get Cora,' he said. As she and Willy took their chairs, Alvirah shrugged off the light fall coat she was wearing. She had bought all new clothes for their river cruise that had ended in early September. This coat was the one she wore when she and Willy left the ship after dinner and took a stroll through the nearby neighborhoods. For an instant she had a keen memory of how much fun that trip had been, but then her mind came back to the present.

Fallowfield returned. 'Before coming down, Cora wants to count the money. I'll take it upstairs–'

'You'll count the money right here,' Willy said firmly, as he put the suitcase on the glass-top coffee table in front of him and Alvirah. Fallowfield was about to object, but when the suitcase popped open and he saw the neat rows of twenty-dollar bills, he changed his tune. 'I'll be right back.'

Alvirah glanced around. The room was pleasant, with two upholstered couches facing each other at opposite ends of the room. On either side of the fireplace there were two armchairs in a striped blue-and-maroon design, and there was an imitation oriental in a cheerful pattern on the floor. What do I care what the room looks like? Alvirah thought to herself, annoyed at her habit of always taking in her surroundings.

She and Willy both sat up straight when they heard footsteps descending from the second floor. A moment later Leslie Fallowfield and Cora came into the room.

Cora's face was very pale, probably because of her years in prison. Her slacks and sweater were loose on her body. Her mud-brown hair was liberally streaked with gray. She looked to be in her late sixties or early seventies. She barely glanced at Willy and Alvirah before her eyes came to rest on the rows of money Willy had stacked on the coffee table. Fallowfield pulled up two chairs for him and Cora.

Cora's smile revealed stained teeth. 'I trust you two, but of course we'll want to count it.'

'Help yourself,' Willy said, 'but keep all of the money on top of the table.'

Willy and Alvirah watched as they got to work. They remind me of kids counting Halloween candy, Alvirah thought. She made a note to share that with Willy on the ride back.

Cora and Fallowfield randomly chose four packets, broke the paper seals and counted out, note by note, the fifty twenty-dollar bills in each one. Satisfied that each bundle contained one thousand dollars, they began to go through the remaining bundles, fanning them like a deck of cards to assure that all of the bills in each bundle were twenties. They stacked these next to the bundles they had counted and compared the height of the bundles until they agreed they were all the same.

'It's nice to do business with honest people,' Cora said, smiling.

Alvirah was not in the mood for conversation. 'Okay, you have the money. Now give us the name of Delaney's birth mother.'

Cora reached into her pocket and unfolded a sheet of paper.

'The mother was seventeen years old. She was

from Hawthorne, New Jersey. Her parents' names were Martin and Rose Ryan. The baby was born on March 16th on Oak Street in Philadelphia. The name of the seventeen-year-old who had her was Betsy. The birth was registered to Jennifer and James Wright from Long Island, New York, as the natural parents. They named the baby Delaney.'

39

Robert Maynard initially called six character witnesses. Two were fellow teachers from Pascack Valley High School, two were neighbors, one was the director of the Villa Marie Claire hospice where Betsy, until three years ago, had devoted hundreds of hours as a volunteer. The last witness was Monsignor Thomas Quinn, the pastor at St. Francis Xavier church, where Betsy attended mass on Sundays.

Each one of them testified that they had known Betsy Grant for many years and had observed her unfailing devotion to her husband.

The monsignor's testimony was particularly compelling.

'Monsignor Quinn, how often did you visit at the Grant home?'

'During the last couple of years, when Dr. Grant was no longer able to attend church, I went to their home every couple of weeks to bring him Communion. Betsy was always there taking care of him.'

'What were your observations of his overall condition during the last year of his life?'

'I observed him sinking deeper and deeper into the horrific effects of Alzheimer's disease. The poor man was terribly afflicted.'

'Did Betsy Grant ever talk to you about putting him in a nursing home?'

'She did on two occasions in the last year. She told me that there had been terrible outbursts and that he had hit her. She said that she wanted very much to keep him at home until the end, but if his behavior deteriorated further, it could become necessary, but *only* as a last resort. She knew that he would be devastated if he was no longer in his own home with her.'

'Monsignor, with respect to Betsy Grant's character, what is her reputation in the community for truth and veracity?'

The monsignor answered substantially as the other witnesses had. 'Everyone who knows Betsy Grant understands that she is a person of good character and credibility.'

'I have no further questions, Your Honor.'

The judge turned to Holmes and said, 'Sir, you may cross-examine.'

Elliot Holmes was a very experienced prosecutor. He knew that there was nothing to be gained in attacking these kinds of witnesses. He formulated his questions carefully and in a respectful tone. He questioned the monsignor in the same manner as he had questioned the other witnesses.

'Monsignor Quinn, you have testified that you visited the home every few weeks during the last couple of years of Dr. Grant's life. Is that correct?'

'Yes, sir. I did.'

'And Monsignor, how much time did you ordinarily spend at the home during these visits?'

'Usually about a half an hour.'

'And Monsignor, is it fair to say that you have no personal knowledge of what went on in that household between your visits every few weeks?'

'That is correct, sir.'

'And is it fair to say that you were not at the birthday gathering the night before the doctor died?'

'Yes, that's correct.'

'So respectfully, Monsignor, you have absolutely no personal knowledge about the events of that evening or the circumstances surrounding Dr. Grant's death?'

'Other than what I have read in the paper, I do not.'

'Thank you, Monsignor, I have no further questions.'

It was now close to the lunch recess. Judge Roth directed the jurors to go back into the jury room and said that he would be with them shortly.

'Mr. Maynard,' the judge said, 'does the defendant intend to testify?'

'Absolutely she does,' he replied.

Judge Roth then addressed Betsy Grant. 'Mrs. Grant, do you understand that you have a constitutional right to either testify or not testify in your case?'

'Yes, Your Honor, I do.'

'Do you understand that if you testify, both

attorneys will question you, and the jury will consider your testimony in the totality of the evidence as they consider their verdict?'

'Yes, I do.'

'Do you understand that if you do *not* testify, I will instruct the jury that your decision not to testify cannot be considered in any way in reaching their verdict?'

'Yes, I do, Your Honor.'

'Finally, have you had enough time to discuss your decision with your attorney, Mr. Maynard?'

'Yes, Judge, I have.'

'Very well, Mr. Maynard. We will begin her testimony after lunch.'

'Your Honor,' Maynard replied, 'it is now Thursday at nearly lunchtime and we are not scheduled to be here tomorrow. Mrs. Grant's testimony will undoubtedly go into Monday morning anyway. I ask Your Honor to allow us until Monday before this critical testimony begins.'

Clearly annoyed, Elliot Holmes briefly objected, knowing that the judge would probably grant the request.

Judge Roth spoke. 'I recognize we are at a very important point in this trial. There is almost no doubt that even if we began this afternoon, this witness would not finish until well into Monday or Tuesday. I will grant the defense request.'

The judge turned to the sheriff's officer standing by the jury door. 'Bring out the jury and I will let them know.'

40

Lisa Clifton began to survey the furniture, bric-a-brac, boxes and rugs she had brought with her when she married Scott.

'Since we're buying a new house, I'd just as soon keep everything separate,' she had told Scott three years ago when they were making wedding plans. 'My grandfather needs to go into a nursing home and he wants me to clear out anything I want from his house. He was a careful collector and had some very nice things.'

Scott had readily concurred. 'My ex, Karen, went on a buying spree the year before we split up. I swear she knew that we were washed up and wanted to stick me with all this modern stuff. There isn't a comfortable chair left in the house.'

They had laughed together. That was when I thought I was going to live happily ever after, Lisa thought. We were for one year, maybe a little longer, and then it changed. He changed. She would have to get new furniture for a living room and bedroom, but otherwise she would be ready to start in her new place when she moved out.

She made a list of everything that she'd stored in the attic, then went downstairs and phoned a moving company. The earliest they could take her was one week. 'That will be all right, but I insist you come around ten o'clock. I'll be looking for an apartment around Morristown. If I

191

don't find one immediately, I'll have to leave everything with you in storage.'

'That will be fine.'

Lisa could not know that as the clerk disconnected the call, he was thinking, Another messy breakup. Wonder if there'll be a fight about the stuff she's grabbing. Well, no matter what, breakups are good for our business!

Scott got home at five thirty. His kiss was warm, his hug tight.

'How's my little girl?' he asked heartily.

His little girl, Lisa thought. Oh, please. I'm nobody's little girl, especially not yours.

She forced a smile. 'I'm fine.' She doubted that he caught the sarcasm in her tone of voice.

As usual, Scott took off his jacket and reached in the foyer closet for his sweater. 'What kind of cocktail may I fix for the lady of the house?' he asked.

My God, how many clichés has he got in him tonight? Lisa wondered, even as she began to realize that her love for her husband had changed to profound hurt and scorn. 'Oh, just a glass of wine,' she said. 'We can have it while watching the six o'clock news. I'm dying to see what Delaney Wright has to say about what went on in court today.'

Scott frowned. 'I really don't want to see or hear anything about the case.'

'Well, then why don't you wait in the living room while it's on?'

She caught Scott's surprised expression. Be careful, she warned herself. Don't let him suspect that you're planning to leave him. She forced a smile. 'Oh, Scott, I'm so sorry. I didn't mean to sound brusque. It's just that I'm so sorry for Betsy and I keep hoping that something will turn up to exonerate her. I don't see how anyone in his right mind could believe Betsy murdered Ted. I mean I didn't get to meet them until Ted was pretty sick, but the way she treated him was so tender, so loving. Even that night when he slapped her, she wasn't angry at him. She was sad.'

'That's not the way some people see it,' Scott snapped as he stomped upstairs, forgetting about a cocktail.

When the segment came on, Lisa watched and listened intently. Her impression was that Delaney Wright was trying to be objective, but when she reported the damning testimony that Dr. Grant could have lived as long as five more years, she did it almost reluctantly. She can't say so, but I think Delaney Wright absolutely believes that no matter what comes up to make it seem as if she's guilty, Betsy could not and would not have killed Ted. Delaney seemed deeply moved by the heartfelt testimony of the character witnesses who had fervently attested to the goodness of Betsy as a human being.

When the broadcast was over at six thirty, Scott came downstairs. 'Sorry to have been so crabby. But you know how hard it is for me to hear any new stories about poor Ted.'

'Yes, I do.'

'All right then. You made a reservation at the club, didn't you?'

'Yes, for seven o'clock.'

'Good, but let's get there a bit early and take

193

two cars. I have to check on some patients at the hospital.'

Or one patient in your love nest, Lisa thought. 'That's fine with me,' she said agreeably.

41

Betsy Grant, accompanied by Robert Maynard, walked out of the courthouse. She was trying to emotionally absorb the testimony that Ted could have lived several more years. She knew that this testimony had been damaging. She hoped that the character witnesses had helped.

She turned to avoid the multiple cameras as she hurried straight to the car. Almost since the beginning, Richie Johnson was the driver who had been bringing her to the courthouse in the morning and taking her home at the end of the day. She had told Robert Maynard that it was absolutely unnecessary for him to drive all the way from Manhattan to Alpine and then back to Hackensack.

Maynard had arranged for him and Singh and Carl to meet her at the curb each morning and walk her into the courthouse. What Betsy had not said to him was that she needed to keep her head clear, and that his tiresome reassurances were distracting and unwelcome.

Tonight as usual she had begged off her friends' dinner invitations or requests to come over and visit for a while. 'I need the sound of silence,' she had said apologetically. 'My head is spinning.'

They had all understood, but she also knew that they were very worried about her.

I'm very worried about me too, she thought despairingly. She knew that Richie sometimes glanced in the rearview mirror to see how she was doing, but if she did not initiate conversation, he didn't either.

When she arrived at the house, Carmen, as usual, was preparing dinner. No amount of persuasion could keep her from being there all day Monday through Friday. Only Betsy's promise to be with friends on the weekend had kept her from being on the job on Saturdays and Sundays as well.

Before Ted's death, Carmen would have his dinner ready for him early, Angela would serve it, and I'd sit with him, Betsy remembered. When he was finished, he usually went to bed. Then she would often go out to the gym or a movie or have dinner with people at the club.

Or with Peter. But at the most, that was twice a month.

'Miss Betsy, make yourself comfortable. I'll have a glass of wine ready for you in the den when you come down.'

Carmen said the same thing every night, but it was oddly comforting to hear it. Someone to watch over me, Betsy thought. And I can't talk to Peter. After that impassioned phone call the day he had been on the stand, she had begged him not to call again until the trial was over. 'Peter, for all I know my phone is tapped,' she had said, 'and maybe yours is too.'

She felt chilled. When she took her jacket off,

195

instead of pulling on a long-sleeve top, she chose a warm, knee-length bathrobe to wear. Betsy tried to push from her mind the terrifying realization that next week she herself would be on the stand.

Carmen had the den ready for her. The lights were on, the thermostat turned up, and a glass of wine was waiting on the cocktail table.

The six o'clock news was coming on. It was hard to concentrate on the local news – a traffic accident on the Verrazano-Narrows Bridge, a mugging in Central Park, a scam by a landlord.

Then Delaney Wright came on camera. With a sinking heart Betsy listened to what she already knew. That Dr. Bevilacqua had testified that Ted could have lived another few years or even longer.

I'm going to be convicted of murdering Ted, she thought. That can't be. That simply can't be. When I go to prison for the rest of my life, will everyone completely forget about me? Or maybe twenty years from now will the Innocence Project help them figure out that I didn't do it, and they'll let me out with a sincere apology? Twenty years. I'll be sixty-three.

She turned off the television after Delaney Wright was finished. The face of the young re-porter filled her mind. When she was summarizing Dr. Bevilacqua's testimony, it looked to Betsy as though she was trying to hide her own distress at the damning answers he had given.

Carmen called her in to dinner, a lamb chop and vegetables. Betsy forced herself to eat. I can't be fainting in the courthouse, she thought. It would probably make me look even more guilty.

As she was pouring coffee, Carmen brought up

the subject of the missing bracelet. 'Miss Betsy, there isn't a place anywhere in the house I haven't looked for it. It's just not in the house. Do you think you ought to report it now? When I picked up the mail, I saw a bill from your insurance company. Isn't that bracelet still insured?'

'Yes, it is. Thank you, Carmen. I'll take care of that. It seems silly to pay to insure jewelry and then not use the insurance when we know we're never going to find it.'

I've barely looked at the mail since the trial started, Betsy thought. I can't ignore everything else. Another task that she wanted to accomplish went through her mind. Years ago, when they started their practice, Ted, Kent and Scott had each bought a set of medical books. When Kent was moving into his new office, he had left his books and other personal effects in storage while it was being renovated. There had been a fire in the storage place and his books had been destroyed.

He had never asked her, but she knew that he would be happy to have the original set that had been Ted's. As she sipped the coffee, Betsy reflected that Kent and his wife, Sarah, had been tried-and-true friends during this whole ordeal. Certainly when they testified they had both emphasized the care she had given Ted and the tenderness she had always shown him.

More than that, in his worst moments, Ted had been grabbing these books from the shelves and throwing them wildly across the room. It was a memory she wanted to erase, and she knew that giving the books to Kent would be the first step in softening that memory.

When she came in to say good night, Betsy said, 'Carmen, you know the medical books on the top two shelves of the library?'

'Yes, I do.'

'After the trial is over, would you please pack them up. We'll have them shipped to Dr. Adams' office.'

'Of course.'

After Carmen left, it occurred to Betsy that Alan might have wanted the books. She scornfully dismissed the possibility. He'd either throw them away or try to sell them, she thought. This is still *my* house. Everything in it belongs to me, either to keep or give away.

If I am found guilty, does Alan take over everything I have? she wondered. For a moment a feeling of all-encompassing loneliness overwhelmed her. She could not call Peter. As it was, the media had gone after him. On page three the headline in the *Post* had been DEAD DOC'S WIFE AND OLD FLAME REIGNITE!

It was only a quarter of eight, but Betsy decided to go upstairs. I'm not sleepy, but if I get into pajamas, maybe I can read for a while in the sitting room, she thought. The room where she and Ted had spent so many quiet, happy hours together.

Just as she had settled into a chair upstairs, the phone rang. She looked at the caller ID and saw that it was her father. The last thing I need is his cheery words of comfort, she thought, as she said flatly, 'Hello, Dad.'

'Bets, it didn't go well for you today in court. I mean having Ted's doctor say that he would have

198

lived another few years didn't look so good for you.'

'I know it didn't.'

'Gert was saying that I really should be there to support you. She said that the grandkids are old enough to understand that these things happen, and it's not as though you're any real relative to them.'

I don't believe I'm hearing this, Betsy thought. I can't believe it. Choosing her words carefully, she said, 'I have repeatedly asked you not to call me "Bets." I don't want you to come to the court-room, but you can thank your beloved wife for making the offer. The one person who might have been a comfort, a so-called "real" relative, is the baby you sold for forty thousand dollars. She's twenty-six years old now and I would love to have her in my corner. Please don't bother to call me again.'

She slammed down the phone and closed her eyes before her father could answer. Her over-whelming need for the daughter she had never known wracked her body and soul. She could feel again the brief moments when the midwife had let her hold her newborn infant.

The feeling passed, and suddenly tired to the bone and soul, Betsy turned off the light and went into the bedroom.

42

Like all other witnesses in the Betsy Grant trial, Alan Grant was under an order of sequestration. The judge had instructed that until the trial was completed witnesses could not discuss their testimony with each other, nor could they be in the courtroom watching other witnesses testify. Witnesses were further forbidden to read or listen to any newspaper or media accounts of the trial.

With the exception of going back into the courtroom, Alan Grant broke all of those rules. He read every newspaper article he could find, and every night he surfed the television channels looking for any reports on the trial. And he had been talking to another witness.

Alan was at the point where he was afraid to check his email or his phone messages. With all the publicity about the disbursements he had received and the inheritance that he would soon get when Betsy was convicted, the pressure was unrelenting. Everybody wanted their money, and they wanted it now. He was able to mollify most of them by telling them that after Betsy was convicted and sentenced, he would be right back in chancery court to get the estate unfrozen and he would quickly get his money. It had also helped when he told each one of them that he would throw in an extra ten thousand-dollar bonus for all of their troubles.

That had been good enough for all of them, except one. That person refused to believe that Alan couldn't come up with any money now, and had angrily told him that he better watch his back.

In the little sleep that Alan had been getting, his dreams were filled with images of his dearly loved father being smashed on the back of his head with the marble pestle.

43

Monday morning Betsy Grant was scheduled to be the final defense witness. Alvirah and Willy had been first on line outside the courtroom door to enter as spectators. They had spoken at length about whether to tell Delaney that Betsy was her mother, and decided to wait until after the verdict was in to break the news to her. They knew how emotional it would be for her, and they understood that once she knew she would have to stop reporting on this trial. When they took their seats in the courtroom, Delaney was sitting in the press row right in front of them.

A bombshell had landed late last evening. A woman in Milwaukee had posted on her Facebook page a picture of an obviously pregnant teenage girl holding up a dress. Beneath the picture the woman had written this caption, 'Almost fainted after realizing that Betsy Grant is the Betsy Ryan who worked in her aunt's dress shop in Milwaukee twenty-six years ago. I knew her aunt from high school and I met Betsy several times. She was a very sweet girl. I snapped this picture of her after she helped me pick out this dress for my sister's wedding. There's no way she killed her husband. She wouldn't hurt a fly.'

The jury remained in the jury room when the proceedings began.

Prosecutor Elliot Holmes stood up. 'Your Honor, we are all aware of the Facebook post that was made at 10 P.M. last night and widely reported on the eleven o'clock news an hour later, and also in the newspapers this morning. I believe that there are two issues before this court.

'As to the first issue, we submit to the court that this photograph is highly relevant evidence. We ask Your Honor to recall Peter Benson's testimony that he dated Betsy Ryan in their junior and senior years of high school. But shortly after graduation her parents told everyone they believed that she was too young to attend college away from home, and that she would spend the year in Milwaukee working at her aunt's dress shop. Mr. Benson testified that he lost contact with her after that.

'Your Honor, it is very obvious that the real reason she delayed college was that she had become pregnant, and went to Milwaukee to keep this pregnancy secret. If the defendant did give birth to a child, I assume the child was put up for adoption.

'Your Honor, ordinarily a pregnancy of the defendant twenty-six years ago would have no relevance in this trial. But we submit strongly that we should be able to inquire of the defendant during her testimony if Peter Benson was the father of this child. As I have argued in my opening statement, and intend to argue in my summation, the state asserts that the primary motive for the defendant to kill her husband was her desire to start a new life with Peter Benson. If he is in fact the father of this child, that would be powerful evidence of an even deeper bond between the defendant and Mr. Benson.

'Finally, with respect to this first issue, if the defendant changes her mind and does *not* testify, then we will seek to recall Peter Benson on rebuttal and question him about this information.'

The prosecutor continued: 'Your Honor, as to the second issue, even though we seek to admit this evidence, we believe it would be appropriate for the court to individually question each juror as to whether they have seen this information, and if so, whether the caption that "she wouldn't hurt a fly" would impact their decision in this case.

Judge Roth turned to Robert Maynard. 'Your thoughts, sir?'

'Your Honor, of course, I have spoken to Betsy Grant about this Facebook post. Like everyone else, we learned about it late last night when it was on the television news. We strongly object to this very late evidence being submitted to the jury.'

Delaney watched as Maynard made his brief and rather feeble argument. It struck her that he did not indicate whether Betsy Grant would admit or deny that Peter Benson was the father. He sounds as if he knows his argument is a lost cause and that the evidence will be heard by the jury, she thought, as she looked over at Betsy Grant, who was staring straight ahead and showing no emotion.

Today she had chosen to wear a blue and white tweed jacket, a navy blue skirt, and black patent leather high heels. A single-strand pearl necklace, small pearl earrings, her wide gold wedding band, and a narrow silver-band watch were the jewelry she had chosen. Throughout the trial she had been wearing her hair pinned back, but today, probably on Robert Maynard's advice, she had let it fall loosely on her shoulders. The result was that she looked even younger, as if she were in her early thirties, and absolutely beautiful.

What on earth can she be thinking? Delaney wondered. If it turns out that Peter Benson is the father of her child, the prosecutor is right – it will show an even deeper bond between them. That could bury her in the minds of the jurors.

Then Judge Roth spoke. 'Counsel, this is certainly late evidence, but it is potentially highly relevant. This is obviously not a circumstance in which a prosecutor previously knew about evidence and didn't turn it over to the defense. If that were the case, I would certainly prohibit it. But this Facebook information was posted late last night. I will question each juror individually as to whether he or she is aware of this information, and if so whether the juror can evaluate the information fairly and make up his or her own mind about the verdict, notwithstanding the comments in the caption.'

Judge Roth spent the next hour and a half separately calling jurors into his chambers. Every one of them had seen or read about the story. Every one of them assured the judge that they would consider the evidence fairly and not be affected by the comment in the caption.

The judge ruled that all jurors could remain, and that if Betsy Grant still wished to testify, this information could be referenced. If she chose *not* to testify, the prosecutor would be permitted to recall Peter Benson on rebuttal.

Maynard stood up again. 'Your Honor, Betsy Grant *is* going to testify.'

Judge Roth ordered that the jury be brought back into the courtroom. When the last juror was seated, Robert Maynard spoke. 'Your Honor, the defense calls Betsy Grant.'

All eyes in the courtroom were upon her as she rose from her chair and walked to the area in front of the bench. The judge directed her to raise her right hand to be sworn in by the clerk. 'Do you swear to tell the truth, the whole truth, and nothing but the truth?' In a low, but firm voice she answered, 'Yes.'

She stepped up to the witness stand and was seated. The sheriff's officer adjusted the microphone in front of her. Robert Maynard initially went through her marriage to Dr. Edward Grant, the details of his lengthy illness and her efforts to give him the best possible care. Then he focused on the major areas that he knew would strongly impact this verdict one way or the other. During the questioning, he always referred to her as 'Mrs. Grant.'

'Mrs. Grant, on the evening prior to your husband's death, did Dr. Grant have an angry outburst during dinner and forcefully slap you across the face?'

'Yes, he did.'

'And did you fall back into your chair sobbing?'

'Yes, I did.'

'And did you say a number of times, "I can't take it anymore"?'

'Yes, I did.'

'And would you tell this jury what you meant by that?'

Betsy turned in her chair and directly faced the jury. 'I had done my best for the more than seven years of my husband's illness to take good care of him. I loved him very deeply. Two years prior to his death, I took a leave of absence from my teaching position and eventually eliminated all of my volunteer work, to stay home and be there for him full-time. But during the last year of his life he assaulted and verbally abused me on several occasions.'

Betsy's voice broke. After a sip of water she continued. 'My own doctor, seeing the impact this was having on me, advised me to put Ted in a nursing home. I had always resisted that advice because I knew it would only add to Ted's depression and anxiety. But after he hit me that last evening, I knew I could not endure any more. I knew in that moment it was time to make that decision.'

'And what decision was that?'

'I knew the time had come to do what I never wanted to do. I was going to put him in a nursing home.'

'Mrs. Grant, before you went to bed that evening, did you turn the alarm system on?'

'I was so upset that night that I simply don't remember. I don't think I did. I couldn't check that because we had an old alarm system that did not keep an electronic record of when it was on or off.'

'Did you normally put the alarm on at night?'

'Normally, either Angela or I turned it on.'

'Mrs. Grant, after the caregiver, the house-keeper and your guests left, did you look in on your husband before going to bed?'

'Yes, I went into his bedroom to check on him. He was in a sound sleep. I knew Angela had given him a sleeping pill after his outburst.'

'What time was that?'

'Around 9:45 P.M.'

'What did you do then?'

'I went into my bedroom, which is down the hall on the ground floor. I immediately went to sleep.'

'When was the next time that you saw your husband?'

'The next time was at about eight o'clock the following morning, right after Angela Watts came into my room and told me that he was dead.'

'Mrs. Grant, evidence has been presented in this trial that the alarm was on when the caregiver arrived that morning. The evidence has also shown that when everyone left the prior evening, you were alone with your husband. Did you hear anyone come into the home that night?'

'No, I did not. But I was so upset that since Ted seemed to be in a deep sleep, I also took a sleeping pill, which I rarely do. I fell into a very deep sleep.'

'Apart from you and the caregiver, who else knew the code to the alarm?'

'Carmen, my housekeeper, of course knew the code. And even though he was very ill, up until a couple of years before he died there were times when Ted would start mumbling the numbers of the code. We had never changed it since the day we moved into the house.'

'Did you ever give Alan Grant the code?'

'I never did, but I don't know if Ted ever told him, or if Ted ever said the numbers in Alan's presence.'

'Who had a key to your home?'

'Of course, Ted and I. Also Carmen and Angela.'

'Did Alan Grant ever have a key?'

'I don't know. I never gave him a key, and Ted never indicated he had given him a key. And I know Angela and Carmen never would have given anyone a key without our permission.'

'As of the time of your husband's death, where was his key?'

'In the last two years of my husband's life, he did not go anywhere on his own. His key was hanging on a hook in the kitchen. Once in a while Ted would take that key off the wall and I would find it on the shelf in the library that had become his bedroom.'

'What would you do with the key when you found it in his bedroom?'

'I would simply put it back on the kitchen wall.'

'When was the last time that you saw that key?'

'Three or four months before Ted died I noticed it was not on the kitchen wall. I expected to find it in the library but I didn't.'

'Did you ever find that key?'

'No, I didn't. Carmen and I looked everywhere, but we never found it.'

'Were you concerned about this missing key?'

'Not particularly. I assumed it was somewhere

in the house, or that he had thrown it in the trash and it was gone.'

'In the last several years of your husband's life, was Alan Grant ever alone with him?'

'Many times. He would sometimes take him for a drive. Sometimes they would just sit by themselves in the den and watch television.'

'Now, Mrs. Grant, I'm going to ask you some questions about the Facebook posting. Let me show you this exhibit. Is that you in this picture?'

'Yes, it is.'

'Are you pregnant in this picture?'

'Yes, I was. About six months pregnant.'

'At that time were you working in your aunt's dress shop in Milwaukee?'

'Yes, I was.'

'When did you go to Milwaukee?'

'I went to Milwaukee in mid-July, after I graduated from high school.'

'When did you become pregnant?'

'In late May, the night of my senior prom.'

'Before you became pregnant, had you planned to go to college that September?'

'Yes, I had been accepted at George Washington University, in Washington, DC.'

'What was your parents' reaction to your pregnancy?'

'They were both extremely upset and embarrassed. My father in particular was very angry at me.'

'Did you change your plans for college?'

'Yes. My parents insisted that with the exception of my mother's sister in Milwaukee, no one should ever know about my pregnancy. My parents told everyone they had decided that I was too young to go away to college and that I should spend the year working with my aunt in Milwaukee.'

'Did you give birth to a child?'

'Yes, I did. A little girl. My daughter was taken from me immediately. On her deathbed my mother admitted to me that my father had sold the baby to the highest bidder. He got forty thousand dollars. It has been a source of intense pain for me since that time.'

'Did you ever tell Dr. Grant that you had had a child?'

'Absolutely. Before we were married. I felt strongly that it was only fair for him to know.'

'What was his reaction?'

'He offered to help me try to find my child.'

'And what did you do?'

'I didn't do anything. I was embarrassed and ashamed. My father had sold my baby. On her deathbed more than twenty years ago, my mother told me that she thought that the money was going to be put toward my college education. Instead, my father used that money to court his present wife, even though my mother was still alive.'

Betsy choked back sobs. 'I have missed my daughter every moment of every day, since her birth. As a teacher I was constantly around students who were the same age as my daughter. I have always wondered where my daughter was.'

'Mrs. Grant, who is the father of your child?'

'Peter Benson is the father.'

'Are you absolutely certain that he is the father?'

'Yes, I am absolutely certain. Peter was the only

boy that I dated in high school.'

'Did you ever tell him that you were pregnant?'

'No, I did not.'

'Did you ever tell him that you had given birth to a child?'

'No, I did not.'

'Why didn't you tell him?'

'Because my parents had banished me to Milwaukee. They did not want Peter, or anyone else, to know about the child. They did not want her, and they did not want Peter's family to possibly seek custody of her. And as I have already told you, my father sold my baby.'

'So you are telling us that from the time you realized you were pregnant to the time this Facebook picture was posted last night, you never told Peter Benson about this child?'

'No, I did not. I am beyond distressed that he has probably seen these reports and knows I gave birth to his daughter.'

'Mrs. Grant, you do not deny that you met Peter Benson for dinner once or twice a month in the couple of years before your husband died?'

'No, I do not.'

'Were you having an affair with Peter Benson?'

'No, I was not.'

'Tell us about this relationship.'

'It was exactly as he explained it when he testified. I bumped into him in a museum in New York a couple of years before Ted died. We were both at a very low point in our lives. He was grieving over the loss of his wife and I was grieving over the loss of the wonderful husband I had had. We were a great comfort to each other.'

'Did you develop strong feelings for Peter Benson?'

'I would be lying if I did not acknowledge that as time went on, my affection grew very deep. As he testified, he felt the same way.'

'Did you discuss the feelings you had for each other?'

'Yes, we did. I told him that I would never be unfaithful to Ted and I would never abandon him.'

'Mrs. Grant, did you do anything to harm your husband on the night of March 21st into March 22nd of last year?'

'Absolutely not. It is certainly true that on that last evening I finally made the decision to put him in a nursing home. But I would never have harmed him.'

'No further questions, Your Honor.'

'Prosecutor, you may cross-examine.'

Elliot Holmes stood up and walked toward the witness stand. 'Mrs. Grant, there is no doubt that as of 9:45 P.M. on March 21st of last year, you were alone in that house with your husband. Is that correct?'

'Yes.'

'And during the night, you never heard anyone come into the home. Is that correct?'

'Yes.'

'And when the caregiver arrived the next morning at 8 A.M. the alarm was on. Is that correct?'

'Yes.'

'And your husband was found dead a couple of minutes later. Is that correct?'

'Yes.'

'And you are aware that the police found no

sign of an intruder breaking in, such as a broken window or a broken door lock?'

'Yes, I am aware of that.'

'Mrs. Grant, you have basically admitted that for the couple of years before your husband's death you were regularly seeing Peter Benson?'

'Yes, I was. I have already said that.'

'Did you ever have dinner in New Jersey?'

'No, we did not.'

'Why not?'

'I wanted the comfort of his friendship, but I knew how it could be perceived if I was seen with him by anyone I knew. I do not deny that I wanted to keep our friendship private. I had enough on my plate. I didn't need gossip as well.'

'Mrs. Grant, isn't it a fact that you killed your husband because you were weary of his illness and all that went with it and you wanted to be with Peter Benson?'

'Mr. Holmes, I was weary. I was sad. I could have accomplished everything you just talked about by putting my husband in a nursing home. If my husband had been in a nursing home, I could have seen Peter Benson much more frequently than I actually did.'

Betsy leaned forward in the witness stand and pointed her finger at the prosecutor, her voice rising.

'If I had put him in a nursing home, I would have introduced Peter to my friends and they would have understood.'

'How long has it been since you have seen or talked to Peter Benson?'

'The last time I saw him was in court the day

213

he testified. He phoned me that night to make sure I was okay. And before that I called Peter the morning that my husband was found dead and–'

The prosecutor interrupted her. 'Did you call him that morning to give him the good news that you were now free?' Holmes asked, his voice dripping with sarcasm.

Betsy flinched and gripped the arms of the witness chair. 'Mr. Holmes, for you to suggest that the death of my husband was good news is despicable.'

'Mrs. Grant, do you think it was despicable to smash the head of a helpless and feeble man who was asleep in his bed?'

Betsy stood up in a rage. 'Yes, I do, but I didn't do it. I did not smash my husband's skull and then go back to bed. I did not kill my husband. I did *not* kill Ted.'

The judge said to Betsy, 'Ma'am, I ask that you sit down.'

Elliot Holmes looked up at Judge Roth. In a dismissive tone he said, 'Your Honor, I have no further questions of this witness.'

The judge turned to Robert Maynard. 'Any further questions?'

'No, Your Honor. Thank you.'

The judge looked at Betsy Grant. 'Mrs. Grant, you may step down.'

Judge Roth's words sounded as if he was saying them to her from a long distance away. She started to stand up, then her legs felt weak and everything went dark.

There were gasps throughout the courtroom as she fainted and fell to the floor. As the sheriff's officers rushed to assist her, the judge ordered the jurors to go back into the jury room and the spectators to leave the courtroom. EMT officers quickly arrived and within ten minutes reported to the judge that Betsy was okay. After speaking with the attorneys, the judge decided to recess the proceedings until Wednesday morning.

The jurors remained in the jury room while Betsy was being treated. Before she left, Robert Maynard consented to the judge bringing out the jury without Betsy Grant being present. The judge told the obviously concerned panel that the defendant was okay and that the trial would resume on Wednesday. He reminded them that their verdict must be decided solely on the evidence and not be based on bias, prejudice or sympathy.

44

Jonathan Cruise had a list of six doctors in Fort Lee that he wanted to interview. He had decided he would identify himself as a reporter for the *Washington Post* and discuss with them their general perceptions of how serious the problem of drug overdoses in northern New Jersey was.

The ones he was really interested in were Doctors Kent Adams and Scott Clifton. The fact that they had been partners with Dr. Ted Grant played on Jon's instincts as a reporter. There's something there was the insistent thought that ran through his mind.

He deliberately saw two of the other doctors first so that his story would be credible to Clifton and Adams.

The first one he saw was Dr. Mario Iovino, an obstetrician who stated that the tragedy was that babies whose mothers had been on crack were often badly damaged: 'You can spot them immediately,' he said. 'Instead of a healthy cry, they mew like cats when they're born. I've only had a few over the years, but my heart sinks when I hear that sound.'

Jon jotted down notes. 'What is the age range of the mothers of those babies?' he asked.

'It runs the whole gamut, from fifteen to forty-five' was the answer.

Jon's next visit was with Dr. Neil Carpenter, a rheumatologist. 'I get calls from patients claiming they fell or are having severe arthritis, or sprained something and the pain is terrible.'

'What do you do when you suspect or know that they're becoming too dependent on their pain-relieving drugs?'

'I recommend heating pads and Extra Strength Tylenol,' he said with a smile.

Jon's next appointment was with Dr. Scott Clifton at two thirty the following day. Dr. Kent Adams had agreed to a meeting, but had indicated his schedule was filled for the next two days.

45

Because of Scott's constant sneering remarks about Betsy Grant, Lisa had not followed her instincts to attend the ongoing trial. She and Sarah Adams had already testified, and both lawyers had indicated that neither would be recalled as a witness. Under those circumstances, the judge had modified the sequestration order as to them, and had ruled that they could attend the court proceedings if they wished to do so.

The prosecutor didn't want them back. Both Sarah and she had been overwhelmingly supportive of Betsy when they were on the stand. There was nothing more that either of them could add to their testimony. Of course, Lisa had not been there when Sarah testified, but that night Scott had bitterly complained. 'From what I heard on the news, you and Sarah were gushing about what a great person Betsy is. Why don't you just phone the Vatican and get her canonized?'

'She *will* be canonized after what's she's been through' had been Lisa's equally caustic response. When she met Betsy and Ted shortly after her marriage to Scott, she had been surprised and pleased to hear that Betsy, like herself, enjoyed doing Bikram yoga. They decided to attend sessions at a hot yoga studio in Westwood, which was about equidistant from Ridgewood and Alpine. They made it a point to meet for workouts once a week, and their friendship grew to where they had lunch together about three times a month.

Those lunches had ended when Betsy was indicted and Lisa was listed as a potential witness at the trial. Even so, Lisa had often thought of how Betsy would speak of Ted with so much tenderness. She missed having Betsy as a friend. As the inevitable break with Scott approached, she read every newspaper account and watched every television report about the trial. She particularly enjoyed Delaney Wright's coverage and her exchanges with the anchor.

The night before Betsy was scheduled to testify, Lisa got very little sleep. She got up early and was in the kitchen before Scott came down to breakfast.

He was still trying to maintain a front of being affectionate. 'Lisa, once this trial is over, I want us to fly down to Santo Domingo for at least a long weekend. After that I bet we won't need to see a marriage counselor.' He added, 'And let me tell you how terrific you always look, day and night.'

'Thank you. And Santo Domingo sounds like a great idea.' She tried to sound amicable as she noticed the increasingly dark circles under his eyes. He's getting even less sleep than I thought.

'And we've got to get around to putting this house on the market and finding a new one,' Scott continued. 'I'm leaning toward that new condo complex they just built in Saddle River. Some members from the club have moved there, and I hear they really like it.'

Get me out of here, Lisa thought. I'm not good at putting up a false front.

When Scott left after giving her a seemingly affectionate kiss, she brushed off her lips and went upstairs to get dressed. As she was taking off her bathrobe, she looked in the mirror. I still look pretty damn good, she thought. She was glad she had cut her wheat-colored hair to a cap around her face. Her hazel eyes were her best feature. Her now shorter hair accentuated her high cheekbones. After showering she put on a lightweight gray jacket and matching slacks that had been her favorite outfit when she was working.

When the courtroom doors opened, she was able to get a seat a few aisles behind the defense table. When Betsy and her lawyers came in, Betsy glanced at the spectators, caught Lisa's eye, and gave her a quick smile. Obviously she was glad to see her.

Betsy was on the stand for hours.

Lisa's stunned reaction to the news about Betsy's baby mirrored the reaction of everyone in the courtroom. Her admission that Peter Benson was the father of her child had left everyone in shock.

When Betsy fainted as she stepped down from the stand, an utterly chagrined Lisa stayed in the courtroom when the judge ordered it cleared. 'I'm a close friend,' she told the sheriff's officers firmly, as one put an oxygen mask over Betsy's face and the other checked her pulse.

When Betsy started to regain consciousness, Lisa was beside her, holding her hand and smoothing back her hair from her forehead. When Betsy came fully awake, tears began to trickle from her eyes. Lisa brushed them away. When the ambulance team arrived, Betsy adamantly refused to go to the hospital. 'I want to go home,' she said. 'Is my driver still here?'

Robert Maynard and his associates had been standing toward the back of the courtroom door. When an EMT informed them that Mrs. Grant wished to go home, they said they would escort her to her car.

Delaney was on the steps of the courthouse watching as she came out. Betsy had dark sunglasses on, but it was obvious that her face was tearstained. Delaney watched as the cameras took picture after picture of Betsy, then gasped as Betsy seemed to sag when the driver opened the car door.

It was a distinct relief to see Lisa Clifton get into the car with Betsy and put her arm around her as the driver pulled away from the curb.

Dr. Scott Clifton had made it very clear on the stand that he thought Betsy killed her husband. But it's obvious his wife doesn't agree with him, Delaney thought.

Suddenly depressed by the events of the day, she waited and then spotted Alvirah and Willy standing off to the side. Delaney waved and they hurried over to her. 'Delaney, why don't you come and have dinner with us at the apartment tonight?'

'I'd love to,' Delaney said.

46

The warm smell of roast beef in the oven greeted Delaney as she entered Alvirah and Willy's apartment after her report on the Betsy Grant trial on the 6 P.M. news. On the air Don Brown had asked her about the courtroom reaction when Betsy Grant fainted. She had chosen her words carefully before she answered. She said that there had been a universal gasp from the spectators and members of the jury. She described how the judge had sent the jury back to the jury room and cleared the courtroom.

'Do you think that the jury is more likely to be sympathetic to her?' Don had asked.

Delaney wanted to say, 'They should be,' but caught herself from sounding so prejudiced. 'They all looked very concerned when she collapsed. I noticed one juror start to cry.'

But when the broadcast was over and they were off the air, she told Don that Betsy Grant was passionate about her innocence, and there was no doubt the jurors had been sympathetic when she fainted. But she also thought that the prosecutor had dealt her a fatal blow when he asked her if she gave Peter Benson the 'good news' that her husband was dead. 'I mean that came right after she had admitted that she was in love with him, and that he was the father of her child. And I don't think Betsy Grant's lawyer has come up with a convincing explanation regarding the alarm being on when the caregiver arrived the morning the body was found.'

Delaney told Alvirah and Willy what she had said to Don.

'What do you think, Willy?' Delaney asked.

'I've said from the beginning that I think she'll be found guilty,' he said quietly.

Even though the roast beef was delicious, Delaney could only pick at it. 'Alvirah, you know how much I love your roast beef and Yorkshire pudding, but I'll be honest. I can't eat much of anything. Every bit of my mind is screaming at me that Betsy Grant is innocent.'

Tears glistened in Delaney's eyes. 'Alvirah, you and I have covered enough of these trials to know what it's like to see the defendants when they have been found guilty of murder or manslaughter and watch as a sheriff's officer handcuffs them and takes them away.'

She gave an apologetic smile. 'It broke my heart when I heard Betsy Grant so passionately say how much she has missed her baby and how much she has ached for her for all these years. I can only wonder if I ever find my birth mother what it would be like to hear her say those words to me.'

Alvirah and Willy looked at each other. Then, as she reached and took Delaney's hand in hers, Alvirah said, 'Delaney, you heard your birth mother say those words this afternoon. Betsy Grant is your mother and Peter Benson is your father.'

47

When Alvirah gave her the stunning news that Betsy Grant was her mother and Peter Benson was her father, Delaney's emotions ran between euphoria and heartbreak. She was convinced that, at the very least, Betsy would be convicted of manslaughter. The overwhelming evidence against her, especially the revelation that Peter Benson was the father of her child, was going to carry more weight with the jury than Betsy's insistence that she would never have hurt her husband.

Her child, Delaney thought. Me.

When she was three years old she had cried because she did not look like anyone else in the family. Now, thinking about Peter Benson, she realized that she had his dark brown and wide-set eyes.

My father, my mother, she thought over and over again after a night of fitful sleep. She got up early, showered and dressed. When she touched up her makeup, she stared in the mirror. Peter Benson is my father, she thought, but my features are more like Betsy's.

She could not do more than swallow a cup of coffee as she thought, Why would anyone want to kill Dr. Grant? The obvious suspect would be Alan Grant. As he had testified, his expenses and debts were very high and he would inherit at least half of Dr. Grant's fifteen-million-dollar estate.

And all of it if Betsy was convicted. He may very well have been told the alarm code by his father. Alan easily could have taken the key off the hook in the kitchen. But he did have a solid alibi for where he was the night of the murder.

Who else could have done it? Carmen Sanchez and Angela Watts each had been left twenty-five thousand dollars in Dr. Grant's will. The estate lawyer had testified to that. But did either of them know that before he died?

What about Dr. Grant's former partners? They had severed their partnership soon after Dr. Grant had been diagnosed with Alzheimer's disease and each had gone his separate way.

There is no other plausible suspect, Delaney thought in despair.

At nine o'clock Tuesday morning she was in the office of the executive producer with the door closed. 'I have to recuse myself from reporting on the Betsy Grant trial,' she began. When she gave her reason, the usually imperturbable expression on Kathleen Gerard's face changed into one of incredulity and then compassion.

'Delaney, of course we have to take you off the trial. And I understand your fear that your mother is going to get convicted.'

Delaney nodded. 'I'm so sure she's innocent and I feel so helpless.'

After a brief pause, she continued. 'I have two requests. Would it be okay if, starting today, I take some personal time, maybe a week?'

Gerard answered quickly. 'Of course, Delaney. Take as much time as you need.'

'Thank you. And right now nobody except you

and two of my close friends know about my relationship to Betsy Grant and Peter Benson. If it's okay, I'd like to keep it that way for the time being.'

'You have my word,' Gerard promised.

48

Peter Benson, reeling from the impact of seeing a Facebook post of a pregnant young Betsy and then hearing the radio reports of the testimony that he was the father, did not know what to do.

Every instinct made him want to drive up to Alpine and be with Betsy, but he knew that at this crucial point in the trial he needed to stay away from her.

She was suffering alone all these years, after being forced to give up our baby and being too ashamed to search for her, he thought. He remembered Betsy's father all too well. In July, the summer after he and Betsy graduated from Hawthorne High School, Mr. Ryan had phoned and told him not to call Betsy again, that she was going to wait a year before starting college. 'She's too young to go away,' Martin Ryan had said, 'and she's too young to be seeing so much of you or of anyone else.'

Peter remembered clearly how angry Betsy's father sounded when he delivered the message. Then he thought about Betsy's mother. She clearly had been browbeaten by her husband and was already suffering from the cancer that took her life six years later.

Peter remembered how he had written to both Betsy and her father to express his sympathy at the time of Mrs. Ryan's death and had not heard back from either one of them.

Then he thought over and over, I have a twenty-six-year-old daughter somewhere out there? Who does she look like? I have brown eyes; Betsy has blue. Doesn't brown usually predominate over blue?

He had taken the day off because ever since he had testified at the trial, he had known that the gossip on campus was all about him and Betsy. He had wanted to be at home when the news reports on her testimony began coming in.

After his wife died, Peter had sold their house and moved to a condo within walking distance of the campus. He and Annette were both disappointed that they had never had a child. They had gone for in vitro three times and she had miscarried every time.

I became a father when I was eighteen, Peter thought. If I had known that, would I have chosen to quit college and get a job? I don't know. I can't picture myself as an eighteen-year-old anymore.

On the witness stand Betsy said she had wanted to keep the baby, but her father had sold her for the highest price. Who got her? Was she even in this country?

At 7 P.M. his mother phoned. Now seventy-three, widowed for four years, she said, 'Oh Peter, how happily Dad and I would have taken the baby. If only we had known. Knowing how close you two were, I was always suspicious of the way Betsy decided to defer college and take off for Milwaukee. If only I had followed my instincts and gone to see her there.'

A few minutes later he could not wait any longer and called Betsy. When she answered the phone, her voice was low and tired and sad. 'Peter, I know I'm going to be found guilty. I hope you will try to find our baby. And if you do, please convince her that her mother is not a murderer.'

49

After ten more burglaries and a winning streak at blackjack in Atlantic City, Tony, as usual, had stayed at the tables too long and given it all back.

At square one again, he thought morosely, as he drove into Saddle River, New Jersey.

He still had the bracelet. Oh, sure, he could get thirty thousand for it from the pawnshop even if it had been reported missing, but then he'd lose his one bargaining chip if he ever got caught doing a job again.

One *big* bargaining chip, he reminded himself.

But now it was time to make another score. He'd been hired as a window washer again. It wasn't hard to get that job. People were having their fall cleanups, and for many that included their twice-a-year window washing.

He was on the third day at one of those big mansions in ritzy Saddle River. When he was doing the windows in the master bedroom, he had taken a quick look around. In one of the closets they had one of those joke safes, exactly like the one in Betsy Grant's bedroom. It would be a cinch to open it.

Tony wasn't sure he was going to do it, but just in case he disconnected one of the balcony doors outside the master bedroom from the alarm system.

But then his boss at the window-washing company asked him when he'd be finished. 'Tomorrow afternoon at the latest,' Tony assured him.

'You'd better be. The family is going on a cruise and they don't want anyone working in the house while they're gone.'

Perfect timing, Tony thought. The stepladder that he always carried in his car was high enough to let him shimmy up to the balcony.

Of course they probably had security cameras all over a place like this. But when he got near the property, he'd stop and cover his license plates with a heavy cloth, and wear dark clothes and a ski mask. It was all in the planning. If the alarm went off, he'd be back on Route 17 before the cops had turned on the engine of a patrol car.

It was tricky. Tony knew that. But he loved the rush of satisfaction that came with beating the system. And if something went wrong, he could always use the bracelet to play *Let's Make a Deal*.

He had waited over the weekend until late Monday night to be sure the family was bye-bye on the cruise, then at one in the morning gone back to the house. When he turned off the highway, he stopped to cover the license plates. Unaware that a patrol car was in the vicinity and observing his actions, he got back in the car and drove to the house he was planning to rob.

The driveway in front of the house was circular, but also continued around to a parking area in the backyard. Tony left his car back there and, carrying his ladder, cautiously made his way to the front of the house. There he unfolded the step-ladder, climbed to the top and hoisted himself up onto the balcony. As he began to pick the door lock, a glaring spotlight was trained on him and a voice boomed through a loudspeaker ordering him to put his hands in the air and freeze.

50

At 1:15 A.M. on Tuesday Tony Sharkey, hand-cuffed in the back of a police car, was driven by the arresting officer to the Saddle River police station. He was taken to the booking area, where he went through a process very familiar to him. He was photographed, fingerprinted and asked the usual questions about his name, date of birth and address.

He was then walked down the hall to the Detective Bureau. Detective William Barrett was waiting for him.

'Mr. Sharkey,' he began, 'I have been informed by the arresting officer that when you were given your Miranda warnings at the scene, you indicated that you wanted to talk to a detective. Is that correct, sir?'

'Yes,' Tony agreed, his tone resigned.

'As the officer told you at the scene, and I will now repeat, you have a right to remain silent. You have a right to an attorney before you answer any questions. If you cannot afford an attorney, one will be appointed for you. Anything you say can and will be used against you in a court of law. And finally, if you choose to answer questions, you may stop answering at any time. Do you understand all of this?'

'Yeah, yeah, I know it by heart.'

'All right, Mr. Sharkey, were you attempting to break into the home where you were arrested?'

'Of course I was. Why do you think I was up on the balcony in the middle of the night? I wasn't picking no apples.'

'I'm sure you weren't picking apples, sir,' the detective replied sarcastically. 'What were you going to do when you got inside the house?'

'Look for some jewelry and cash.'

'Was anybody else with you?'

'No, I'm always the Lone Ranger.'

'So, sir, what is it you want to tell me?'

'You know that big trial going on in Hackensack where they charged that rich lady with killing her husband? You know, that dude with Alzheimer's?'

'I'm familiar with the trial,' Barrett said crisply. 'What about it?'

'I had worked at the house washing the windows a couple of days before. I was in the house the night the doctor got whacked. I didn't do it, but I don't think his wife did it either.'

230

'You were in the house that night?' Barrett asked incredulously. 'What were you doing there?'

'I was helping myself to a piece of jewelry. I took a bracelet. I still have it.'

'You still have it? Where is it?'

'It's at my pad in Moonachie. The cop who arrested me took my keys. You can go there right now and get it. It's stuffed with diamonds and emeralds.'

'Where will we find it?'

'It's in a paper bag under a loose tile in the floor, under the bathroom sink.'

Detective William Barrett had no idea whether Tony Sharkey was crazy or really had something important. But there was no question they had to check it out immediately.

He turned to the other officer in the room. 'Get me the keys from his property envelope. Mr. Sharkey, please sign this consent form.'

Tony quickly scribbled his signature on the form.

'Okay, we'll send the officers to your apartment right now. I'll talk to you again when we see if they find anything.'

'Good,' Tony replied. 'And tell them there's nothing else in the apartment. Don't mess up my décor.'

Rolling his eyes, Barrett said, 'We'll take you to the holding cell now.'

'Oh, one more thing. After you get the bracelet, call Wally's Window Washers in Paramus. Ask them to send you the names of the guys who were working at Grant's house in Alpine the two days before the dude died.'

51

Ninety minutes later, at 3:15 A.M., the officers were back from Moonachie and meeting with Detective Barrett. He was examining the bracelet they had recovered under the loose tile beneath the bathroom sink – exactly where Tony had said it would be. 'Get him from the holding cell,' he said.

Tony smiled as he sat down at the table across from Barrett and saw the bracelet in his hands. 'Didn't I tell ya? And look at the initials, TG and BG. Ted and Betsy Grant. So sweet.'

'Okay, so this part of what you said panned out,' Detective Barrett said cautiously. 'I can't get that window-wash place until the morning. Their office isn't open in the middle of the night.'

'That will pan out too, guaranteed.'

Barrett knew that Prosecutor Elliot Holmes had to be informed about this right away. All of the police departments had his contact numbers for emergencies. I guess this qualifies, Barrett thought. He stepped out of the room and, with a bad feeling in the pit of his stomach, dialed the prosecutor's home number. Elliot Holmes, awakened from a deep sleep, answered the phone.

'Sir, I apologize for calling you at this hour. I would only do so under extreme circumstances. But I thought it was necessary.'

'All right – what have you got?'

Barrett told him of Tony's arrest, the recovery of the initialed bracelet and Tony's claim that he had been in the home on the night of the murder. Holmes listened, incredulous at what he was hearing. 'When was the bracelet reported missing?'

'Here's the crazy part, sir. It never was. I called the Alpine Police before I called you. They have no such report on file.'

'So if he did go into the house, there's no proof of when he did.'

'That's right, sir. He does claim that he worked there washing windows a few days before the doctor died. I can't confirm one way or the other until the place opens in the morning.'

Seething, Holmes knew that he had to talk to Sharkey and then notify Maynard. 'Get him to my office at 8 A.M. and I'll talk to him. I really need this garbage when we're ready to do the summations.' Without another word, Holmes hung up.

Five hours later, Holmes entered the interrogation room at the prosecutor's office and sat down at the conference table. Tony had just been brought in by Detective Barrett. Two of the homicide detectives who had worked on the trial sat down next to the prosecutor and looked at Tony with contempt.

Holmes began, his voice riddled with sarcasm. 'So, Mr. Sharkey...'

'Call me Tony. Everybody else does,' he replied cheerfully.

Holmes ignored his answer. 'Mr. Sharkey, I understand that you have received your Miranda warnings and want to talk to me. Is that correct?'

'That's why I'm here. You got a nice office.'

'Do you understand those warnings? I should add that I assume you do. Your criminal record is atrocious so I also assume that you've received those warnings quite a few times before.'

'Yeah, lots of times. I understand all of it. No problem.'

'I am informed by Detective Barrett that you claim that you were in the Alpine home the night the doctor was murdered. The first time you tell the police about this is when they arrest you trying to break into a house. Then you produce a bracelet that may or may not come from the Alpine house but was never reported stolen.'

Holmes was about to continue when another detective entered the room and whispered in his ear. Holmes grimaced as he listened.

Holmes resumed. 'I was just informed that the window-washing company has confirmed you worked at the Alpine house for a couple of days before the doctor was murdered.'

Tony turned to Detective Barrett, looking triumphant. 'See, I told ya.'

Holmes, furious, said, 'How does this convince me that you were there when the doctor was killed?'

'I came back to go into the house the night after I was finished breaking my back washing their fancy windows. I had seen the safe in the master bedroom upstairs and I knew it would be a piece of cake to get into.'

'How did you get in?'

'When I was there doing the windows, I disconnected the alarm wire in the window in that room. I went through that window when I came back and I twisted the wire again when I left, to make it look like it was still connected, but it really wasn't. So I didn't set off the alarm when I left. It was a real joke system. Easy to get around.'

'You told Detective Barrett that you saw a car pulling away?'

'Well, yeah but this is where we gotta talk turkey. I want you to give me probation before I spill any more beans.'

Prosecutor Elliot Holmes stood up. 'You want probation? You want probation? You are a career criminal. You were caught a few hours ago at a burglary. The bracelet was never reported stolen. Even if it was taken from that house, and whether you took it or not, that will be another charge at the very least of possession of stolen property. You can't prove you were in the house that night. And you won't tell me anything about this mystery car you supposedly saw.'

Elliot Holmes could barely contain his fury. 'You will get nothing from me except more indictments. I have an obligation to immediately notify the defense counsel, Mr. Maynard, of what you have said. If he buys into your garbage, then he can ask to call you as a witness. I promise you that I will destroy you on the stand.'

Turning to his two detectives he barked, 'Get him out of my sight.'

52

Robert Maynard arrived in his skyscraper office at a few minutes before nine. Even though he was not going to court, he was fully dressed in a suit and tie. His shirt had cuff links and his shoes were shined. He was planning to prepare his summation today. He knew that the evidence against Betsy Grant was virtually insurmountable and his best hope was for a hung jury, and if not, then a conviction for manslaughter. Not five minutes later his secretary buzzed him that the prosecutor was on the phone.

'Hello, Elliot. I can honestly say that you're the last person I would expect to be calling me.'

'Hello, Robert. And you are the last person that I thought I would be calling. But I have an obligation to inform you of some developments.'

Dumbfounded, Maynard listened to the details of Tony Sharkey's arrest, the recovery of the bracelet, and his claim that he had been in the home the night of the murder. 'So there it is,' Elliot said. 'You can go see him at the Bergen County Jail. Given all of these circumstances, I am forced to consent if you ask the judge to reopen your case and put him on the stand. I really hope that you do. I'll annihilate him. He wanted probation in exchange for destroying my case.'

Robert Maynard took a moment to digest what he had just heard. Last-minute surprise witnesses only happened on bad cops-and-robbers TV shows, he thought. His voice suddenly more confident, he said, 'Elliot, I don't know where this is going. But if destroying your case means that my innocent client is exonerated, well that's just too bad. I'll get to the jail within an hour and talk to him. I will call you after I do and let you know whether I intend to use him.'

'Okay. Do that. If you intend to call him, we'll have to see the judge this afternoon. This guy does not want a lawyer, and I know the judge will first want to question him on the record about his decision to testify and what kind of prison time he's exposed to.'

'All right. After I speak to him, I have to talk to Betsy about what we do. I should be able to get back to you by noon.'

'That's fine.' Speaking with a little less hostility, Holmes then commented, 'I have been doing this for a long time and this is a first for something like this at the end of a murder trial.'

'Well, I've been doing this about twenty years longer than you and this is a first for me too.'

Robert Maynard hung up the phone. Skeptical though he was about the potential witness that he was about to meet, for the first time he allowed himself to seriously consider the possibility that Betsy might actually be innocent.

On the ride to Hackensack he telephoned Betsy and told her what had occurred. Startled to hear of Tony's claim that he had been in her home the night Ted died, she gasped, 'Robert, do you know what this means? I have never thought that you believed I was innocent. I have no idea when that bracelet went missing. I only realized that it was missing a couple of months after Ted died. I hadn't worn any of my expensive jewelry in a very long time. Carmen and I scoured the house and finally decided Ted must have thrown it out, just like the key. I never dreamed it was stolen because all of my other valuable jewelry was in the safe. I was just about to file an insurance claim for it.

'Wait a minute, Robert,' Betsy said. 'Carmen is trying to tell me something. What is it, Carmen?'

Carmen grabbed the phone from her hand. 'Mr. Maynard, I wanted to say this in court but the judge kept telling me to only answer the question. I wanted to tell him that there was dirt on the rug in the master bedroom when I went to vacuum right after Dr. Ted died.'

'Did you ever tell anyone this?'

'No. I kept trying to tell myself that I must have missed it. But I checked all the rooms to make sure they were clean after the window washers left. There was no dirt on that rug then. I'm sure of it. I was so upset that Dr. Ted was gone that I thought maybe I had missed it. But I know I didn't.'

'Carmen, are you absolutely sure about this? This could be very important.'

'Yes, Mr. Maynard. I felt bad when I didn't say it at the trial. But like I said, the judge just told me to answer the question.'

Betsy grabbed the phone back.

'This may be a very big help,' Maynard told her.

'Let's hope so, Robert.'

'Betsy, I'm going to meet with this guy in the

next hour. I have to get a sense of whether he could help us or maybe kill us. I will call you after I see him.'

'Okay. Pray God, this is the miracle I have been waiting for.'

Robert Maynard had phoned ahead to the Bergen County Jail to ask them to have Sharkey available to him as soon as he got there. After going through security, he was led to a small attorney conference room. It consisted of a table with two chairs. A couple of minutes later, he watched as Tony Sharkey was led in, accompanied by two sheriff's officers. One of them spoke. 'We will be right outside the door. Let us know when you are finished.'

As he sat across from him, Maynard immediately sensed that Tony Sharkey was worried. Holmes had told him that he wouldn't give him any deal. If anything, Holmes was now out to get him.

'Mr. Sharkey—'

'Call me Tony.'

'Okay, Tony. You must understand that my sole obligation as an attorney is to my client Betsy Grant. Whatever I do, as far as using you is concerned, depends on whether or not I consider it to be in her best interest.'

'Agreed,' Tony replied. 'It's your solemn duty and all that kind of thing.'

'You must understand that you are entitled to a lawyer.'

'I've heard that about six times. I don't want one. The last genius who represented me got me four years in prison.'

'All right. That's up to you. You must also understand that I cannot force the prosecutor to give you probation or less time in prison.'

'So he told me,' Tony replied sarcastically. 'A real gem of a guy.'

'What I *can* promise you is my strong belief that if your testimony results in the real killer being identified, or at least if it shows that Betsy didn't do it, the prosecutor, who will certainly be embarrassed, will be under a lot of pressure to give you much less time in prison. And Betsy certainly won't want you prosecuted for going into her house. You will just have to deal with getting caught at the Saddle River house. That's how I see it.'

Tony listened intently and nodded his head. 'Listening to you go through this, I guess that's my best shot.'

Maynard replied, 'But of course you must go through everything with me now and tell me everything you know. That's the only way I can decide whether to call you. I don't want any surprises if you testify. If you double-cross me, we will have you fully prosecuted for the stolen bracelet also. Do you understand that?'

'Yeah, sure. Tell that doll not to worry. With what I know, I'm her new best friend.'

Maynard then went through every detail of what Tony had told the police and the prosecutor. After that, he went into the details that Tony would *not* tell the prosecutor.

'You said you saw a car pulling away from the home in the middle of the night. What kind of car was it?'

'It was a fancy Mercedes. Maybe a couple of years old.'

'What color was it?'

'It was dark out but it looked like it was black.'

'Could you see the driver?'

'I saw someone behind the wheel, but couldn't make out anything more.'

'What about the license plate?'

'A Jersey plate, definite on that.'

'Did you see any of the numbers or letters on the plate?'

'No, too dark. Just too dark.'

'What did you do after that?'

'I did what I went there to do. I climbed in the window and took the bracelet from the safe. I had talked to the doll while I was there washing her fancy windows. She was nice enough. Then I talked to the housekeeper. We were there a couple of days. She told us we could leave the equipment anywhere upstairs overnight because everybody slept downstairs. I couldn't believe my luck. When I came back to hit the safe, I knew I wouldn't be tripping over nobody upstairs.'

Maynard knew that it would be a gamble to call Tony as a witness, but it was a gamble that could pay off big-time. He also knew that without taking this risk, Betsy was almost sure to be convicted.

'Mr. Sharkey, I will strongly advise my client to agree that you should be called. I am virtually certain that she will take my advice. I am now going to leave and call her. I will also call the prosecutor. We agreed that if you were going to testify, we would notify the judge immediately and arrange to have you brought to court this afternoon so that he can question you on the record. You are doing all of this without a lawyer and I know he will want to see you first.'

'Sure thing,' Tony replied. 'I read in the paper the judge was Roth. I'll say hello to him again. He's the one who did my last sentence when I got four years.'

'See you later, Tony,' Maynard replied as he signaled to the officers standing outside that he was ready to leave.

His first call was to Betsy. 'Get down here at twelve thirty. Meet me in the parking lot and we can talk in my car before we walk in together. I am calling the prosecutor, then the judge.' He paused. 'Betsy, try not to get your hopes up too much. My gut tells me that he is telling the truth. But he's a low-life, no doubt about that. It's hard to predict how the jury will react to him.'

'All right, Robert. I'll take a chance. Maybe this is my only chance. Don't you agree?'

'I do. One more thing, Betsy, do you know anyone who owns a new or recent black Mercedes with a New Jersey license plate?'

Betsy paused, then answered. 'Yes. I do. For openers, both Kent Adams and Scott Clifton have black Mercedes. But it would be absurd to think that either one of them could ever hurt Ted. And of course, a lot of people in this area have black Mercedes.'

Maynard listened, trying not to get too optimistic. 'See you in a little while, Betsy.'

53

At one o'clock Elliot Holmes and Robert Maynard were huddled in chambers with Judge Roth. Betsy Grant was seated on a bench outside the courtroom with Maynard's associate. She was wearing a scarf which covered much of her face. The trial was in recess today and she had been able to walk into the courthouse with Robert Maynard virtually unnoticed. But her anonymity was about to be lost.

Tony Sharkey sat in the holding cell adjacent to Judge Roth's courtroom. Chatting with the sheriff's officers, and within hearing distance of other inmates and their attorneys, he boasted that he was here to tell the judge that he was going to 'blow the Betsy Grant trial wide open.'

Word began to spread throughout the courthouse and to the pressroom that something big was going to happen in court in just a few minutes.

At precisely one thirty, the doors to the courtroom were unlocked. Betsy Grant, now surrounded by a small crowd that included the court newspaper reporter, walked slowly into the courtroom, ignoring questions that were being shouted at her as to why she was there. The prosecutor and the defense counsel were already seated at their tables. Betsy sat down next to Robert Maynard and folded her hands on the table. Maynard gently patted her shoulder, then looked through his notes as they awaited the judge.

Two minutes later Judge Roth took his place on the bench. The gravity in the tone of his voice was evident. 'In the matter of *State v. Betsy Grant,* I note that the attorneys are here and the defendant is here.

'Counsel, I will first briefly note that this trial was in recess today. The defense rested yesterday and summations were scheduled to begin tomorrow morning at 9 A.M.

'I will now memorialize on the record the developments of the last few hours. I was contacted at 11:45 A.M. today by both counsel and spoke to them via conference call. I was informed that at approximately 1 A.M. today, an individual named Tony Sharkey was arrested by the Saddle River police during an alleged attempted burglary of a home. I was told that Mr. Sharkey was initially interviewed by the police, and within several hours thereafter by Prosecutor Holmes, and thereafter by Mr. Maynard. He is currently an inmate at the Bergen County Jail.

'After speaking with both counsel, I scheduled this emergent session in court, so that I may address the issues that have arisen. Mr. Maynard, I will hear you, sir.'

'Thank you, Your Honor. Judge, there have been extraordinary developments over the last few hours wherein evidence has been uncovered that is critical to my client's defense. We beseech Your Honor to allow the defense to reopen its case and to call Mr. Sharkey, and also to recall both Carmen Sanchez and Betsy Grant. Please allow me to give the court a brief proffer of the testimony they would offer in support of my motion.'

'Please do that,' Judge Roth replied.

'Mr. Sharkey will testify that he was in the home of Dr. Edward Grant and Betsy Grant on the night of the murder. He will admit that he was there as a burglar. He will testify as to how he was able to bypass the alarm, which he had tampered with when he was at the home working for a window-washer company in the two days prior.

'After his arrest in Saddle River, he consented, indeed strongly requested, that the police go to his apartment in Moonachie to recover the diamond bracelet that he took from the Grant home on the night that the doctor died. He will testify that as he approached the home, prior to his entry, he saw a black Mercedes leaving from the immediate area outside the home. He estimates the time to have been approximately 2 A.M.

'I further proffer that Carmen Sanchez, upon being informed today of these new developments, told me for the first time and told Betsy Grant for the first time that she saw dirt on the rug of the upstairs bedroom the morning that Dr. Grant was found dead. The dirt was located beneath the very window that Tony Sharkey will testify that he climbed through. Finally, Betsy Grant will explain that she never reported that bracelet stolen because she seldom wore it and only realized it was missing a couple of months after the doctor's death. Both she and Carmen Sanchez will testify that they searched for it and finally concluded that the doctor, afflicted with Alzheimer's disease, had probably thrown it out.

'Your Honor, Tony Sharkey has been given his Miranda warnings several times since his arrest in Saddle River. He insists that he does not want to have a lawyer appointed for him. Of course we understand that the court would wish to voir dire him before he testifies.'

Judge Roth turned toward the prosecutor. 'Mr. Holmes?'

'Your Honor, I personally interviewed Mr. Sharkey. He demanded that I promise him probation in exchange for his testimony, testimony that we believe to be, for the most part, categorically false. I recognize that given the enormous consequences of a murder conviction, Your Honor is virtually compelled to allow this testimony. Again, we strongly take the position that Mr. Sharkey is a liar, and I look forward to cross-examination. As to Carmen Sanchez and Betsy Grant, I also look forward to further cross-examination of them.'

Judge Roth turned to the sheriff's officer standing by the holding cell door. 'Bring out Mr. Sharkey.'

The spectators in the courtroom murmured as Tony was led out in handcuffs and seated at the defense table. 'Quiet in the courtroom,' the judge said sternly.

The judge then addressed Sharkey. 'Mr. Sharkey, please stand up.'

'Sure thing, Judge. You remember me? How have you been?'

'Mr. Sharkey, how old are you?'

'Thirty-seven. I'll be thirty-eight next Tuesday.'

'How far did you go in school?'

'I dropped out in tenth grade.' Tony chuckled.

'I never did the homework.'

'Mr. Sharkey, it is my understanding that you wish to testify as a witness for the defense in this matter, is that correct?'

'I sure do, Judge. I know that this pretty lady didn't kill her husband.'

'Mr. Sharkey, do you understand that you do not have to testify? You have a fifth amendment privilege against self-incrimination. Neither side could call you as a witness unless you consented. Do you understand that?'

'Yeah, Judge. I've heard those Miranda warnings more than a few times over the years.'

'Do you understand that if you wanted, I would immediately have a public defender appointed for you so that you could discuss with him or her whether you should decide to testify or not in this trial?'

'I don't want no lawyer, Judge. I think I make out better on my own.'

'Sir, do you realize that you have a charge for attempted burglary in Saddle River and you may be charged with burglary or possession of stolen property with regard to a bracelet allegedly taken from the Grant home in Alpine? Do you understand that your testimony here could be used against you in those cases and you could get up to five years on each of those charges, for a total of ten years in prison?'

Tony swallowed hard. 'I do.'

'Finally, do you understand that the prosecutor here is making no promises to you? Indeed he intends to fully prosecute you on all charges brought. Do you understand that?'

Elliot Holmes glared as Tony responded. 'Yeah, but I think he will change his mind.'

'But if he doesn't change his mind, and it certainly appears that he has no intention of doing so, do you understand that you would be facing that kind of time in prison?'

'Yes, Judge. I know I'm rolling the dice.'

Judge Roth paused, then spoke. 'I am satisfied that Mr. Sharkey is deciding to testify freely and voluntarily and with full knowledge of his rights. He is thirty-seven years old, attended high school but did not graduate and has been involved in the criminal justice system for many years. I reference his prior record for the purpose of emphasizing that he understands these proceedings and understands his constitutional rights.

'He has been told repeatedly that a lawyer would immediately be appointed for him. He does not want a lawyer. He is entitled to waive a lawyer. My function is to ensure that whatever decision he makes is voluntary and informed. I am so satisfied. He may testify.'

Robert Maynard stood up again. 'Thank you, Your Honor. Judge, I beg one more indulgence from the court. I am now, on very short notice, in the position of having to call Mr. Sharkey and recall Mrs. Grant and Ms. Sanchez. I know we were supposed to resume tomorrow morning. I fervently request that you allow us an additional day to prepare and resume on Thursday, the day after tomorrow.'

Elliot Holmes, exasperated, started to object but then, resigned, said, 'Your Honor, I am ready to resume tomorrow, but I defer to the court.'

The judge replied. 'I never want to delay a jury, but these circumstances are virtually unprecedented. My chambers will contact each juror and inform them that there is an additional one-day delay and we will resume this trial the day after tomorrow at 9 A.M. I note, of course, that the jurors would not be given any further information. They have been repeatedly instructed not to read newspapers or listen to media accounts of this trial. I have no doubt that there will be widespread coverage of today's court proceeding. That is all, counsel.'

54

Dr. Scott Clifton arrived at the Fort Lee office which he had once shared with Ted Grant and Kent Adams. Since then he had been a sole practitioner, and the waiting room was empty.

He had a first-time patient, State Senator Brian McElroy, scheduled at 9 A.M. and it was now five of nine. All new patients were asked to arrive at least twenty minutes early in order to fill out necessary forms.

He looked at his new receptionist, Heidi Groner. Without greeting her, he asked, 'Have you heard from Senator McElroy? He's not here yet.'

Groner answered timidly, 'He called last night and got the answering service. He canceled.'

'Did he give any reason?'

Twenty-two years old and looking even younger,

she replied haltingly, 'He said that after the way his friend's operation turned out, he wouldn't let you touch him with a ten-foot pole.'

Scott stared at her, his gaze withering.

'I'm sorry, Doctor, but you did ask me.'

Scott turned abruptly, went into his private office and slammed the door. That means only one other patient appointment later this morning, he thought bitterly. He had been sure he was in good shape the morning he had operated on Darrell Hopkins.

State Senator Brian McElroy was viewed as a rising star in New Jersey politics. It was unfortunate that he knew Darrell Hopkins, the patient who had come in for a routine knee replacement a month ago. Scott knew that he had been distracted. He hadn't put in the artificial knee properly and an infection had followed. The operation was being redone by another orthopedic surgeon, Dr. Kent Adams.

The office was running at a loss. The overhead was crushing. In addition to the high rent and his increasingly expensive medical malpractice insurance, he employed a nurse, a part-time X-ray technician and a full-time receptionist to handle appointments and insurance forms.

His phone rang. Heidi Groner's voice came over the intercom. 'Doctor, your ex-wife is on the phone.'

Karen, he thought angrily as he picked up the receiver. She'll bleed me dry. His greeting to the mother of his three children was 'How much do you want now?'

His afternoon appointment was not a patient. It

was a reporter for the *Washington Post* who was interviewing doctors about the drug problem in New Jersey. The last thing he wanted to do was talk to a reporter, but when Jonathan Cruise had called, he told him that he had already spoken with Dr. Mario Iovino, an obstetrician, about the impact of drug abuse on the unborn child, and Dr. Neil Carpenter, a rheumatologist, about the addictive nature of pain medications. Both were highly respected in their specialties and Scott could see no reason for refusing the appointment.

At ten minutes of three Heidi's voice came on the speakerphone in his office. 'A Mr. Cruise is here to see you. He apologizes for coming early. But I told him you weren't busy and you don't have any other appointments this afternoon.'

'Send him in,' Scott barked.

Scott put forth his most cordial self when Jonathan Cruise was escorted into his office. He already knew what he was going to say. In the next half hour he explained that, of course, the practice of orthopedic medicine included doctors routinely ordering pain medication for patients following surgery. 'We have to keep a very close eye on when it is necessary to either renew prescriptions or cut them back. We are very careful with all patients but have to be especially diligent with younger ones who too easily can become addicted to painkillers such as Percocet and Vicodin. That is our responsibility. Those of us in the practice of orthopedic medicine are very much aware of it.'

Jon's impression of Clifton was that he was a good-looking man in his late fifties who appeared to be a concerned and caring doctor. However, when he again walked through the empty waiting room he had a sense almost akin to desolation. I wonder how many patients chose to go with Dr. Adams when they broke up their practice, he thought.

As soon as the door closed behind Cruise, Scott turned to Heidi Groner. 'Ms. Groner, it is obvious that you are far too immature for this position,' he said. 'When my former spouse phoned, you should not have referred to her as "my ex." And when I receive a visitor, it is not proper to share with him my appointment schedule for the balance of the day. You can consider yourself terminated effective immediately. You will be paid through the end of next week and your check will be mailed to you.'

Heidi Groner was already on the verge of quitting herself. There was too little to do and she thoroughly disliked Dr. Scott Clifton. As she rose from the desk she slipped into her pocket the business card the reporter had given her.

Could I give him an earful, she thought, smiling to herself.

55

Alan Grant had lost ten pounds since the trial began. Testifying had been a harrowing experience. Seeing Betsy at the defense table had made him wonder how he would feel in her place. Why couldn't Dad have just died of a heart attack? Why did it have to come to this?

He was asked to go to Georgia to do a prestigious and lucrative photo shoot for *Happening* magazine. The original photographer had been delayed on another job in Buenos Aires.

Alan knew that even though this job would pay very well, and he certainly needed the money, he had to turn it down. As a witness who could be potentially recalled, he had been instructed not to attend the trial. But when the jury completed its deliberations, he could be in court to hear the verdict. She'll be found guilty, he promised himself. There's no way she'll be let off. Then the nightmares will be over.

It had gotten to the point where every night he dreamt of his father's skull being crushed by that pestle. And often other events filtered into his consciousness. Sobbing with his father at his mother's grave. His father buying him the condominium. And the best photography equipment. His father rejoicing as he started to get good reviews for his work.

When Alan woke up, he would be shivering. The trouble was that even though I'm good at photography, I hate it, he thought. When he got his money from the estate, he would figure out what else he could do. He realized that he never again wanted to be owing money, having creditors dunning him. He hadn't filed a tax return for years. And he had just received a notice from the IRS demanding that he contact them immediately.

This pressure is too much, he thought. When Betsy is convicted, I'll go to the chancery court

253

right away and request enough money to pay everybody.

But when he fell asleep, the nightmares began again.

At 4:00 in the morning he had taken two Ambien, or was it three? He slept until almost 2:00 in the afternoon. After turning on the small TV in the kitchen, he put two pieces of bread in the toaster. When the newscaster said, 'new development in the Betsy Grant case,' he moved closer and turned up the volume. He stared ahead in shock as he heard that a man just arrested for burglary claims to have seen a car leaving the Grant property at 2:00 in the morning on the night his father was murdered.

56

Her tone was flirtatious as she said, 'Mr. Cruise, I hope you remember me. I met you at Dr. Scott Clifton's office yesterday. On your way in, you gave me your card.'

'Yes, of course. How can I help you?'

'I don't want to talk over the phone, but I'd like to meet you. I have some very interesting information that you should know.'

'Of course, I'll meet you,' Jon said. 'Do you want to pick a place near your office in Fort Lee?'

'I no longer work in Fort Lee. I was fired right after you left.'

'I'm sorry to hear that.' Now Jon was even more intrigued about what the former receptionist wanted to tell him. People who have been fired are usually willing to share a lot more than those who are worried about keeping their jobs.

He continued, 'Where would you like to meet?'

'I live with my parents in Tenafly. The Clinton Inn is in the middle of town. Will that be all right?'

'Yes. Would six o'clock tonight be okay?'

'Okay, and after what I tell you, you're going to want to buy me dinner.'

After he finished his conversation with Groner, Jon called Delaney. 'We'll have to meet later this evening, Delaney,' he began. 'A few minutes ago I received a phone call from Heidi Groner, a receptionist who was just fired by Dr. Scott Clifton. She claims she has important information and wants to share it. I have no idea what it's about. This may be a case of a disgruntled employee who wants to vent after getting fired, and I'll be honest, I think she's a bit of an airhead–'

'Jon, you have to see her,' Delaney said immediately.

She had been planning to tell Jon at dinner that Betsy Grant and Peter Benson were her parents. But that could wait.

'Jon, I am still stunned about that guy who was arrested in Saddle River and claims he was in Dr. Grant's home the night he was murdered.'

'It's an astonishing development,' Jon said.

'I know the prosecutor doesn't believe him, but the defense attorney is going to call him as a witness. Jon, do you realize what this could mean for Betsy Grant?'

'Yes, I do. And I know how strongly you feel about her. But Delaney, so many nuts love the limelight, and Tony Sharkey may be one of them. They'll say or do anything to get attention.'

'I know you're right,' Delaney said, 'but I think there's something to this.'

57

On Tuesday afternoon Lisa Clifton met with the real estate agent in Morristown and found a four-room condo in a luxurious new building with an available rental. It was exactly what she had in mind, a large two-bedroom unit with plenty of windows.

As she signed the lease, she felt a sensation of relief wash over her. Why did I stay in the marriage this long? she asked herself. I've been miserable for at least two years. Now I just want to get away from him.

She got back in her car, pleased to have been successful in apartment hunting. A few days more, she thought, I can't wait. Can't wait to get out of that house with its dreary modern furniture. And the fact that Scott was being so affectionate was making it worse. Last night, after she left Betsy's home, they had met friends for dinner. He had called her 'Dear' so often he had sounded silly. Was he worried that if they broke up, she would go after more than was in the prenup? She had, after all, given up her well-paid job at his specific request. I wish I could tell him not to worry about that, she thought. I'm not looking for any of his money. I just want out!

While driving home, she heard about the thief who claimed to have been in Betsy's house the night of Ted's murder and who had seen a black Mercedes leaving the grounds. Lisa gripped the wheel. She distinctly remembered that night. After she and Scott got home from the dinner party, he had told her that he was too upset after the scene in the dining room to go to bed. When she came down the next morning, he was asleep on the couch in the den. She had not questioned his story for a minute. He claimed that he had had a few drinks to help him calm down and that's why he fell asleep there.

He *had* been upset that night.

And they *did have* a black Mercedes.

But why would Scott have any reason to hurt Ted? The partnership had broken up years ago.

That question led to another one. Ted had lunged across the table, Lisa thought. I was sitting next to Scott. Was Ted lunging at Scott and not me? In that poor failing brain of his, was he aware of something Scott had done that infuriated him?

Lisa did not notice how quickly the trip had gone until she pulled into the driveway.

Home!

To her surprise Scott was in the living room. He greeted her with one of his affectionate kisses. 'Hey, I tried to get you, but you didn't answer your phone.'

Lisa felt a chill go through her body as his arms

tightened around her. 'I forgot my phone,' she said, 'and I went shopping. Nordstrom and Neiman Marcus are both having big sales.'

Scott relaxed his grip. 'Hope you treated yourself.'

'I did. I ordered two suits that are being altered. They'll be ready in a week.'

And I'll be out of here by then, she thought.

58

Delaney had gone home after her meeting with Kathleen Gerard yesterday. She had spent much of yesterday and today rereading her notes from the courtroom, reports she had filed, and reviewing news accounts of the trial on websites to see if she had missed anything that might be helpful. Just before Jon had called, she had been trying to decide whether or not to call Lisa Clifton. Lisa was obviously so supportive of Betsy, and Scott Clifton obviously so hostile. Was this taking a toll on their marriage?

How could there not be some strain between them? she asked herself. Maybe if I told Lisa that Betsy is my mother, she would be more open to me. There's no harm in trying, she thought. There is no harm in trying anything that might help Betsy, she decided.

As she tried looking up the phone number, she was surprised to see that there was a listing for a Lisa Clifton in Ridgewood, New Jersey, but nothing for a Scott Clifton. Is it odd that the family phone number is in the wife's name or is that how doctors do it? she asked herself.

Lisa answered the phone on the first ring. What Delaney could not know was that Lisa had been waiting for the clerk from the moving and storage company to verify exactly the time they would pick up furniture on Friday morning.

Delaney, after identifying herself, came straight to the point. 'Mrs. Clifton, from what I observed in court, you are very sympathetic to Betsy Grant.'

'I am and always have been. There has to be a better explanation for what happened that night, and I think I may know it.'

'Mrs. Clifton, may I come out and talk to you?'

'It's Lisa. Yes, you can. I've been watching your coverage of the trial and you've been very fair. But I can't do it today. I have an appointment I can't break this afternoon, and my husband and I are going to dinner with friends.'

'Mrs. Clifton, Lisa, this trial is coming to an end so quickly. If you have information that may help exonerate Betsy Grant, I beg you to share it now.'

'It's not proof. It's only a feeling. But I'll be happy to see you tomorrow.'

'What time can we–?'

'I'm sorry. I have to go. Please call me tomorrow morning.'

After she hung up the phone, Delaney felt helpless and aimless. Lisa had just said that she had a different idea about what really happened to Ted Grant but had no proof. I'll bet she means Alan Grant, she thought. Of course, he is the logical choice. But there is absolutely no proof that he was the killer and he has an airtight alibi.

Airtight alibi! He had it because he had gone to the home of a former girlfriend, Josie Mason, and spent the night with her. The security cameras verified that he had not left her apartment that night. Delaney wondered if Alan had seen that woman again. Or could it be that he had paid her to let him stay at her apartment?

Rather than ignore any possible avenue, Delaney reviewed her trial notes. Mason was a hairdresser at Louis & David, a salon on East 50th Street. She looked up the phone number and dialed it. A voice that turned cross at the mention of Alan's name reluctantly agreed to meet her for a drink at 5 P.M. Mason suggested the Peacock Alley bar in the Waldorf Astoria.

The popular cocktail lounge was almost full. It always has a festive air, Delaney thought. I wish to God I could feel festive!

Josie was already waiting at a small table to the left of the bar. Delaney recognized her because she had testified in court. Josie was a shapely blonde, about thirty years old, with hair barely touching the top of her shoulders. She wore a low-cut white blouse and black slacks.

Delaney took a seat beside her. Now that they were only a few feet apart she could tell that Mason's unlined face had probably benefited from some Botox treatments. The tiny creases around her mouth suggested that she was a heavy smoker.

'Hi, Josie, thanks for meeting me,' Delaney said as a waitress arrived to take her order. Mason was already drinking an apple martini and Delaney decided to join her in one.

After she ordered, Josie began to reach into her pocketbook, then stopped and shrugged. 'I don't get this stupid rule that you can't have a cigarette with a drink. It drives me crazy.'

'I never smoked, but I have friends who feel the same way,' Delaney said agreeably.

'I like the way you've been covering the trial,' Josie remarked. 'I mean you're fair, not like some of those nuts on the radio shows who think they're smarter than God and keep screaming that Betsy Grant smashed her husband's head.'

Sound and fury signifying nothing, Delaney thought, but she answered, 'I couldn't agree more.'

'Those guys are sure nailing Betsy Grant,' Josie said. 'I mean they all keep whining about how she killed her sick, helpless husband because she wanted to be with her boyfriend. I saw his picture in the newspapers. He's gorgeous. And he's a widower!'

We're talking about my father, Delaney thought, but then trying to get to what she was probing for, she said, 'Alan testified on the stand that you two had planned to meet for a drink around ten o'clock, after he got back from the party at his father's house.'

'That's about what happened,' Josie said with a shrug.

'What do you mean by *about?*'

'Me and Alan would go out for a while. We'd break up. He'd call me out of the blue and we'd start going out again. About six months before his father died we had a big fight. I mean he's good-looking and he's classy. But he was always whining about how broke he was. I even started picking up the checks. My girlfriends told me I was stupid, and I eventually figured out that they were right. So I said to him go make some money and then call me back. But then a few months later we started going out again for dinners and stuff. About a week before the dinner at his father's house, he told me how hard it would be for him to see his father so sick. He asked if we could meet for a drink around ten o'clock, after he got back from New Jersey.'

'So you made a date to see him that night?'

'Yeah. We agreed to meet for a drink. I was already there. He was okay in the beginning, but then he got to be a real downer. He was depressed and almost started crying. He told me he felt so alone, he might be having a nervous breakdown, he's so worried about his father and stepmother, his father's so sick and he's slipping... He said he didn't want to be alone that night, could he stay with me?'

Josie shrugged. 'I'm always a sucker for a sob story, so I said, "Sure. Okay."'

Delaney chose her words carefully. 'Josie, I know the security cameras saw him come in with you around midnight and leave around eight o'clock the following morning. Does that mean you're absolutely certain he was in your apartment all night?'

'Oh, he sure was with me all night. He spent half the night crying. I thought I'd go nuts.'

'Did you see much of him in the year and a half

since his father died?'

'Some. Listen. I know he's going to inherit big money. When he gets it and he stops talking about his troubles, who knows if I'll be interested? But wouldn't you think that after I miss time from work, get on the witness stand and give him a rock-solid alibi for the night his father died, he'd at least call and thank me? I mean if he'd gone back to his place alone, who would have believed him?'

Josie tilted her head back and downed the last sip of her martini. 'That calls for one more,' she said as she raised her hand to signal the waitress.

Delaney was frantic to leave. I think it's a good bet that Alan deliberately set up his sometimes girlfriend to give himself an alibi because he knew somebody was going to murder Dr. Grant that night.

As Delaney was paying the check, Josie started to laugh. 'One really funny thing happened that night. I had just two days before adopted a shelter cat.'

Please get to your point. I don't have time for pet stories, Delaney thought.

'I didn't know it, but Alan's really allergic to cats.'

'And he still stayed over?'

'Yeah, he took several Contacs and sneezed his way through.'

'Did you tell this to the police?'

'No. We didn't talk about it. Why would the police care about somebody's allergies?'

59

Trying not to look impatient, Jonathan Cruise waited at the Clinton Inn in Tenafly for Heidi Groner. She was already fifteen minutes late and he was beginning to wonder if she would show up. Five minutes later, she appeared.

'Sorry to be late,' she said. There was nothing apologetic in her tone of voice or her broad smile. In the office her hair had been pinned up. Now it was loose and fell at least three inches below her shoulders. She was carefully made up and her hazel eyes were accentuated by mascara and liner.

Jon recognized that she was a very pretty girl, something he had not noticed at the brief meeting in Dr. Clifton's office. Expecting they would be having dinner, he had intended to keep the initial conversation general. But Heidi got right to the point. 'I told you I got fired yesterday.'

'Yes, I'm sorry.'

'Don't be. I was about to quit. That place was like a morgue. The night before you were in talking to Dr. Clifton, State Senator McElroy called and left a message to cancel his appointment. Dr. Clifton operated on his friend a few weeks ago, a knee replacement. He got it wrong and the guy has to have it redone.'

'Did that sort of thing happen often?'

'I wasn't there long enough to know. But I'll tell

you this, he could rent out his waiting room.'

A waiter was hovering at the table. 'What would you like to drink?'

'Oh, just a glass of Chardonnay. I'm not a big fan of the strong stuff.'

'Make that two Chardonnays, please,' Jon told the waiter, then looked back at Heidi. 'My understanding is there's a big overhead in most medical practices.'

'Oh, sure there is. I was full-time. There were also part-timers, a nurse and an X-ray technician. He wasn't seeing enough patients or doing enough surgeries to pay our salaries. I'm sure he's peddling drugs.'

Jon felt himself tense up. 'What makes you think that?'

'He has a disposable phone. You know the kind where it has just so many minutes on it.'

'I know what that is.'

'Well, I could hear that one ringing two or three times a day. And one time, last week when his office door was open, I heard him make an appointment to meet in a parking lot near the office.'

'And you think he was meeting people to sell them drugs?'

'Sure, I do. Or at least prescriptions for drugs. Why else would he meet someone in a parking lot?'

Jon thought of how Scott Clifton's office had seemed so desolate.

'I'm saving the best for last,' Heidi said, her tone conspiratorial. 'Did you read about that Hollywood director's son who overdosed last week?'

'Yes, I'm familiar with that story.'

'Wasn't his first name Steven?'

'Yes, it was.'

'Well, when Dr. Clifton was on that other phone last week, as he was getting off I heard him say, "Good-bye, Steven."'

60

Straight from his dinner with Heidi Groner, Jon drove to Delaney's apartment. It was ten o'clock. He listened as she told him that she thought Josie Mason had been set up to be Alan's alibi for the night his father died.

'It makes sense, doesn't it, Jon? That way, he's pretty much in the clear.'

'It does make sense,' Jon agreed, 'but of course it means that someone else other than Alan committed the murder. Now let me tell you what I found out today.'

Delaney listened. 'You mean that Dr. Clifton is selling illegal drugs?' she asked.

'Most likely he's selling prescriptions for *legal* drugs. There are pharmacists who know a doctor is writing too many scripts, but they don't report it or ask any questions. The people who are getting these prescriptions filled, the addicts, are paying cash. It's a big moneymaker for the doctor and the pharmacist.'

'But none of that would give Scott any reason to kill his former partner.'

'No, it wouldn't,' Jonathan admitted. 'Unless tomorrow Tony Sharkey can come up with something more than saying he saw a black Mercedes, I don't think his testimony helps Betsy Grant.'

'And the prosecutor and Maynard will be doing their closing arguments on Friday and the case will be going to the jury,' Delaney said as her eyes filled with tears.

Jonathan put his arm around her. 'Hey, Delaney, I'm surprised at you. You've reported on so many trials. I can't believe you let yourself get so emotionally involved in this one.'

It was time to tell him. 'Jon, how would you feel if you just found out Betsy Grant is your mother?'

61

On Thursday morning, the trial resumed. The courtroom was packed with press and spectators as the judge came out and ordered the jurors to be brought into the room.

After they were seated, the judge turned to the jurors and said, 'Ladies and gentlemen, I told you on Monday that the attorneys would be presenting their summations to you this morning. On Tuesday, it was brought to my attention that, due to additional developments, the defense counsel wished to reopen his case. I am going to allow him to do that.

'It is my understanding that a person who has not previously testified will now be called. His name is Tony Sharkey. He lives in Moonachie. If anyone knows this person, please raise your hand.' The judge paused. 'Okay, good, no one knows him. Mr. Maynard will also recall Carmen Sanchez, who has previously testified, and Betsy Grant, who has previously testified.

'Ladies and gentlemen, Mr. Maynard will question these witnesses and then Prosecutor Holmes will cross-examine them. When these witnesses are finished, Mr. Maynard will rest his case again and we will recess until tomorrow morning, when the attorneys will argue their summations to you. After that, I will instruct you on the law and then you will begin your deliberations.

'Mr. Maynard, you may call your first witness.'

'Thank you, Your Honor. The defense calls Tony Sharkey.'

Tony Sharkey looked around the courtroom as he entered through the holding cell door. He was wearing a suit and tie that Maynard's associate had hastily purchased for him. He was escorted by sheriff's officers on either side of him. After being sworn in, he stepped onto the witness stand and sat down.

Maynard began his questioning by asking Tony about his age, his address and his employment as a window washer. 'Mr. Sharkey, when and where was the first time that I met you?'

'Tuesday. In the can. The jail.'

'Were you arrested in Saddle River the previous evening?'

'Yeah. I got caught doing a break-in. The cop saw me on the balcony.'

'Did you go to the police station after that?'

'Yeah. That's when I talked to a detective. Told him I got some good info for him.'

'Did the police, at your request and with your consent, go to your apartment in Moonachie?'

'Yeah. I told them to go there. They took my key.'

'What were they looking for?'

'I told them that a bracelet I took from the Grant house in Alpine last year, the same night as when the doctor got whacked, was under a loose tile in the bathroom.'

Betsy visibly grimaced as Tony spoke of her husband being 'whacked.'

'Mr. Sharkey, I am showing you a bracelet that has been marked as Defense Exhibit 10. Is this the bracelet that was under that tile?'

'Yeah, no doubt. Look at the initials. TG and BG. They brought it back to the police station and the detective showed it to me.'

'What did you tell the detective?'

'I told him that I didn't think that this little lady killed her husband. I told him that I took the bracelet that night. Before I went in, I seen a black Mercedes – right next to the house – hauling out of there.'

'What time was it?'

'Two, maybe two thirty in the morning. I wondered what the hell that was all about.'

'What happened next?'

The jurors sat mesmerized as Tony related how he had been there as a window washer, had tampered with the alarm and had taken the bracelet.

'Mr. Sharkey, why did you only take one bracelet from the safe?'

'When I do a job, I just take one, maybe two good pieces. Then the people in the house don't realize that anyone's been there. When they realize it's gone, they don't call the cops 'cause they think they forgot to put it back where it should be. That way, they don't report it to the police and have them crawling all over the house looking for fingerprints.'

'Mr. Sharkey, have you been promised anything for your testimony here today?'

'Nope. I'm getting zilch from the prosecutor. You told me that the lovely lady here would let bygones be bygones about me taking the bracelet.'

'Your Honor, I have no further questions.'

'Cross-examine, Prosecutor,' said the judge.

'Mr. Sharkey, isn't it a fact that you have six prior felony convictions?'

'Yeah. I ain't proud of it. My mother sure ain't proud of it.'

'And you know that the judge will instruct the jury that they can consider those prior convictions when they evaluate the credibility of your testimony, in other words whether they believe you.'

'Yeah I know. I been through this before.'

'Mr. Sharkey, when is the first time you met me?'

'Early Tuesday morning. You looked real pleased to meet me.'

'And you told me some of what you said here today, correct?'

'Right.'

'But when I asked you to describe the car you

supposedly saw fleeing from the home, you wouldn't tell me. Is that correct?'

'That's the truth.'

'As a matter of fact, you demanded that I promise you probation for your testimony before you would say any more. Is that correct?'

'Yeah. I figured that was fair if I'm gonna come in here.'

'And I told you, based upon what you had said, that I am not promising you anything except full prosecution for the attempted burglary in Saddle River, and full prosecution for the burglary of the Grant home, even if Mrs. Grant now forgives you because you're trying to help her get off on this murder charge. Is that correct?'

'That's pretty much it.'

'Mr. Sharkey, you say that you stole this bracelet in March of last year. Correct?'

'Yeah. That's when it happened.'

'Mr. Sharkey, I went through some of your previous sentencing reports. Is it not true that you have a severe gambling addiction and work somewhat sporadically for the window-washing companies?'

'I won't deny that I go to Atlantic City whenever I got some cash. I work at window-wash places whenever they have jobs for me. They ain't the busiest places.'

'Then, if you're short on money, why did you hang on to this bracelet all this time? Why didn't you fence it and get thousands of dollars for it?'

'Because I figured I might find myself in a bind like I'm in now. I figured I could use it to get some time off my sentence.'

'So you are here just trying to help yourself. Correct?'

'Sure. But I'm telling it straight about what happened.'

'But if you hadn't been arrested in Saddle River the other night, you wouldn't be here all worried about Betsy Grant, would you?'

'No, I can't say I would be. But I always felt bad for her since she was arrested.'

'Mr. Sharkey, you have no proof that you were in the home that exact night, do you?'

'No but add it up. I window-washed the two days before. I know the company sent you that info. And I got the bracelet. And check that alarm. It's older than I am. Anybody could get around it.'

'And you just happened to see a mystery car fleeing the scene?'

'No mystery. It was dark. I told you what I saw.'

'Your Honor, I have no further questions.'

Tony slowly left the witness stand with the sinking feeling that it hadn't gone well. Robert Maynard had the same feeling.

'Call your next witness, Mr. Maynard,' the judge said.

'The defense calls Carmen Sanchez.'

Carmen walked from the entrance door slowly up toward the witness stand. The judge told her that she had been previously sworn in and was still under oath. Maynard took her through her account of the dirt on the rug and how she had helped Betsy look for the bracelet.

Elliot Holmes then began cross-examination.

'Ms. Sanchez, let's talk about the supposed dirt on the rug. You pride yourself on being a meticulous housekeeper. Correct?'

'If you mean do I clean good, yes.'

'And you say that you saw dirt on the rug the morning that the doctor was found dead?'

'Yes. But I was so upset.'

'But you say you had cleaned and vacuumed this area the day or two before?'

'Yes. That's why I was so surprised.'

'Ms. Sanchez, you are very close to Betsy Grant. Correct?'

'Yes. She is always good to me.'

'And you care about her a great deal, correct?'

'Yes. Yes. Very much.'

'And she was arrested for the murder of her husband within two weeks of his death?'

'Yes. I was so sad.'

'And you knew that she was alone in the house with her husband that night, correct?'

'Yes. I knew that.'

'But you believed that someone else did it, correct?'

'Yes. Yes.'

'So that would mean that someone came into the house during the night, correct?'

'I guess. I don't know what happened.'

'And it never occurred to you to talk about this dirt on the rug that might have been left by the unknown intruder?'

'No. I don't know why. I don't know. I only really thought about it when I did my testimony. But the judge said just answer the question.'

'But even after that, you said nothing to Mrs. Grant or to Mr. Maynard until Mr. Sharkey suddenly popped up two days ago, correct?'

'What do you mean by popped up?'

'I mean you said nothing until Mr. Maynard learned about Mr. Sharkey two days ago.'

'No. I don't know why. I was embarrassed that maybe I missed the dirt when I vacuumed the day before.'

'Ms. Sanchez, let's move on to a different topic. You say you helped Mrs. Grant look for this bracelet over a long period of time. Correct?'

'Yes. We could not find it.'

'But you don't know when it was stolen, do you?'

'No.'

'I have no further questions, Your Honor.'

Robert Maynard stood up. 'Your Honor, I now recall Betsy Grant.'

When she was seated on the witness stand, he spoke gently. 'Mrs. Grant, this is your bracelet, isn't it?'

Betsy's voice broke. 'Yes. Ted gave it to me for our first anniversary.'

'Are your initials and his initials engraved on it?'

'Yes.'

'When did you first realize it was missing?'

'A few weeks after my husband's death.'

'Did you report it stolen?'

'No. I had no reason to believe it had been stolen. There was no other jewelry missing.'

'Did you report it as lost to your insurance company?'

'No. I thought Ted may have taken it and put it somewhere in the house. I did not want to report it lost, get money from the insurance company and then find it later on. Carmen and I looked everywhere for it. I wanted very much to find it. It meant a lot to me. I had just decided the other day to report it lost, but before I got a chance to do it, all of this happened.'

'No further questions, Your Honor.'

Elliot Holmes walked up to the witness stand. 'Mrs. Grant, you have no idea when this bracelet was stolen, do you?'

'Not specifically. I had not worn it in the last year before I realized it was missing. Ted couldn't go out anymore so there wasn't much occasion to wear this kind of bracelet. I think I last wore it to a charity dinner.'

'Did you ever wear this very sentimental item in the dozens of times you had dinner in New York with Peter Benson?'

Betsy wanted to scream. 'No I did not!' she shouted.

'So, it could have been stolen anytime in that year, correct?'

'I was not aware it had been stolen, so obviously I don't know the exact moment. But Mr. Sharkey had never worked at my house until the two days before Ted died. How would he have known about my house before that?'

Holmes snapped, 'Mrs. Grant. Just answer the question.'

'I told you. I had not worn it in the year before Ted died and I didn't realize it was missing.'

'And after you were arrested, your longtime housekeeper never told you about dirt on the rug under the upstairs window. Correct?'

'No she did not. I wish that she had. She feels very sorry about that.'

Smirking, Holmes said, 'I have no further questions.'

Betsy stepped down from the witness stand and slowly walked back to the defense table. Robert Maynard pulled her chair back for her and she sat down.

'Judge, the defense rests.'

'Any rebuttal, Prosecutor?'

'No, Judge.'

The judge turned to the jurors, told them that the presentation of evidence was complete and that they should return at nine o'clock tomorrow for the summations and legal instruction.

62

Thursday was Josie's day off. She slept late, but as she got up, she was thinking how happy she was that she had met Delaney Wright. It had opened a new way of thinking for her.

What if I got a meeting with the prosecutor and told him that after thinking it over, I realized that Alan had set me up to be his alibi. In her mind she ticked off what she would tell the prosecutor. One, she hadn't even talked to Alan for six months when suddenly he called, then told her how much he missed her. For about a month before his father died they went out at least three times a week. Then one night he started whining how worried he was about his father and how lonely he had been feeling. He said he knew he would be really depressed after the birthday party for his father, and would need somebody to talk to. I said okay, and agreed to meet him for a drink at ten o'clock at O'Malley's, one block away from my apartment. For the next hour and a half I listened to his sob story. Then he said he didn't want to be alone. He begged me to stay at his apartment, but knowing what a slob he is, I had told him to come to my place instead.

Like I told Delaney Wright, she thought, I didn't know Alan was allergic to cats, and he didn't know I had adopted one. He started to wheeze the minute he walked through the door, but even so, he stayed. And what a coincidence it was that his father was murdered that very night. Bingo, I'm his alibi!

Since his father died, Alan and I have been getting together at least once a week, but it was nothing more than a pretense of dating. Look, I've been around and I know if a guy is interested, she thought. And did he even thank me for backing up his story when I was on the witness stand? No. I covered his tail and that was all he wanted.

I can tell the prosecutor all of this, Josie thought. I'll be recalled to the stand. I'll knock the wind out of that whining jerk who was so crazy about his father but stood to inherit millions when he died.

As she petted her cat, Josie thought, I'll call Alan and tell him to come up with a million bucks or I dial the prosecutor. I'll tell him to get a loan. He'll get all his father's money when his stepmother is convicted, but I wouldn't trust him that I'll see any of it once the trial is over.

You thought I was too dumb to figure this out, Alan, Josie thought. It took me a little time, but now I have it straight.

She smiled, and the cat began to purr.

63

When the phone rang Thursday afternoon and he saw it was Josie, Alan almost didn't pick it up. But she had backed him up one hundred percent on his alibi. That was more important than ever now. He needed to keep her happy.

'Hi, Josie,' he said warmly. 'How's my best girl?'

'Your best girl has been doing a lot of thinking,' Josie answered, a smile in her voice. 'Now let me explain to you what I've been thinking about.'

Alan's fingers became clammy as she told him what she wanted. 'Josie, there is no way in the world I can get you one million dollars in the next twenty-four hours. And I can't sign anything saying I owe you that kind of money.'

They haggled back and forth for the next ten minutes before Alan was able to persuade her to accept a compromise. He told her he would make an appointment at his lawyer's office. He'd meet her there and make her a joint owner of his condo. He was pretty sure that would be easy to do. If anyone asked, he could say he loved Josie and wanted to show her how serious he was about their relationship. When the trial was over and he got his money, he'd give her the other half of the condo.

After Josie hung up, Alan slammed his cell phone down on the table. What next? Even if he got the whole fifteen million, he had already promised Scott twenty percent of it. And he had botched the job, Alan thought. He was supposed to go back to the house after the dinner and inject Dad with something that would make it look like a heart attack. Instead Dad woke up and started to strangle him. Scott grabbed the pestle and smashed the back of his head.

Alan picked up the phone and called his lawyer. After that he called Josie back and told her to meet him at his lawyer's office at four o'clock.

64

Delaney wanted to go to court on Thursday morning to watch Tony Sharkey testify but was even more interested in meeting Lisa Clifton. She had been surprised when she received an 8 A.M. call suggesting that instead of meeting at her house they have coffee at a restaurant in Allendale, two towns away.

If Lisa Clifton's expression had been compassionate when she attended to Betsy, today it was anxious. Lisa's eyes scanned the room as though she were looking for someone.

At ten o'clock, when Delaney arrived at the restaurant, most of the breakfast crowd had left. Lisa was sitting in a booth near the back.

The reporter in Delaney always studied the appearance of anyone she was interviewing. She had observed in court that Lisa had a slender body and short dark blonde hair. Now she could see that her angular face was attractive. There was no mistaking the tension in her voice.

'Delaney,' she began, 'as I'm sure you noticed yesterday, I am very concerned about Betsy Grant. She is my dear friend, and she no more killed her husband than you or I did.'

'I absolutely agree,' Delaney said. 'It's very clear to me that Dr. Clifton believes Betsy Grant is guilty. I'll be honest. I've wondered if that has caused tension between you two.'

Lisa Clifton's eyes scanned the room. 'Delaney, my marriage is over. It was a mistake from day one. I saw a real estate agent. I signed a lease on an apartment in Morristown. I have my old job back at Johnson & Johnson. I'm moving my things out of the Ridgewood house tomorrow.'

'I'm sorry,' Delaney said.

'Don't be,' Lisa said. 'Before I say anything, Delaney, tell me who you think killed Ted.'

Delaney didn't hesitate. 'Alan Grant. I know he has a perfect alibi, but that's the point. It's too perfect. He arranges to see an old girlfriend for a drink on the night of the dinner party. He prevails on her to let him stay the night at her apartment because he's lonely. In the process he gets the security cameras in her building and her as his alibi. Alan didn't kill his father, but there's no doubt in my mind that he was working with whoever did.'

Lisa paused and looked around the room again,

but said nothing.

Lisa knows something, Delaney thought. This might be my only chance to get her to talk. 'Lisa, you have heard that a burglar is swearing he was in Betsy's house and stole her bracelet the night her husband was murdered and that he saw a black Mercedes leaving the property.'

'Yes, I heard that on the radio.'

'His testimony is too vague. I have enough experience in court to know the prosecutor is going to blow this guy away.'

'I'm afraid that's what is going to happen.'

'And tomorrow the prosecutor and Betsy's defense lawyer are going to sum up, then the case goes to the jury and Betsy Grant is going to be convicted,' Delaney said, her voice rising.

She waited. When Lisa said nothing, Delaney burst out, 'Lisa, I'm sure you don't know that I'm adopted. I had some friends try to see if they could trace my birth parents. On Monday night these friends told me that Betsy Grant is my mother and Peter Benson is my father.'

Startled, Lisa studied Delaney's face. 'I can see your resemblance to them,' she said. Again she looked fearfully around the small dining room. 'Delaney, I swore my husband was home all night, the night Ted died. And I thought he was. But I went upstairs to bed and he said he was going to watch television in the den, have a scotch and unwind. When I went down in the morning he was asleep on the couch fully dressed. He could have gone out and come back in the middle of the night, I simply don't know. And he has a feeling I'm up to something. When I came back from

281

seeing the real estate agent he had come home early from the office and wanted to know where I had been. That's why I asked you to meet me here instead of at my house.'

Delaney stared at her. 'You think your husband might have murdered Dr. Grant?'

'I think it's more than a possibility. In the weeks before Ted died, Scott and Alan Grant met for lunch several times. Now I'm wondering if Alan offered him money to kill Ted. Alan could easily have found out the alarm code from his father and taken that missing key and given it to Scott.'

None of this will be allowed in court, Delaney thought. It's all supposition. Lisa already testified that Scott was home that night. When it comes out that they're divorcing, it will look like a spiteful ex-wife trying to damage her former husband's reputation by adding these extra details about him sleeping on the couch that night.

'Lisa,' she asked, 'would you consider staying with Scott until an investigator tries to find if there is any reason he might have wanted to kill Dr. Grant?'

Lisa shook her head vehemently. 'I can't. There's something about Scott. I'm afraid of him. I can't stay there anymore.'

Delaney knew there was no way she could ask Lisa not to move. 'I understand, but please keep in touch with me.'

'I will. I promise.'

Delaney had to settle for that.

65

Betsy's blazing hope, that Tony Sharkey's testimony would make a difference, had faded away. That night, lying in bed, she tried to make sense of the day's events.

Even if Sharkey proved he was in the house, she thought, it doesn't mean that he was here at the same time as whoever was in the black Mercedes. Scott has one. So does Kent. So do a lot of the residents of Alpine. And what if there never was a black Mercedes?

I am going to prison. I know I am. Her mouth went dry as she pictured being told to stand and listen to the foreman of the jury give the verdict. If it's murder, I'll be sentenced to thirty years to life. If it's manslaughter, it will be ten years.

I know I am innocent. Would it be so bad to decide not to go that route? Some of Ted's pills are still in the bathroom in the library. Would it be too awful to take a handful of them and be finished with it?

The thought was oddly comforting and she fell asleep.

66

Peter Benson could not just sit home and watch media reports of the final two days of the trial. If he couldn't be with Betsy, he had to be near her. He looked up a hotel near the courthouse, and wearing dark glasses and a baseball cap over his dark hair, he checked in early Thursday morning. As soon as he had closed the door behind him, he turned on the television. There had been such widespread interest in the trial that the closing two days of it were being broadcast live on the local channel, News 12 New Jersey.

Filled with hope, he watched Tony Sharkey begin to testify. That hope was shattered when the prosecutor with biting sarcasm tore apart Sharkey's story of seeing a black Mercedes exit the driveway the night Dr. Grant was murdered.

When the camera was on Betsy, Peter was anguished to see how impassive she seemed to the testimony, as though she were building a shock wall around her. But she seemed much more emotional as he watched her testify about the lost bracelet.

After the judge adjourned court for the day and said that closing arguments would begin in the morning, Peter tried to decide whether or not to drive to Alpine and see Betsy. Caution prevailed. If the media got a picture of him going into her house the day before the summations, it would look terrible for her.

But he could phone her. At 10 P.M. he assumed she would be alone and he made the call. He knew his name would come up on her cell phone, but she did not answer. And the answer message she always had on her phone was turned off.

He kept calling every few minutes until a sleepy voice answered, 'Peter.'

'Betsy, why didn't you answer? Are you all right?'

'I took a sleeping pill. I needed it.'

'Of course you did. But are you sure you're all right?'

Betsy looked at the bottle of pills on the night table that she had been trying to get up the courage to swallow.

'Yes, I am, Peter, I promise.'

Betsy was falling back to sleep. 'Yes, I am, Peter, I promise I'm okay.'

67

'Why are you so jumpy?' Scott asked Lisa Friday morning. 'You can't even swallow a bite of toast and your hands are shaking.'

Lisa was sure that the truth was the best way of answering. 'Scott, you certainly know that either today or next week Betsy will probably be found guilty of murder or manslaughter. And you should know I'm very fond of her and sure she is innocent.'

'And you surely know that she killed my close friend, partner and colleague of thirty years when she smashed his head in?'

Across the table they looked at each other, then Scott said, 'Lisa, despite the fact that we bitterly disagree on this subject, I love you dearly and I'm looking forward to having this behind us and going away together.'

'I am too,' Lisa answered and tried to smile. Especially, the *going away* part, she thought to herself. She wanted to scream. Go to the office and please God, stay there! The movers will be here at ten o'clock, she thought.

'I'm surprised you're not going to court to hear the summations,' Scott said, his eyes searching her face.

'I can't,' she said simply. 'I don't want to listen to that prosecutor trying to put Betsy in prison.'

'Well, the next time you'll get a chance to see her will be in the state prison.' Scott downed a final gulp of coffee and got up. 'In a way I admire your loyalty, even when it's misplaced.'

Lisa hoped he did not feel her body stiffen as he caressed her cheek and kissed her forehead.

Then he was gone. She rushed upstairs to shower and dress. Her suitcases were in the attic. She had to get out of here. She hurried up to the attic and turned on the light. The matching pieces of luggage were stacked in a far corner, past the rugs and furniture she was planning to take. As she picked up the largest suitcase, she saw a glint on something overhead in the rafter. Curious, she reached up, took it down, then gasped.

It was a black marble pestle.

She knew beyond doubt that it was the one missing from Ted Grant's bedroom.

68

At 9:15 A.M. Delaney, running late after being stuck in a traffic jam, was being driven to the courthouse in an Uber car when her cell phone rang. Surprised, she greeted her quickly. 'Hello, Lisa.'

Lisa's voice was high-pitched and nervous. 'Delaney, I was packing to leave. I've got to get out of here today. The movers are coming in an hour. When I was getting my suitcases from the attic, I saw something on a rafter right across the room. Delaney, it's the pestle. I'm sure it's the one that matches the mortar bowl in Ted's room. That's why Scott stayed downstairs the night Ted died. He was planning to kill Ted.'

'Lisa, calm down. Where is Scott now?'

'He's at the office. He had a patient at nine o'clock.'

'Get in your car and drive to the courthouse,' Delaney said. Then she thought, Lisa's so upset she might have an accident.

'No, don't do that,' she said quickly, 'I'm on Route 4. I can be at your house in ten minutes. I'll pick you up and take you to the courthouse. While I'm on the way, take a picture of the pestle with the background of something in the house

287

so we can prove it was there. I'll call you back with a number to send it to.'

She dialed the prosecutor's office and reached the homicide unit. After tersely explaining who she was, she said, 'I'm going to send a text with a picture. It's critical to the outcome of the Betsy Grant trial. It's the murder weapon.'

The skeptical assistant prosecutor shot back, 'Send it to this number. We'll look at it. The defense summation has already begun.'

Seconds later she was back on the phone with Lisa.

'Send the picture to the prosecutor. Can you remember this number?'

'I think I can remember but I'll write it down. And please get here fast.'

Should I have her get out of the house and go to a neighbor? Delaney wondered. But it was only nine twenty-five and she said that Scott has a nine o'clock patient in his office in Fort Lee.

At nine thirty, the driver stopped in front of 522 Cleveland Avenue. 'I'll only be a minute,' she said. 'Please wait.'

As she hurried up the walk, Lisa threw the door open. She was holding her phone and her pocket-book. 'Delaney, I didn't get that number you gave me right. I tried to send but it didn't go through.'

'It's all right. I can send it.'

Lisa reached into her pocketbook and took out the pestle. 'The cell phone reception here is bad,' she said, her voice trembling. 'It's better in the kitchen.'

I'm holding the murder weapon, Delaney thought, as she rushed down the hall. In the kitchen she propped the pestle against the row of decorative canisters and took the picture. When she tried sending, the first attempt did not go through, nor did the second one. Finally, the third try was successfully sent to Holmes' office.

Before she started back down the hall, she heard the front door open and then Scott Clifton ask, 'Are you going out, Lisa?'

Delaney dialed 911. 'Help. Killer at 522 Cleveland Avenue. Stay on the line. Record what's happening here.'

Before the operator could answer and without breaking the connection, Delaney held the phone out toward where they were speaking.

Delaney could hear their voices clearly. Lisa was trying not to sound upset. 'Oh, Scott, I thought you had a patient.'

'He changed the time of the appointment. Where were you going?' His voice was rising.

'To the hairdresser. Silver threads among the gold.'

He looked at her. 'Not that many, Lisa. I asked you, where are you going?'

Delaney thought to herself, good job, Lisa. Keep stalling him. 'Scott, I hoped to avoid this scene. The moving van will be here at ten to take all my things from the attic out of here. I left my wedding and engagement rings on the dresser.'

'I thought there was something up. Why don't we go check the attic to make sure you haven't helped yourself to anything of mine.'

As he pushed Lisa up the stairs, Delaney crept silently into the hall as she heard Scott shout, 'I know you have it. Where is it?'

Lisa ran down from the attic screaming, 'You murderer. You would let Betsy go to prison for something you did. You killed Ted.' Delaney stepped back into the living room to avoid being seen. Her heart racing, she prayed, 'Please get here fast. Please.'

Lisa tried to open the front door but Scott yanked her back. He had his hands on her throat, shouting as he was choking her. 'Give it to me. Why couldn't you just stay out of it?'

Delaney slipped the cell phone into her jacket pocket and rushed back into the foyer.

Scott's hands tightened on Lisa's throat. 'Alan promised me over a million dollars. It would have been twice that when Betsy was convicted.'

Delaney knew there was only one thing she could do. She lifted the pestle and slammed it on the side of Scott's head. He dropped his grip on Lisa, turned and lunged at her. Blood was spewing from a gash on his forehead.

Desperately, she swung the pestle again, this time hitting the side of his face. With a snarl he tore the pestle out of her hand and raised it to strike her.

She stumbled back and the pestle missed her by inches. Then, as Scott raised it again, the door burst open and three cops, their guns drawn, rushed in.

'Freeze, and put your hands up,' one of them shouted.

Delaney pulled her phone out of her jacket. Her voice almost incoherent, she asked, 'Did you get all that? Did you get that?'

The 9-1-1 operator's voice was adamant, 'I sure

did, loud and clear, ma'am. I sure did.'

Delaney exhaled. 'Send your recording of this call to the following number right now. It's the prosecutor's office.'

69

Elliot Holmes, tasting victory in the most publicized case in his career, was listening to Robert Maynard's fiery summation. He was itching for it to finish so that he could get up and deliver his own.

All of a sudden, the door to the courtroom flew open and an assistant prosecutor rushed to where he was sitting. Furious, he snarled, 'This had better be important.'

Visibly annoyed, Judge Roth said, 'This is an unfair distraction to the defense attorney and to the jury.'

Prosecutor Holmes stood up. 'I most sincerely apologize to the court, the jury and the defense counsel. Please give me just one moment.'

Holmes took the cell phone from the assistant and looked at a picture of Scott Clifton surrounded by Ridgewood policemen. One of the police officers was holding the pestle. The text explained what had occurred. Elliot Holmes knew that his case was over.

'Your Honor, I request a fifteen-minute break to listen to a recording that is on this phone. This may be critical to the outcome of this case.'

The judge realized that something enormous must have happened. 'We will take a brief break. I instruct the jury not to discuss what you have just seen.'

Robert Maynard sat next to Betsy during the recess. 'Betsy, I don't know what is happening, but my gut tells me that it is good for us. Otherwise, they wouldn't dare interrupt my summation like this.'

Twenty minutes later, a shell-shocked Elliot Holmes addressed the court. 'Your Honor, the prosecutor's office always diligently seeks to ensure justice. I have been informed that Dr. Scott Clifton has been arrested at his home in the last hour and the marble pestle has been recovered there. I have also listened to an audio recording of the events surrounding his arrest, where he made certain admissions regarding the murder of Dr. Edward Grant. He has implicated both himself and Alan Grant.'

Holmes's voice broke. 'Your Honor, I must conclude that there has been a tragic miscarriage of justice. The state no longer believes that Betsy Grant killed her husband or was involved in any way. The state deeply regrets the suffering she has endured.

'Your Honor, the state moves to dismiss the indictment.'

Cheers erupted in the courtroom. The judge gently instructed the spectators to remain quiet.

All Betsy could think of was how close she had come to swallowing the pills last night.

Judge Roth spoke. 'I have listened to the prosecutor's representations of the extraordinary developments which have occurred, literally, in the last hour. The prosecutor is satisfied that, based upon these developments, the defendant Betsy Grant is innocent. The prosecutor has acknowledged that there has been a terrible miscarriage of justice. Fortunately, this new evidence has come to light prior to a verdict in this case, which, if guilty, would have resulted in lengthy incarceration.' The judge paused. 'This indictment is dismissed. Mrs. Grant, with the best wishes of the court, you are free to go.'

As cheers erupted again, Betsy tried to absorb those words. Free to go. Free to go.

As she slowly stood up, Robert Maynard's arm around her shoulder, she thanked the judge. Peter Benson, who had been watching Robert Maynard's summation in his hotel room, had raced down to the courthouse when Elliot Holmes requested the brief break to evaluate the information that had just been received. Peter had slipped into the back row of the courtroom just as Holmes started to tell the judge what had occurred and his reasons for asking that the indictment be dismissed.

As soon as the judge told Betsy that she was free to go, Peter hurried forward toward the defense table. A sheriff's officer briefly began to intercept him, but Judge Roth waved him off. Betsy and Maynard turned to leave the courtroom. They had just taken a couple of steps when Betsy saw Peter coming toward her. Maynard stepped aside as Peter put his arm under hers and said, 'I'll take care of her now.' He looked into Betsy's eyes. 'And always.'

70

Delaney waited three days before she called Betsy and asked if she could stop over and see her. 'Of course, you can,' Betsy said. 'I know how you were rooting for me. I wondered why you didn't cover the last week of the trial.'

'I promise I'll explain that to you,' Delaney answered. 'By any chance will Mr. Benson also be there?' As she expected, the reply was yes.

Her heart was in her throat as she drove to Alpine. She exchanged greetings with Betsy and Peter, and they went into the living room and sat down. Delaney leaned forward, clasped her hands and in a voice trembling with emotion said, 'I have something to tell you. It's something I learned only a few days ago. Betsy, you said on the witness stand how you have yearned for your child every day of your life. In exactly the same way I have yearned for my birth mother.' Delaney looked from one to the other. 'And now I have found not only my mother, but my father too.'

As Betsy and Peter, incredulous, tried to comprehend what she was saying, Delaney continued. 'I was born at 22 Oak Street in Philadelphia on March 16th, twenty-six years ago. My grandparents were Martin and Rose Ryan...'

Epilogue

Six months later

Alan Grant and Dr. Scott Clifton are awaiting trial on an indictment charging them with the murder of Dr. Edward Grant. Dr. Clifton is also charged with the attempted murder of Lisa Clifton. Their lawyers have tried to cut deals for them by offering to testify against each other. Both face life in prison.

Jonathan's investigation uncovered evidence that Dr. Clifton provided the drugs that had caused Steven Harwin to overdose. Dr. Clifton is awaiting trial on a second indictment in that case.

Tony Sharkey received three years in prison for the attempted burglary of the Saddle River home. At Betsy Grant's request, he was not prosecuted for the burglary of her home. He told Judge Roth at his sentence that 'All things considered, this ain't so bad.'

A week after the trial ended, as Carmen was packing the medical books to send to Dr. Adams, she found one with a hollow center. It contained three prescriptions pads in Dr. Ted Grant's name, filled out and signed supposedly by him. Were these pads what he so desperately wanted to *find?*

Alvirah had called Sam to say that she really didn't need to retile her apartment, but she insisted on sending him a five-thousand-dollar check to show her gratitude for his priceless information. Sam thanked her profusely and assured her that if she ever really *does* need new tile...

Betsy and Peter were married by Monsignor Quinn at St. Francis Xavier. As Betsy, lovely in a champagne-lace gown, and Peter, handsome and distinguished in a dark blue suit and silver tie, exchanged their vows, Delaney blinked back happy tears. My mother, my father, she thought.

Delaney was Betsy's maid-of-honor. Peter's closest friend, Professor Frank Reeves, was his best man.

The reception was at Betsy's house in Alpine. As a wedding gift Jennifer Wright compiled an album of pictures of Delaney starting when she was a few days old. 'This way you can follow her from the beginning.' She smiled as she handed it to Betsy.

Delaney had asked Betsy and Peter if it would be all right to call them by their first names. They had understood immediately. There had been visible happiness on Jennifer's face when she knew she was the only one Delaney would ever call 'Mom.'

That evening was a wedding celebration and a reunion. The people they cared most about were there. Jennifer and James Wright, Delaney's big brothers and their wives, Peter's mother, Alvirah and Willy who had made this day possible, Lisa Clifton and Delaney's beloved nanny Bridget O'Keefe. My family, Delaney thought joyfully.

Jon came over to her carrying two glasses of champagne. 'It doesn't get any better than this,' he said.

Then as she sipped champagne, Delaney looked

across the room at Bridget who was deep in conversation with Alvirah. She remembered Bridget's warning, *When things seem so good, there's trouble on the way.*

Not this time, Bridget, she thought happily. As you also said when you were positive about something, *'I can feel it in my bones.'*

The publishers hope that this book has given you enjoyable reading. Large Print Books are especially designed to be as easy to see and hold as possible. If you wish a complete list of our books please ask at your local library or write directly to:

Magna Large Print Books
Magna House, Long Preston,
Skipton, North Yorkshire.
BD23 4ND

This Large Print Book for the partially sighted, who cannot read normal print, is published under the auspices of

THE ULVERSCROFT FOUNDATION

THE ULVERSCROFT FOUNDATION

... we hope that you have enjoyed this Large Print Book. Please think for a moment about those people who have worse eyesight problems than you ... and are unable to even read or enjoy Large Print, without great difficulty.

You can help them by sending a donation, large or small to:

**The Ulverscroft Foundation,
1, The Green, Bradgate Road,
Anstey, Leicestershire, LE7 7FU,
England.**
or request a copy of our brochure for more details.

The Foundation will use all your help to assist those people who are handicapped by various sight problems and need special attention.

Thank you very much for your help.